DEATH BY ASSOCIATION

D1598650

DEATH BY ASSOCIATION

A Captain Heimrich Mystery

Richard and Frances Lockridge

Chivers Press
Bath, Avon, England • Thorndike Press
Thorndike, Maine USA

BC MM NW

This Large Print edition is published by Chivers Press, England and by Thorndike Press, USA.

Published in 1995 in the U.K. by arrangement with the authors

Published in 1995 in the U.S. by arrangement with HarperCollins Publishers, Inc.

U.K. Hardcover ISBN 0–7451–2658–8 (Chivers Large Print)
U.S. Softcover   ISBN 1–56054–306–X (General Series Edition)

Copyright © 1952, by Richard and Frances Lockridge

All rights reserved.

The text of this Large Print edition is unabridged.
Other aspects of the book may vary from the original edition.

Set in 16 pt. New Times Roman.

Printed in Great Britain on acid-free paper.

British Library Cataloguing in Publication Data available

Library of Congress Cataloging-in-Publication Data

Lockridge, Richard, 1898–
  Death by association: a Captain Heimrich mystery / by Richard and
    Frances Lockridge
  p.   cm.
  ISBN 1–56054–306–X (alk. paper : lg. print)
  1. Heimrich, M. L. (Fictitious character)—Fiction.   2. Police—
New York (State)—Fiction.   I. Lockridge, Frances Louise Davis.
II. Title.
[PS3523.O245D4   1995]   94–25980
813′.52—dc20

CHAPTER ONE

There was not time to see, to see for remembering, all the pictures made by sea and land, by the many bridges and by the fishers on the bridges; the pictures clear in sunlight which was bright yet somehow soft; the pictures glimpsed and then hurled past, hurled backward by the ponderous, headlong progression of the bus. She could look ahead and see a bridge, with men and women— variously, sometimes grotesquely, now and then brightly, costumed—fishing from it and then they were on the bridge, seemed to be brushing the fishers, threatening to hurl them into the blue water or mangle them against the concrete guard wall over which they leaned. But when she looked back the fishers were still there, unperturbed, standing on, but now and then perilously backing from, a narrow concrete ledge between rail and roadway. She looked back once and a woman in a red shirt and tight blue trousers was leaning forward toward the rail, partly over it, and was pulling up a fish which wriggled silver in the sun.

If only she could remember that; if only there were time to remember any of it. But when the bus slowed, when it stopped, it was always on a key where the road ran only straight, like a road anywhere, with frame

1

buildings on either side and gasoline pumps and signs offering fried shrimp, and jewfish and lime pie. There were pictures everywhere, there were pictures even where the bus stopped—at Tavernier, on Key Largo; at Marathon, on Key Vacas; at the lower toll gate, on Big Pine Key—but the best pictures went backward at sixty miles an hour, on straightaways at seventy. The bus had no time for pictures. The bus was implacable. It hurled itself south, not taking breath, and hurled itself toward the sea—toward the southernmost end of everything. It had started where the road started, she thought—in Maine the road started, didn't it?—and forced its way the length of the seaboard. 'From Northern pines to Southern palms.' As it neared the end of its unrelenting journey it went faster, through a swirl of pictures, of light and color, toward the final blueness of the sea. It would not stop when the road ended; it could not stop. It would continue to the end of the springboard and off it, into blue water. It would plunge into the water and throw up great waves on either side, and at the top the waves would break into spray and sparkle in the sun. Then the bus would go on, with blueness all around, and fish would swim outside the windows and look in at the people and—

She was not asleep, had not been asleep. Yet, nevertheless, she awoke and took herself in hand. The bus had not started in Maine. It had

2

started in Miami. It was not going to the southernmost end of the world, but only down a chain of keys to the endmost key, the southernmost and westernmost key. To, specifically, Key West, where there was an absolute guarantee against frost; where there had never been a frost. The bus would not fall off the end of the North American continent and continue under water toward Cuba. It would turn docile in a town, creep through traffic, bungle its way around corners, finally draw up to a curb. She could see the pictures ahead; see the bus, now merely ponderous, now meek, almost embarrassed, turning a corner too sharp for it in a street too small. It would be careful not to knock over palm trees. She had a picture of the bus sidling grotesquely around a palm tree, trying to make itself smaller. It was a sharp picture, and a satisfying one, although, having never been in Key West and being only recently familiar with palm trees anywhere, Mary Wister was forced to invent detail. This she did by detaching, from the other pictures in her mind, such fragments as seemed suitable...

Already the bus appeared to be losing confidence. It went more slowly; it no longer seemed to brush aside other vehicles as it had done for a hundred and fifty miles, from the outskirts of Miami (and the last too highly colored, too modern, too self-conscious house) to this area of thickening traffic. Mary Wister looked at her watch. It was time for the traffic to thicken; time for Key West. Mary Wister looked out her window, which was on the left as one faced forward in the bus, and there was a high wire fence, there was a gate with Marines on guard, beyond there were the bloated forms of tethered blimps. That would be the naval station, or, at any rate, part of it. That would be Boca Chica. A jet plane shot violently up from somewhere, screaming, a comet with an angry lashing tail. The bus, suddenly old, decrepit, an uncertain hulk, went across another bridge and into town. It went, now like a bull on lead from a nose ring, down a broad street, between palm trees—down, she saw from the street signs, Roosevelt Boulevard. But soon it was on Truman Avenue, which was busier but rather less impressive. Then the bus turned into a narrow street, bungled its way—as she had foreseen—around several corners and stopped at a curb.

'Well, here we are, folks,' the driver said, and opened the door of the bus. 'Key West, folks,' he added, to relieve any stubborn doubt.

When it was her turn, Mary Wister got out of the bus. When it was her turn, she retrieved her luggage. She said, 'Yes, please' to a man who said, 'Taxi, miss?' She said, 'Yes,' again when he said, 'The Coral Isle, miss?' and got into the cab. When the driver had stowed her two bags and portfolio case and got behind the wheel, when he had started the car, she said,

4

'How did you know?'

'Just look like it, I guess, miss,' he said, and made a right turn and then another and then a third. 'One way streets,' he told her. 'Get so's we can tell, generally. Some looks like The Coral Isle and some looks like The Keys.'

There was nothing in particular to say to that except 'oh,' which Mary Wister said, dutifully.

'Since the railroad blew down, you can't tell by buses,' he said, cryptically. 'Anybody can come by bus.'

She said 'oh' again, and looked at pictures of old houses behind walls, and at square frame buildings housing obviously fifth rate groceries, at cottages which might have been anywhere and at pink stucco oddities which should have been in Miami's outskirts or in Los Angeles. The cab turned left and went along for two blocks of nondescript structures and then passed, unexpectedly, an ancient square mansion, keeping itself to itself behind a high brick wall. The cab stopped at lights and then crossed Truman Avenue. For the next several blocks most of the houses were recent; many were bright, most seemed to hug the coral earth, clutching its substance against another such hurricane as had blown down the railroad.

The cab turned, after a few blocks, into a wide gateway and along a circling drive toward a porte-cochere. The cab was forced to stop part way along the drive to wait while a chauffeur-driven car ahead was unloaded of two men and luggage. One of the men was tall and thin and, although obviously not old moved with something like the carefulness of age. The other was a square man, with a square face, older than the other, having the appearance of great physical solidity, but— which was unexpected—also moving with somewhat exaggerated care. He, indeed, got out of the car awkwardly, as if not all of him were functioning.

Alert young men in red jackets swooped on bags. The two men, the tall and thin one first, went into The Coral Isles and resilient youth, jacketed in red, followed after with bags. The big car rolled away, then, and the cab rolled in. A tall man in uniform opened the door, beamed at Mary Wister, said 'good afternoon, miss' and gave her unrequired assistance in getting out. He got her bags and case from the cab and put them on steps to a porch and another young man in a red jacket came out at a trot to welcome them. Mary paid and tipped and smiled and followed.

There was a great deal of lobby, extending to right and left of the entrance. Looking straight ahead, before she turned to follow the red coat right toward the desk, she saw the picture of palm trees through french windows, and beyond the palms the sea. She waited briefly behind the solid man, who waited behind the tall, thin man. 'Boy,' the clerk said, and resilient youth—they all looked like football players of the trimmer sort, Mary Wister thought—took key and bags and tall, thin man away. The queue of three was a queue of two; the clerk smiled at her over the solid man, and smiled, simultaneously, at the solid man.

'Heimrich,' the solid man said. 'M. L. I have a reservation, naturally.'

The clerk beamed; he asked to be allowed a moment, he turned back to the desk in triumph and with key. He said again, 'Boy!' and the solid man followed boy and bags down the long lobby.

'Now!' the clerk said to Mary Wister. 'Now!' It was a moment for which he had been waiting, perhaps all his life.

'Mary Wister,' she said. 'The Florida Associates.'

'Of course,' the clerk said, a clerk who should have known. 'Of *course*!' He turned away, turned back almost instantly with key in hand. 'Boy,' he commanded. 'Take Miss Wister to two-oh-two. On the ocean side, Miss Wister. A lovely vista.'

'Yes,' Mary said. 'Thank you.'

She turned from the desk after the youth in red jacket. She turned almost into a man in tennis shorts, a sweater draped over his shoulders, wrapping its arms around his neck. He carried a racket; he smiled and was sorry he had almost been bumped into. And only then

7

did Mary Wister realize that, in early February, she had come on summer. It was, she thought, as if until that moment—that moment of the picture of a man in tennis clothes, red from exercise, sweating a little from exercise—shc was still enveloped in the North's cold; had brought the cold with her, in her tweed suit, her light but still too heavy top-coat, in her skin. Until that moment she simply had not noticed warmth. She had not noticed in Miami, between train and bus station or—which of course was the way it truly was—had taken for granted. But now she felt the warmth of summer. She thought of New York, and shivered. She followed the boy down the lobby, past chairs and sofas which were, with no exceptions, empty. She followed the boy into an elevator, and out of it on the second floor, and down a long corridor—it was, evidently, a hotel of distances—and into a small, square room, with an outsized window filling most of one wall.

The boy was busy. He opened the window. He opened the door to a bathroom which was almost as large as the small room. He opened another door and said, 'Quite a closet, miss,' and waited comment.

'For heaven's sake!' Mary Wister said, and spoke sincerely. The closet was a cavern; it appeared to be half again as large as the room it adjoined. Involuntarily, she looked at her two, not large, bags. The youth beamed at her.

'Hits everybody,' he said. 'Some closet, isn't it? Used to be, everybody who came here fished. Had a lot of stuff, you know. They gave 'em closets, they gave 'em closets.'

'Yes,' Mary Wister said. 'They did, didn't they?' She looked around the bedroom, which now seemed very small.

'I'll tell you,' the youth said, 'you won't spend any time in it, except to sleep. Nobody does. Anything else, miss?'

There was nothing else, except a tip. Then there was quiet in a small room with a large window, with a late sun pouring in the window. She looked through the window at palm trees, at a lawn with chairs and chaises, at a parapet beyond and, beyond the parapet, sand and the sea. And far out on the water, seemingly stationary but from its smoke trail certainly at work, there was a little ship. Then, as she watched, there was a roaring in the air and a jet plane knifed in from the sea, very low, at, but then by an unnervingly narrow margin, over The Coral Isles. After the plane passed, it was very quiet; she thought she could hear the sea. She stood for several minutes by the window, breathing warm air, looking at pictures in blue and green, before she unpacked and went into the enormous bathroom for a shower, and came out into the room, the cold washed from her skin and the softness of summer caressing it. Then she dressed, not this time in tweeds, and after a time went out to see. For the

9

moment, the disappointment, the emptiness, was hardly there at all.

She found a stairway before she found the elevator, which appeared to have hidden itself willfully, and went down a single flight to the lobby. It was not so empty now; around a piano men in white dinner jackets with instrument cases were gathering; in one corner, formed by a sofa and a deep chair, surrounding a table, two couples were waiting, thirst evident in their faces, while a young man in a white jacket listened to their orders. Mary walked past them, along the lobby toward the desk, the newsstand, the glass cases of violent shirts for, she assumed, men maddened by February warmth. But before she reached the desk and the newsstand, she saw french doors open at her left and went through them onto a wide porch.

Here there were people, in the sun of late afternoon. Here a man in a city suit sat on a chaise and smoked a cigar and read a *Wall Street Journal*; here two plump women in their fifties knitted with quick needles and spoke with quicker tongues, and spoke in the accents of Georgia. Or was it South Carolina? Pictures were always so much clearer than sounds, so much more revealing: the needles darting, one through dark red wool, the other through white; the yellow circles—they looked like quoits—on the dress of one of the women; the shape of the women; the way one of them, her

10

turn to speak awaited, showed the tip of a red tongue between white teeth, as if it were held there captive, forced to bide its time. One of the women, the one whose tongue was not in the white trap of teeth, smiled up at Mary Wister, and the smile was friendly, a welcome to warmth, to summer in February.

Mary went across the porch, after smiling appreciation of her welcome, and down a cement walk toward the parapet and the sea. Reaching the parapet, which was broken for a stairway to the beach itself, she paused, the sun warm through her thin dress, a summer coat light on her arm, and looked out over the water. Gulls rose and fell over it; the little ship had taken itself off. But a powerboat, going somewhere in a sputtering hurry, shot by, bouncing in the quiet water. Light bounced from the water, from the powerboat's spray. She turned back and looked toward the hotel. After all, whatever else she got, she must get some part of the hotel itself—something bright and welcoming, and distinctive of this hotel only, which would, some day, some place, make a woman say to a man, or a man to a woman, 'That's where we want to go. That looks wonderful.'

Well, Mary Wister thought, that won't be hard. It does look wonderful.

The sun was on the façade she faced. A hundred windows flashed in it. The sun reached into the covered porch, stretched

11

diagonal, shortening panels on the porch floor. The hotel was grayish white in the sun, red roofed. Bougainvillaea climbed between the windows. It was a long hotel, stretching itself parallel to the sea. There was a central section along which the porch ran; at either end there was a wing and each wing, angling widely from the central section, reached toward the water, so that the lawn and the palm trees were held lightly in an open cup. Mary Wister looked at the hotel and thought in pictures, as she had thought for so long as she could remember. She looked to her left and saw the flat green surface of tennis courts. There were high hedges at either end of the courts and, beyond the hedge at the more distant end, there was—only partly to be seen from where she stood—what was evidently a dance floor, since several couples were dancing on it, to rhumba rhythms.

Along the side of the tennis court nearest her, there was a railed area, roofed and shaded by green and white canvas; there were tables in the area and several men and women, dressed for tennis, rackets piled on tables, were watching four men play doubles with energy but with only moderate skill, with red faces and—their voices carried—frequent ejaculations, most of them self-addressed and delivered in tones of hopeless fury. They were all, evidently, having a wonderful time. The rest of the sentence forced its way into a mind which sought to bar it. But she didn't, Mary

12

Wister told herself; she didn't at all. She didn't wish anybody there. There wasn't anybody. She was harsh with her mind. Not *anybody*. But the picture formed, in spite of her—the short, broad jaw, the intense blueness of the eyes, the brown hair which so often needed cutting.

Mary shook her own head to shake the picture from it, and the sun was bright on her own dark brown hair, so that the hair looked polished. What she needed was a drink. She started up the walk toward the welcoming porch, and heard music from the lounge beyond. But Lee walked with her, step by step. Well, this was always the worst time of the day. They had most often met at this hour, and sat in a corner of a bar where they were known, and drinks were brought to them without the need of ordering—a daiquiri without sugar for her; a scotch for him. And then they had talked. How they had talked; how many evenings they had talked, forgetting to drink; sitting for an hour over the first drink, while it warmed in glasses; forgetting to order again and not needing anything but talk. The best hour of the day, then, and now the worst—now an hour to be got through somehow, anyhow.

Mary Wister, brown haired and brown eyed, slim in green linen, walking quickly in brown pumps of lizard skin, twenty-six years old, commercial artist by trade, competent in all she did, dressed by Saks' and Bonwit's and

13

Bergdorf's, shoes by Delman, pretty lady on top of the world, climbed the steps to the porch and went across it, step by step with a man named Lee, who could be seen by no one—a six-foot-two man (needing a haircut) who wasn't there any more, and would never be there again, and, when you thought about it, never had been there at all. Oh damn, oh damn, oh damn, oh damn, Mary Wister thought. She pushed open the screen of the french door.

The lounge, deserted an hour before, was full now—it was full of music from a five piece orchestra; it was bursting with the music of a five piece orchestra. It was filled with people, in chairs and on sofas, perching on ottomans, surrounding low tables. It was filled, but from raised hands, snapping fingers, agonized expressions on the faces of those parching and ignored, insufficiently filled, with white-jacketed youths, trotting with trays. The people, as Mary had expected, came two by two; a cocktail lounge as neatly proportioned as an Ark. Male and female they had been created, one of each for each, and the lounge of The Coral Isles certainly rubbed it in. Mary hesitated, looked for a place into which she might intrude. A single place.

She saw only one. It was a chair which shared a table with a small sofa, and the small sofa was occupied—occupied by the tall thin man who had moved like an older man, and the solid man who had moved a little as if he expected to break. Well, that would be better than a couple from the Ark. She crossed the room to the chair, stood in front of the chair and said, 'Is this—?'

'Not at all,' the tall, thin man—who was also a pale man, almost a gaunt man—said in a soft voice, in an oddly gentle voice. 'Please do.'

Mary Wister did. The pale man smiled at her, encouragingly. There was gentleness in his smile, and almost an offer of friendship, although there was no reason he should think she needed friendship, or encouragement. It was because she was only half a pair. That was it. He was encouraging her not to mind that she broke the pattern of the Ark. He was being gentle with the forsaken. 'A long drink of water,' Mary thought, in a phrase which jumped into her mind suddenly, out of childhood. 'Nothing but a long drink of water.' Who was he to be sorry for her? She could beckon and men that would make two of him would—

Well, she had, and a man hadn't. She had spent two years falling deeper and deeper into love, and had ended by being liked. Just liked. She had ended by being somebody to talk to. Fine. Wonderful. Then she felt that, ridiculously, she was flushing. That was all that was needed; to blush like a schoolgirl because a man told her, in a gentle voice, that an unoccupied chair was also unclaimed. She looked away from both the men, from the pale

15

one who had spoken and the one with a square, weathered face who had merely, faintly, smiled and nodded and who had then, sleepily, closed his eyes. She caught the eye of a passing waiter; when he came, she ordered a drink—a martini, not a daiquiri without sugar—in a crisply casual voice, a voice from the best New York bars.

'Very dry, please,' she said. 'With lemon peel.'

'It seems a pleasant place,' the thin man said to the man who sat beside him, although the man beside him had his eyes closed and might have been thought to be asleep. Possibly, Mary Wister found herself thinking, the music hurt his eyes. She realized she was looking at the solid man, trying idly to remember the name she had overheard him give at the desk, and looked away sharply.

'They,' the solid man said, without opening his eyes, 'tell me the food is good. The people seem peaceful.'

It seemed to Mary, who had to overhear, but who continued resolutely to look away, who turned a little in her chair the more comfortably to move away, to withdraw—it seemed to Mary an odd thing for the solid man to say. The people were not noticeably peaceful; they were noticeably animated. The orchestra was not peaceful. By what association with what violence were they, then, to be described as peculiarly people of peace?

16

By a man but now home from war? The solid man, she thought, looked a little old for that. The thin, pale man—

The waiter brought her drink. He set it, on a square of paper, ornamented with a palm tree, on the table. She had to turn in her chair, sit straight in her chair, if she was to reach the glass. She turned and the pale man was reaching a long hand, a long white hand, for his own glass. How pale the hand was, how fragile! (She saw a square hand, a blunt hand, hard with bone and muscle. As if it were actually there, she closed her eyes against it, but only for a moment. That got you nowhere.)

As she and the thin man leaned simultaneously toward the table, there was nothing which could keep their eyes from meeting. His eyes were brown; they were brown and they seemed to be tired. He smiled. The smile asked nothing, said nothing, yet it was not merely of the lips. Mary felt her own lips move, as if without her will, arranging themselves in the shape of something socially like a smile. Now he would speak, the long drink of water.

'You've just arrived too,' he said, in the same curiously gentle voice. 'Almost when we did. We were just agreeing it seems a pleasant place.'

'I'm sure it is,' Mary Wister said, in a voice which said nothing, in a tone which ended it then and there. She took her glass from the table and moved back into her chair, withdrew into her chair. The long drink of water, she thought, as if that childhood phrase were pinned in her mind, fluttered there. But at the same time she thought, why am I doing this? What difference does it make? What's the matter with me, anyway?

She sipped her drink, and looked away from the pale man and the solid man, looked at people safely distant. The men in the lounge were, for the most part, wearing sports jackets—only a few of which competed with the blaring music—and slacks. Here and there a man wore a white dinner jacket. The women were dressed more variously. The plumper were in flowered prints; a few were in dinner frocks; one or two were only partly in their dinner frocks. They must come, Mary thought—faces and bodies becoming pictures in her mind—from almost everywhere; from New York and from Des Moines; from Atlanta and Milwaukee; from the Upper East Side and, at a remove or two, from the lower. Some had been long in the sun and were brown from it, and some were newly red and a few— like the thin man at whom she did not look— were pale from the North, as she was herself. And they had come from the cold which shrinks the body to find the solace of the sun.

Bernstein had explained what the place would be like when he had offered her a job, saying at the same time she probably wouldn't take it, and that he wouldn't blame her. But he had thought of her, all the same, and thought there could be no harm in making the offer. They couldn't, he told her, pay her rates.

'However,' he added, and grinned, teeth strongly white in a lively brown face, 'we can offer you room and board. And a chance to get out of this.'

He had gestured, then, toward the window of his office, twenty stories up on Madison Avenue. Sleet beat against the glass, rattled against the glass.

He had realized that, while she was absent from New York, there would almost certainly be better jobs and she would miss them. His own agency would almost certainly have better, and others might. She would take herself out of circulation—oh, until late March, perhaps early April. But it was hers if she wanted it.

Half a dozen Florida hotels wanted to do a 'thing.' 'This thing,' he told her. The hotels were pretty much of a kind; he'd call it medium-luxury. Rates from, say, twenty to thirty or thirty-five a person, American. Not 'Gold Coast,' although one of the hotels was on the beach. Not Boca Raton. Not Palm Beach.

'Pleasant places, they sound like,' he said. 'Pleasant people, maybe. Anyhow, it ought to be warm.'

The half dozen hotels wanted to do 'this

thing' as a group, although they were not under a single management. They wanted text, which wasn't Mary Wister's problem, and pictures, which were, if she chose. Good pictures. Water color or, if she wanted, oil. If she wanted any part of it, as he supposed she wouldn't. So?

'Yes,' Mary Wister said. 'I'd like it, Bernie.'

'You're probably being a fool,' he said. 'I can't do better than I said.'

'I'd like it,' Mary repeated. 'I'm—tired of New York, Bernie.'

He looked at her quickly with his warm dark eyes. But then he smiled and said he saw her point; said that New York was lousy in February. Particularly in February. He said she could start anywhere she liked, but that if he were in her place he'd start with The Coral Isles in Key West, and come north with the spring. 'If any,' he added, looking again through the window at the driving storm. He had said he'd see to her plane tickets.

'Train,' she had told him then, and had learned that there was no train beyond Miami, only the air or the highway. Train and a bedroom and then, because it seemed simpler, Greyhound bus. She found out afterward that The Coral Isles would have sent a car, but the bus had been fine. For the three hours or so, she hadn't felt lonely in the bus, and the pictures had been bright. When the bus reached Key West, the people who had been on it vanished. It was as if they had never been;

20

they lived for three hours or so, to surround Mary Wister with an abstraction of humanity, and then the abstraction disintegrated. 'No aftertaste,' Bernie probably would say.

Here, actually in The Coral Isles, it was obviously not so simple. The job would take her a week or more (at a guess) and humanity, not in the abstract, would impinge, if she let it. She didn't, of course, have to let it. The long drink of water could smile and smile, and see where it got him.

The long drink of water was not smiling, at least at her. He was talking to the man beside him.

'It troubles you,' he was saying, to the solid man. 'It shouldn't.'

'Not as you mean it,' the solid man said. 'It has to happen from time to time. It goes with the job, you see. In this case there was no alternative. Or, none that I could accept, naturally. None that I could see in time.' The solid man paused and closed his eyes. 'Perhaps that troubles me,' he said. 'That I let it go too far; let it go until there wasn't an alternative. However—' He paused. 'He's dead and I'm here,' he said. He paused for a longer time. 'He was twenty-one,' he added.

'It shouldn't worry you,' the thin man said, in his gentle voice. 'How about another drink?' He smiled at his companion. 'I prescribe it,' he said. He raised a long, thin hand to a passing waiter, who veered.

21

This was a different waiter. It was inevitable that he should consider the three of them together, inevitable that he should look, first and expectantly, at Mary Wister, that he should, quite without realizing it, offer himself as a catalyst. The thin man, the sleepy man, waited too.

'Nothing, thank you,' Mary Wister said, wanting another drink, holding an empty glass. And, unreasonably, she was furious. Even so simple a transaction as buying a drink was impossible of achievement. You moved an inch, you nodded your head, you said, 'Martini, please,' and you locked with others. People grappled with you.

The thin man smiled faintly and ordered for himself and the solid man.

'If I could have my check, please?' Mary said.

Because this was the wrong waiter, a check took time, which Mary Wister was left to sit through, ignored (politely) yet uncomfortably conscious of herself, flushed by the consciousness of herself; as annoyed, now, with herself as with the long drink of water and the man who couldn't bother to keep his eyes open. It had all become ridiculous, and she had become ridiculous. She had become the properly brought up young woman who couldn't speak to strange men. That was the way they locked with you, grappled you in. They made you childish, made you absurd. They—

The check came and she signed it—and had to search her bag for her room key, because she had forgotten the room number, and could not write it in its allotted space. Prudish—and, in addition, incompetent. She wrote her name, hating the thin man for having created a situation out of—out of nothing.

'Miss Wister?' a football player in a red jacket asked, solicitously, with hope. She nodded. 'Mr. Grogan would be very happy if you would have a drink with him,' the red jacket told her. 'Mr. Grogan, the manager.'

'Of course,' Mary Wister said, and started to get up and found, because she had been sitting awkwardly, one foot was numb. It needed that, she thought, and stamped the foot. She followed the red jacket.

'Pretty girl,' the thin man said to the sleepy one. 'Or didn't you notice?'

'Naturally,' the sleepy man said.

'Very stand-offish,' the thin man said. 'Just toward us, do you suppose?'

'Wants to keep herself to herself,' the sleepy man said.

'Wary of wolves,' the thin man said. 'Disconcerted when her foot went to sleep.'

'Naturally,' the sleepy man said, and closed his eyes.

CHAPTER TWO

She had gone to bed early, after a drink with Mr. Grogan, who was large and red faced and white haired, who was hearty, who said, 'Any way you want to do it, lady. Any way at all,' and had seemed to mean it; after an admirable dinner at a table by a window in a big dining room, presided over by a wiry headwaiter in a frenzy about, so far as Mary could see, nothing in particular, since the service was almost as excellent as the food. She had gone out for only a little time into the soft night, and seen moonlight on the sea and on the façade of the hotel and on the bougainvillaea and softly colored lights at the bases of palm trees; had heard music from beyond the tennis courts and had gone close enough to see a patio with tables around it and couples dancing. But then she had gone up early to bed.

She had not gone immediately to sleep, because irritation remained in her mind. But now the irritation was not with the long drink of water, nor with the sleepy man, but with Mary Wister herself. For no reason at all, by getting off on the wrong foot—probably, she thought, the one which subsequently had gone to sleep—she had behaved absurdly in a situation too trivial to require behavior of any kind. That was the heart of it, she had thought,

24

stretched in bed, under a light blanket, moonlight sifting through venetian blinds onto the bed. She had made an issue where there was no issue; adopted an 'attitude' in circumstances which required nothing so positive. Nobody was trying to get to her, to impinge upon her. A man of no importance was trying to sit peaceably and have a drink, accepting with tolerance but without special interest the fact that others, including a brown-haired young woman in a green dress, were near by, also having drinks. She herself, for no reason whatever, out of a clear sky, had made a 'thing' of it. There's only to be said of me, Mary thought, that the sky wasn't clear, won't be clear for—oh, for a long time.

But then, having slept not too well on the train, having ridden a long distance in the bus, Mary had evaded the question—whatever it was—by going to sleep, and it had still been only a little after ten. Music, softened by distance, was drifting through the open window, with the moonlight, with the soft air. She had slept with few dreams, although once she had dreamed for an instant—or an hour?—of a brown hand clenched in a fist. She had awakened, and it was not yet eight o'clock.

She had put on a white sleeveless dress, with the light coat over it. She had packed up her sketch pad and carried it through silent corridors and down the stairs and through the empty lounge, past the closed piano, the tables bare of drinks. She had gone to the porch, bright now in sunlight, and found it almost empty too—but not quite empty. On a chaise longue, in the sun, the thin man was lying. Dark glasses hid his eyes. Already, the sun was reddening his face. He was very long and very thin, and stretched there, his white hands folded in his lap, he was defenseless.

Mary started across the porch and then was conscious that he had turned his head to one side and was looking at her; conscious that, once again, he was faintly smiling. She took another step and hesitated, and turned toward him.

'Good morning,' Mary said. 'It's a nice morning.'

He took off his glasses and started to sit straight. But Mary shook her head and smiled, and then walked on. Things were evened up; everything was all right again. All right, tied up and put away.

'Very,' the thin man said after her.

She forgot the long man as she walked out into the bright morning. The sea rolled in gently toward the land, and sparkled as it rolled. She went along a walk and past the tennis courts and came to a deserted, sheltered area by a sandy beach. Beach chairs and chaises were arranged there neatly, waiting for those who, later, would come to sun themselves. But now there was no one; she had it to herself. She walked out on a long pier

26

which led away from the beach and over the sparkle of the water; she passed ladders which led down from the pier into water so clear it seemed to have no depth. She stopped and watched a hundred, or a thousand, tiny fish, none longer than an inch, swimming in formation. They swam, each seemingly at a prescribed distance from the tiny fish on either side, the tiny fish before and behind, away from the land. Then there was a signal—there must have been a signal. On an instant, the little fish half turned, swimming at an angle to the land; turned again and swam toward the land; about-faced, then, faster than they could be seen to turn, and swam away again in the shallow, bright water, above the sand.

She left the little fish, still engaged in their intricate manoeuvres, and walked to the very end of the pier. She looked back, then, across the water at The Coral Isles itself, long and sprawling in the sun, seeming to reach arms out toward the sea. Now several more people were sitting, or lying, on the chairs and chaises on the porch, toasting in the sun. A hotel servant was moving about on the porch, attentive to needs which, from her distance, were not apparent, and his red jacket was bright in the sunlight. Mary Wister sat on a bench at the end of the pier and began, quickly, to sketch. She would look at things today and get them down, roughly, in black and white. The next day, or the day after, her choices made, she would

27

begin in color. One or two of the color sketches would serve, back in New York, as foundations for more finished work. For once, she had time, which was rare in her trade.

Having time, being at her trade, she forgot time. It was almost two hours before she remembered breakfast; it was another fifteen minutes before the thought of breakfast became imperative. She walked back along the pier, then. She stopped for a moment where she had seen the tiny fish, but now they were making their patterns somewhere else. She went through the sheltered area of beach, and already half a dozen sun worshippers were lying in it, wearing as little as possible and, in the cases of two women, burning as red as seemed likely or desirable. There was, Mary Wister thought, walking on, some magnification in intense coloration of the skin; surely, the woman lying face down on a chaise, did not in fact have such massive shoulders.

She went along a walk, around the tennis courts, and saw, at one side of the deserted dancing floor, tables set in sun and shade. At the same time, she saw Mr. Grogan, as large and red faced and cordial as he had been the evening before. He was sitting at a table with—yes, with the solid man of the cocktail lounge. Mr. Grogan saw her, arose beaming, and beckoned. He urged her not to tell him that she had not had breakfast. When she could not tell him this, he was all a puller out of chairs, urger

28

on of waiters.

'You've been at work already,' he told her, accusingly. 'You New Yorkers.'

Mr. Grogan was, and happened to tell her the evening before, a New Yorker himself. At least, he passed through New York, and sometimes hesitated briefly, as the season of hotel management took him from Key West to New Hampshire, and back again.

'Here's another,' Grogan told her, as she prepared to take the offered chair. 'Miss Wister, this is Captain Heimrich. Got in yesterday too. Captain, Miss Wister.'

The solid man stood up. His eyes were open now, and extremely blue. He was agreeable to meeting Miss Wister, and proved it by keeping his eyes open for several minutes. He was on orange juice; Mr. Grogan was on coffee. Mary caught up with the captain. She heard her purpose there explained, her art extolled; learned that she was going to capture some of the unspoiled beauty, the leisurely charm, of The Coral Isles.

'It must be very interesting,' Captain Heimrich said. 'Getting things down as they look.'

He said this, which was certainly commonplace enough, as if he had been thinking about the matter and had reached a conclusion. He looked at her through the very blue eyes and nodded slowly, confirming his assertion.

For a moment, then, Mary felt again as if she were being grappled with; as if something she sought to maintain were being challenged. But the feeling now was only a flicker of uneasiness, of doubt, and not, as it had been the evening before, a compulsion. She smiled at Captain Heimrich, and said it was interesting enough, and difficult enough, and that it usually didn't come out right. To which he said, 'Naturally,' and nodded again, and finished his orange juice.

'Navy?' Mary Wister asked, putting together Key West's naval base, the captain's age and air of authority and, perhaps, the very blue eyes, to make a guess.

Heimrich repeated the word. Then he said, 'Oh—no, not Navy, Miss Wister. Police.' He closed his eyes then, as if the subject tired him.

'New York State police,' Mr. Grogan said. 'Very well known man, the captain here.'

Heimrich opened his eyes briefly to look at Mr. Grogan, and closed them again.

'How interesting,' Mary Wister said, and felt like a schoolgirl. But what should she say? 'My God?'

'Now Miss Wister,' Heimrich said, and opened his eyes again. 'Now Miss Wister. Why should it be? Your work is. No doubt Mr. Grogan's is. I merely—follow people around. Wait for them to make mistakes.'

'Nonsense,' Mr. Grogan said. 'Don't let him talk that way, Miss Wister. Murderers. He's down here now convalescing. Shot it out with a murderer. Got his man. Right, captain?'

Captain Heimrich looked rather tired.

'A crazy kid,' he said, with his eyes closed. 'I shouldn't have let it come to that, naturally. Just a crazy kid.'

'With a gun,' Grogan said, and Heimrich said, his voice tired, 'Oh yes, with a gun, naturally.' It was clear that he regarded the subject as exhausted, and considered that, as a subject, it had started out very tired. He looked away, at the other tables, and the few people sitting at them, at the shelter beside the tennis court, where two couples had appeared. He was, Mary Wister thought, looking for another subject, for a distraction. Apparently he found it. There was a just perceptible change in his solid, not-mobile, face.

'Well,' he said, 'you have celebrities here, Mr. Grogan.'

'Oh yes,' Grogan said, and was pleased. 'Many.'

He looked in the direction Heimrich had been looking.

'Oh,' he said. 'You mean Wells?'

'Bronson Wells,' Heimrich said. 'Yes.'

Mary Wister was looking now—looking at a man who was facing them and talking to another man, whose back was to them. He was talking forcefully, and seemed to feel little need to listen. He was a tall man in a blue linen sports jacket, pale tan slacks. His hair was

31

black and smooth. His face was long, tapering from a massive forehead, converging as it passed a formidable nose, ending in a pointed chin. He had a small mouth and narrow lips; he had dark eyes noticeably deep set and as he talked to the man who faced him it was evident that he was looking the other in the eyes—to, Mary thought, the point of transfixation. So that was Bronson Wells. She would have known him from his pictures; his many pictures. The man who—what was it Lee had said? The man who had 'made a career out of an aberration.' Bronson Wells the lecturer, the author of books, the favorite of congressional committees. The man who could always, somewhere, find just one more subversive. The man who so often testified, so gravely testified, 'I cannot say, of my own knowledge, that Mr. So-and-So was actually a *member* of the Communist Party,' and, so saying, left Mr. So-and-So mangled in the roadway. Mr. Bronson Wells, the Source.

As she watched, Bronson Wells finished with the other man. He shook a finger at him and turned and strode away, dark head high, gaze no doubt still penetrating.

'Is he looking for them *here*?' Mary said, and Mr. Grogan for a moment looked shocked and Captain Heimrich amused.

'Oh,' Mr. Grogan said, 'there wouldn't be any of them *here*.' He spoke as a housewife might of insects of loathsome appearance and

32

annoying habits. 'He's been on tour. Here for a rest.' He paused. 'A very charming man,' he said. 'Doing great good.'

'Oh,' Captain Heimrich said. 'Naturally.'

The fact was, Mary Wister thought, Bronson Wells was doing good, perhaps even much good. He was a man of zeal; having himself sinned—by being, admittedly, a member of 'the party'—he now was a scourge of sinners. It was not necessary that he recognize gradations of sin. He was relentless in exposing those presently active in the Communist cause; he was harsh also against those who had, like himself, repented, but who had done so less vociferously. It might be true, as Lee had once pointed out, that some of the men Bronson Wells denounced had been quicker than Wells himself to see that what they had once considered an ideal had been transformed into a degradation. It could only be assumed that Wells's repentence had been more thorough, as it had certainly been more profitable. It was possible that a few relatively innocent men had been left mangled behind Mr. Wells's war chariot. But men who did not recognize human degradation when they worked for it had also been publicly liquidated. No doubt the balance was in Mr. Wells's favor. All the same, Mary thought, I wish he had a kinder mouth.

'A very interesting man,' Mr. Grogan told them. 'You must meet him.' Mr. Grogan paused. 'He is—' Mr. Grogan said, and paused again. 'Very impressive,' Mr. Grogan said, after thought. 'Very—magnetic. I think that's the word.'

Captain Heimrich had closed his eyes, and made no reply to this beyond a slow nodding of the head.

Breakfast came then—English muffins, very hot and very crisp; eggs very fresh, coffee obviously dripped through paper filters; marmalade with the flavor both of orange and of lime. Somehow, the question whether they would meet Mr. Wells and be magnetized was lost in the waiter's quick movements, the removal of covers from muffins, the pouring of coffee. Mr. Grogan himself seemed not to notice the disappearance of his suggestion. He told Mary that he hoped she would find time to get in a little tennis, or some swimming. Surely some swimming. He reminded her of the regrettable result of all work and no play.

Nevertheless, she spent the day working, conscious as the day passed, as she sketched the hotel from the parapet, the sweep of lawn and palm trees from the hotel porch, the tennis courts and the dancing enclosure beyond them, that she was watched curiously by almost everyone. She was accustomed to this and, unless the back of her neck was breathed upon, unless comments were loud behind her, she did not mind. Long ago she had learned that next, as exhibits, after working steam shovels came working artists. It was four o'clock when, finally, she snapped her pad case closed— almost catching a nose in it—and walked from the pier along the walks, among the palm trees, to her room. Then, remembering Mr. Grogan's warning, she changed into a white bathing suit, put a white robe over it, and walked back again, climbed down a ladder from the pier and swam, for a quarter of an hour or so, not too energetically, in the bright water.

When she walked back, the sun bathers were collecting themselves—and their hats and towels, their unguents, their dark glasses—and preparing to abandon the sun, as it was abandoning them. As she crossed the porch on the way back to her room, she passed the pale man, who now was appreciably less pale, who had continued to pinken in the sun. He was much where she had seen him in the morning; he was reading, but looked up as she passed. This time she smiled at him, but did not stop.

It was a little after six when she went back down to the lounge, wearing this time a silk print of pale yellow, accented in black, and looked around again for a single chair. But as she looked, Heimrich and the pale man came up from behind her and the captain, who now had his eyes open, said, 'Good evening,' in a deep, tranquil voice, and then, 'Won't you have a drink with us?'

She hesitated for an instant.

'This is Doctor MacDonald,' Heimrich said. 'Miss Wister, doctor.'

The pale man held out a long pale hand. She accepted it, and discovered it was not limp as she had thought it would be, but thinly strong. Dr. MacDonald smiled at her over their joined hands, and released hers and said, 'You've had a busy day.' He looked at her. 'You've burned the back of your neck,' he added. There was, she realized, easiness about Dr. MacDonald—doctor of what, she wondered? He demanded nothing, insisted on nothing; his interest in her neck was detached, but friendly.

'The sun's unexpected,' she said. 'I mean—'

But he nodded, and she did not need to finish. A very easy man, she thought, if still a long drink of water. She said, to Heimrich, that a drink would be fine, and went with the tall, pale Dr. MacDonald and the solid captain of police toward a corner made by a sofa and chairs.

She sat in one of the chairs while they waited, and watched as Dr. MacDonald lowered himself into a chair beside her with a kind of caution, as if he considered himself breakable. She watched as Captain Heimrich put a hand on the arm of the sofa as he prepared to sit and then, rather awkwardly, withdrew the hand and sit slowly and a little awkwardly without steadying himself.

'We both,' Dr. MacDonald said, 'seem about to fall apart, don't we, Miss Wister?'

36

His voice was amused.

'Well—' Mary said.

'The captain here,' Dr. MacDonald told her, 'is recovering from a bullet through the right shoulder, earned in line of duty. I, on the other hand, merely turned my car over, with internal—' he paused. 'Dislocations,' he finished. He regarded Mary Wister. 'I like to avoid mysteries,' he told her. 'You'll have a martini?' He looked reflectively at, apparently, the ceiling. 'Very dry, very cold, lemon peel,' he told her. 'As yesterday?' He looked down from the ceiling. 'I listened,' he said.

She said, 'Please.'

It was Dr. MacDonald who repeated her order to the waiter, added, 'Scotch and soda,' and looked at Captain Heimrich. Heimrich had closed his eyes, which apparently did not affect his vision. 'Bourbon,' Heimrich said. 'Plain water.' He paused and added, 'Naturally.'

'Why?' Dr. MacDonald said, with evident interest. 'Why "naturally"?'

'Now doctor,' Heimrich said. 'Now doctor. I really don't know, nat—' He stopped. He opened his eyes. Then he laughed.

'Now this is very comfortable,' Mr. Grogan said, over the back of Heimrich's sofa. 'Mind if we join you?'

The three of them looked up—looked at Grogan, red faced, white haired, at Bronson Wells, whose dark face seemed untouched by

37

sun, whose hair was very black. (And whose mouth, Mary Wister noted, was still very small.)

'By all means,' MacDonald said, and stood up. After a moment, Heimrich also stood up. Bronson Wells was passed to the doctor, passed to Mary Wister. They partook of Mr. Wells, who regarded them intently from dark eyes and spoke to them in a voice trained for the platform. It was hardly possible, indeed, to realize that a voice so modulated, so impressive, was being used for no greater purpose than to acknowledge, and conventionally to approve, the existence of Miss Mary Wister, Dr. Barclay MacDonald and Captain Heimrich.

Mr. Grogan and Mr. Wells sat, Grogan on the sofa—and a little on the edge of the sofa; Wells in a chair half facing Mary's. Mr. Grogan sat as he did, Mary thought, so that he might better keep an eye on things, which he resolutely did. A waiter approached at just under a dead run and said, 'Yes sir,' hurriedly, with a slight gasp. 'As usual, Jimmy,' Grogan said. 'Mr. Wells?'

'Ginger ale,' Mr. Wells said, as if in benediction, and Mary was conscious of looking at him with some surprise, and that Dr. MacDonald looked at the scourge of the unrighteous with something which might have been almost consternation. Captain Heimrich looked at nothing, being again engaged in resting his eyes.

'Yes *sir*,' the waiter said, in a tone of gratification. He went off at a trot.

'Are you *the* Bronson Wells?' Dr. MacDonald enquired.

'Yes,' Bronson Wells said, with no hesitation. Well, Mary Wister thought, he is, of course. What should he say?

'Oh,' Dr. MacDonald said. He paused, considering. 'It must be interesting,' he said. 'You have revealed a great deal, Mr. Wells.'

'Termites,' Bronson Wells said. 'Yes. You— that is to say, of course, *we*—in this country have been living in a fool's paradise, unaware of the force against us—of the deviousness, of the danger.'

He fixed his eyes sternly on Dr. MacDonald, who nodded acceptance of the statement or who, at any rate, nodded.

'Now Mr. Wells,' Captain Heimrich said, 'we are being warned, aren't we? Have been, wouldn't you say?'

Wells turned a stern gaze on Heimrich, who responded by opening his eyes briefly and then closing them again.

'I am surprised to hear you say that, sir,' Wells said, his voice vibrating. 'You—a police officer. You who should know the danger.' He shook his head. 'The conspiracy is vast,' he said. 'Our whole society is honeycombed.'

Mr. Grogan looked uneasily around the lounge of his hotel, bright with people at their ease, with waiters darting among them; the waiters conscious of Mr. Grogan's managerially roving eye, unaware that, at that moment, he was speculating about honeycombers rather than the efficiency of the staff.

'I have no doubt,' Dr. MacDonald said, 'that you know a great deal of which the rest of us are ignorant.'

'I do,' said Bronson Wells. 'I do indeed.'

Mr. Wells turned back toward Heimrich and seemed about to continue. But then his dark gaze fixed itself on something more distant. He stood up. He said, his voice not raised but carrying with practiced ease, 'Oh—*Shepard*!'

They all looked, dutifully. They looked at a thin, wiry man. Probably in his late thirties. He had neatly parted blond hair, which lay quietly on his head; he should, Mary Wister instantly thought, be wearing a neat blue suit, probably double-breasted, with a white handkerchief neatly pointing from the breast pocket. (Or had she read somewhere that handkerchiefs no longer appeared in peaks, but in a mere piping of white?) He was, however, wearing a yellow shirt and a tie of deeper yellow, above gray slacks, to be sure, but under a sports jacket which seemed, although profusely colored, to be, by majority vote, dark green. Mr. Shepard (or Shepard Something?) looked like a New Yorker who had, resolutely, gone native.

He had stopped at Wells's call. Now he turned and came toward them, smiling. When

40

he was close enough he said, 'Oh, here you are, Wells.'

'I,' said Bronson Wells, 'expected you yesterday.'

There was nothing precisely in Bronson Well's voice to justify Mary's feeling that the gayly costumed man was undergoing rebuke. Wells's voice was modulated; he was polite and even gracious. Mary Wister was nevertheless left feeling that Shepard would have been advised to have arrived the day before.

Shepard—Paul Shepard, as it turned out—did not appear to be a man rebuked, so, Mary decided, she had been imagining things. A habit of mine, she told herself; oh, certainly, a habit of mine. Shepard merely said, as he shook hands with Bronson Wells, that things had held him up in New York; shaking hands around with the others, giving each of the men a precise handshake, measured out; giving Mary herself the smallest, most complimentary, of dividends, he expressed his pleasure crisply and with confidence. He had, Mary discovered, gray eyes set wide apart. Mary changed her half-reached opinion of him. The rather flamboyant clothes he wore were not, as she had at first assumed, compensation for an inner feeling of inadequacy. Watching the wiry blond man, so unassertively competent in movement through the social ordeal (as it always was to her, at any rate) of multiple introduction, she thought the unmodulated vigor of his costume might, more accurately than the blue suit she still was sure he commonly wore, express what Mr. Paul Shepard was all about. He wore plumage when he could, and it was not a disguise. Perhaps it was a revelation.

But she was guessing, of course, and guessing on no evidence. Shepard sat by Grogan on the long sofa and talked to both, and more drinks came. Also, more people came. A dark-haired girl with deep blue eyes, wearing a summer evening frock, quite young and reasonably beautiful, appeared out of nowhere, and was Mrs. Paul Shepard. It was easy to understand, of course, what had brought her there, but it was not so easy to get clearly in the mind the relationship to the rest of another couple, both man and woman tall and middle-aged, both revealing the South in speech, but with accent overlaid, modified by less regional idioms. Mary had been talking to Barclay MacDonald, very pleasantly, about nothing in particular, sipping a second drink, and Judge and Mrs. Robert Sibley were part of the expanding group. But who had brought them into it was not apparent.

They widened the circle; a waiter moved chairs into the circle; he found another table and further ash trays, and took orders for further drinks. 'My round,' Paul Shepard told everybody, and raised a firm, commanding hand against the murmur. 'My round,' he repeated, and made a circle with his hand, which included everyone. The waiter checked glasses, trotted off.

'Actually,' MacDonald said to Mary, taking up where he had left off, 'I'm a country doctor.'

She did not believe him; she said so.

'But I am,' he said. 'Outside New Haven. In the country.'

'And Yale,' she said. 'Aren't you?'

'Primarily a country doctor,' he insisted. 'Unused to the intellectual life.'

'This?' she said, and indicated.

'Gentlemen of distinction,' he told her, his voice solemn. 'A famous lecturer. A gentleman Up for Confirmation.' His voice provided the capitalization. He indicated Sibley.

'Is he?' Mary said. 'What for?'

But that Dr. MacDonald had been trying to remember, and had not been successful in remembering. Something big enough to make a committee wrangle over him; probably, therefore, something diplomatic. MacDonald reiterated that he himself lived a secluded life. 'Measles,' he told her. 'Now and then mumps. Upset tummies.

'I,' he told her, 'am ill at ease with greatness. Did you put something on your sunburn?'

She told him she tanned, with luck. She looked and said, 'Here's another.'

The newcomer to the expanding party was a tall, ruddy man, hair crew-cut, powerful shoulders slanting athletically under the fabric

43

of a gray jacket from Brooks Brothers. He had been, fifteen years or so ago, at Princeton or Harvard or Yale or, if not to one of them, at Dartmouth or Cornell or Brown. Why, thought Mary Wister, he's almost anybody I grew up with, almost everybody. He had been walking by, with the easy air of a man going no place much and in no hurry to get there, and this time—Mary was almost sure—it was Grogan who had signaled him into their harborage. He came in easily, powerful but manageable. He was William Oslen; he was 'Bill Oslen, everybody,' since it was no longer practicable that the circle be manoeuvred. He made a casual, friendly gesture, and found lodgement on an ottoman, which he himself pulled to the fringe of the circle.

'Now there,' Dr. Barclay MacDonald said, for Mary's ear, 'is an anomaly. What would you pick him as?'

'As?' Mary repeated. 'Oh—somebody in Wall Street?'

'You see?' MacDonald said. 'An anomaly. Actually, he's a concert pianist. I've heard him play.'

'In your native village,' Mary told him.

'At New Haven,' MacDonald said, 'we are very musical. We hold the standards high.'

Mary looked at the tall, thin doctor; at his long, expressive face; saw the faintest of lines between his brows.

'You'd think he'd be out concerting at this

time of year,' MacDonald said. 'However.'

He dismissed it. He was casual, detached, interested.

'This is a very lively place,' he told Mary Wister. 'If we sit here long enough, we'll meet everybody. Did you know that former President Hoover comes here to get his hair cut?'

'For heaven's sake,' Mary said.

'Off his yacht,' MacDonald told her. 'Mr. Grogan is very pleased.' He paused. 'Naturally,' he said. He looked at Heimrich, then, but Heimrich was being talked to by Bronson Wells. Mary looked also. The police captain had his eyes open.

'Is that *the* William Oslen?' the slim and reasonably beautiful young woman who was—wait a minute, now—who was Mrs. Paul Shepard, said from Dr. MacDonald's right. She was there unexpectedly, perched on the arm of someone else's chair. 'The pianist?'

It was, MacDonald told her, turning toward her; it assuredly was. His voice was grave, polite. He remained turned toward the reasonably beautiful Mrs. Shepard. Mary listened elsewhere; listened, as was easy, to Bronson Wells's projected voice. She turned toward Heimrich and Bronson Wells, and Heimrich opened his blue eyes briefly, as if to let her in. He closed them, then, and continued to listen.

'—an aroused citizenry,' Bronson Wells was

45

saying. 'That, you will admit, is essential. These are not ordinary times.'

Heimrich lighted a cigarette and offered one to Wells. Wells refused it with a sharp, rather impatient, movement of his head. 'Don't use them,' Wells said.

'Possibly,' Heimrich said, 'no times ever were. But I see what you mean, naturally.'

'Apathy,' Bronson Wells said. 'A willingness to let things slide. What we face is a conspiracy. I know. Once I was part of it. A conspiracy of fanatics.'

'I merely said,' Heimrich told him, speaking still with his eyes closed, 'that we have policemen. Of one kind and another, for one special purpose and another. We have laws. Naturally, I'm not without prejudice—prejudice in favor of law.' He opened his eyes. 'And in favor of policemen,' he added, and smiled.

Bronson Wells did not smile. Fleetingly, Mary Wister wondered if he ever did; if he ever had.

'You are like the rest,' Wells said. 'We've lived soft; we've always lived soft. They're right in saying that. We temporize, give everybody his say, fritter away the little time we have. What we have to do first, before anything, is to save our way of life. I tell you, I *know*!'

Heimrich closed his eyes again, and nodded. But then he opened his eyes again.

'Only,' he said, 'that *is* our way of life, isn't it,

46

Mr. Wells? To let everybody have his say, hold him responsible for his actions? Police his actions, under law? Isn't that how we differ from them?' He turned toward Mary, slowly, his eyes still open. 'I'm afraid Mr. Wells thinks I'm apathetic,' he told her.

'It's not personal,' Wells said. 'I merely wonder whether you, and men like you, are able to face reality. If I have a mission, it is to wake up people like you.'

There was, Mary thought, something strange, obscurely worrying, in Wells's use, in so matter of fact a fashion, of the word 'mission.' It was such a heavy word; it was too heavy for everyday; certainly too heavy for a casual drinking group in a resort hotel, in a place where it was warm in February.

'Well,' said Heimrich, 'I'm just a policeman, you know. I just try to help enforce the laws we've got.' His manner ended it and Wells, after a moment of scrutiny, accepted an ending. He said, across Heimrich, 'You mustn't think I'm a man of one idea, Miss Wister.' He regarded her. 'Although perhaps I am,' he said. 'I—'

But there was a stir, then, and he did not try, against it, to continue. Grogan, who had been talking to Shepard and, beyond him, to the dignified Mrs. Sibley, looked at his watch and announced, generally, that he had to get to work. It was, he said, sometimes hard to remember that he worked there; nevertheless,

47

he did. He stood up and there was that slight uncertainty through the group, that sympathetic consultation of watches, which heralds disintegration. Mary looked at her own watch; it was not yet seven o'clock, hence half an hour, at least, from dinner.

But Grogan, standing, was taking care of things. A waiter trotted across the lounge and was told that it would be the same around for everybody, on Grogan. Mrs. Sibley looked doubtfully at her half-empty glass; William Oslen, on the other hand, looked with interest at his empty one. Mary shared Mrs. Sibley's doubt, being midway of her second. But, she thought, I worked all day.

'Do you good,' Dr. MacDonald said from beside her. 'Dry work, listening.'

The premonitory fidgeting died out; relaxed, they watched Mr. Grogan go toward his managerial chores, stopping from time to time along the way to greet. The waiter jotted notations and departed for the bar. Captain Heimrich appeared to fall asleep; Bronson Wells turned to Paul Shepard on his left. It seemed to Mary that he turned with decision, as if he had been waiting for the time to come.

'Do you like turtles?' Dr. MacDonald asked, with his air of detached interest.

Mary repeated, 'Turtles?'

'There's a marine museum in town,' he told her. 'Went there this afternoon, while the frivolous swam and tennised. Very instructive.'

48

She looked at him.

'Well,' he said, 'the turtles were large. They have barracudas, too. Very savage-looking.' He considered. 'I'm against barracudas,' he said. 'For turtles, in a mild way, but against barracudas.' He looked, so far as she could tell, absently, toward Bronson Wells. He looked back toward her. 'I'm beginning to feel better,' he said. 'Makes me silly, probably, but all the same—' He finished his drink. He looked at the empty glass. 'I'm afraid this is very bad for me,' he told her. 'Have you been in town yet?'

She shook her head, watching his face. Without in any sense leaving her, withdrawing from her, he was still very evidently conscious of the others around them—of the sleepy Heimrich, of Robert Sibley, who was talking with dignity to Oslen, who looked so little like a pianist; of Paul Shepard, who had turned partly away from his wife—who had joined him on the long sofa—and was listening to Bronson Wells, his face expressionless. Mrs. Shepard was talking to Mrs. Sibley. Everybody was accounted for, taken care of. The waiter arrived, and took further care of everybody. Mary hesitated momentarily, but let him leave a fresh martini in front of her.

'It's quite a mixture,' MacDonald said. He tasted his new drink. 'The town, I mean. Several honky-tonks. Do you like honky-tonks?'

'Not terribly,' she said.

49

He shook his head.

'One of them,' he said, 'has twenty beautiful girls under twenty. It says so in lights. Don't you want to look at twenty beautiful girls under twenty?'

'Not terribly,' she said again. 'Should I?'

'I can't think of any reason why,' he said. 'I remember now about Sibley. It's some kind of a U.N. job. He's under suspicion of not believing in Chiang Kai-shek. He—' But then Dr. MacDonald stopped, and shrugged.

It was as if there had been a signal, but there had been none. With MacDonald's sudden silence, there was a general silence in the circle—a silence which one voice broke. Characteristically, Mary Wister thought, the voice was Bronson Wells's.

'I'd advise you to think about it again, Shepard,' Wells said. 'I'd advise it most seriously.'

Paul Shepard merely looked at him. If he answered, it was by an expression in his eyes.

CHAPTER THREE

That was the first of the incidents, if one could call it an incident. Words broke clear in a sudden, accidental silence; words which probably meant nothing in particular. No doubt Bronson Wells, so evidently a serious man, frequently admonished even chance acquaintances to think again about something, to seek to bring their ideas into accord with his, which was to say in accord with the truth. No doubt he often so advised in a tone which lacked little, if it lacked anything, of warning. It was, after all, his career to warn. Perhaps Paul Shepard had, in some fashion, displayed apathy.

The general talk resumed; it seemed to Mary that it was resumed quickly, almost nervously. Mrs. Shepard spoke first, her voice a little raised, to Mrs. Sibley, and she spoke of a shop she had found on Duval Street—a small and charming shop, a shop of blouses and gay Guatemalan skirts, of the most delightfully impossible of summery hats. They, she and Mrs. Sibley, must go tomorrow. They—

'—how closely they actually listen, I can't say, of course,' William Oslen said. 'What it means to them, I don't know. What they really hear—who knows? All I can say is—'

That was another snatch. Now there were snatches everywhere. 'So keyed-up I have to take two every night,' Penny Shepard told Mrs. Sibley, who said, 'Oh—my dear!' Then Barclay MacDonald said, 'I have the greatest trouble getting women to listen to me. They always wander off.'

She turned to him, said she was sorry. He smiled and shook his head.

'Of course,' he said, 'it is quite possible that I

am not an interesting man. I've often speculated about that.'

He looked as if he expected comment.

'Oh,' Mary said. 'I'm sure—'

'Don't say you're sure I am,' he told her. 'You have no data. The chances are very high that I would, on further acquaintance, bore you excessively. I have, for example, an almost irresistible inclination to discuss cation reactions and many people find them dull. Would you be interested in cation reactions?'

She hadn't, she said, the faintest idea. He regarded her with attention and shook his head. He told her he doubted it very much.

'I can't,' he said, 'even interest the captain, although I told him something to watch out for. A way of poisoning. He considered it too involved.' He regarded Heimrich. 'Although he is, actually, an imaginative man.'

Heimrich gave no indication of hearing this. His eyes were, however, open. He was regarding William Oslen, but there was nothing in his face to indicate to what purpose. Mary looked at Oslen, who was listening to Sibley and now and then nodding in agreement. She turned back to MacDonald and said, 'Tell me about—what is it?—cations?'

'I shall be—' MacDonald began, and stopped. William Oslen stood up suddenly, apparently in a middle of one of Sibley's sentences, and looked with evident surprise at

52

a slight, dark girl who was coming along the aisle left down the center of the lounge. She was a black-haired young woman, untanned and almost pale; her mouth bright against the pallor of her face; her dark eyes very wide apart. I never, Mary Wister thought, saw anyone so vivid.

'Rachel!' Oslen said. 'Of all people— Rachel!'

She smiled at him.

'The last person,' Oslen said, his voice a little raised. 'I thought you were—' He stopped and shook his head, while he took a step toward the small, vivid girl and held out a hand. He did not say where he had thought her to be, if that was what he had planned to say.

'Hello, William,' the girl said, and took his hand. 'I hadn't the faintest idea you were here. Not the faintest.'

And her voice, also, was a little raised as if, Mary thought, she spoke not only to Oslen, but to all around, sharing with them all her surprise at this, evidently, most improbable of chance meetings. Involuntarily, Mary looked at Barclay MacDonald, and saw his eyebrows rise, just perceptibly. It was only as she saw the lifted brows that Mary realized why she had, as if for confirmation, turned to the thin, tall man beside her. Sharing, without words, his suggested question whether the pianist and the girl were not both, somehow, a little overdoing astonishment, Mary realized for the first time the question in her own mind.

But then the men were pushing aside tables, and standing while Oslen brought the dark, vivid girl into the circle, reiterating his astonishment that she should be there at all. Introducing her, he managed to get back into the character he had, to Mary at any rate, temporarily stepped out of. He was, again, the maturing graduate of a good Eastern school; he was at once assured, yet modest, almost diffident. He turned out, also, to have an extraordinarily good memory for names. The girl was Rachel Jones. She was poised, assured, smiling, repeating names as they were offered her. She was light and graceful then, on an ottoman between William Oslen and Robert Sibley.

'You could,' MacDonald said, for Mary's ear only, 'have knocked him over with a feather.' He regarded her. 'Sometimes,' he said, 'I notice a lack in myself. I would have been less surprised by—by a zebra. I mean, a zebra dropping in for cocktails. Have I lost my sense of wonder?'

'It did seem rather dramatic,' Mary said.

'Yes,' MacDonald said. 'Or—dramatized?' He looked at Heimrich and, this time, Heimrich turned toward them.

'Now doctor,' Heimrich said. 'Why would they do that, do you think?'

MacDonald shook his head.

'No,' Heimrich said. 'I don't either.

Although, you may be right, I think.' He paused. 'Or half right, naturally.'

The conversation was general again; it was possible again for two or three to draw a small, enclosing circle around themselves. Mary found that she was in such a circle with Barclay MacDonald and, momentarily, with Heimrich. But then Heimrich closed his eyes again and merely sat, comfortably enough, apparently quite contented, and Barclay MacDonald told her that the reaction was an exchange of ions, under controlled conditions, in elements. She listened and did not understand a word of it, and sipped her drink and did not wonder about anything, except, mildly, about cations, which this long drink of water, this pleasant man, was not really trying to explain to her, but was merely talking about, with a kind of detached happiness. It was, she thought, surprising how interested one could become in something about which one did not understand a word.

'—because of the positive charge,' Barclay MacDonald said.

'Oh yes,' Mary said, 'I understand that,' but did not.

'With the exchange reaction set up—' MacDonald said, and Mary Wister listened to the end of the sentence, and nodded to show that she understood, which was not in the slightest degree the case. The long, thin face of the country doctor from outside New Haven took on animation as he talked of cations. Mary found herself thinking of them as soft furred, with paws, although she assumed that this was not the case with them.

Then, suddenly, relaxation was again broken in upon, as it had been first when Wells had spoken to Paul Shepard in what was so nearly a tone of warning and, for a second time, when the concert pianist who looked like a stockbroker had greeted the vivid Rachel Jones with such surprise. This time it was broken by a sudden, high giggle from, incongruously, Mrs. Robert Sibley. The giggle had an almost shattering quality. Mrs. Robert Sibley, dignified wife of, presumably, a potential diplomat, had much too evidently had much too much to drink. The situation was unnerving.

Mrs. Sibley still sat erect in her chair; her gray hair remained in dignified order. But Mrs. Sibley's face was unbecomingly red and her giggle was embarrassing. She looked across the circle at Bronson Wells and said, in a high, clear voice, 'You're a funny man. A funny, funny, *funny* man.' Then she giggled again. '*Every*body thinks you're a funny man,' she told Bronson Wells, for everybody to hear. Wells looked at her, his face unchanged, his eyes intent.

'Don't *look* at me like that!' Mrs. Sibley said, and now her voice was too loud for the circle, was almost loud enough for the whole of the

56

lounge. She stood as she spoke, and in standing knocked over the glass in front of her.

By that time, Judge Sibley was beside her, had a firm hand on her arm. His touch seemed to sober her; she looked around at the others with a strange, unbelieving expression on her face.

'Time we had some dinner, Florence,' Sibley said. 'Time we both had some dinner.'

And he did not, either by word or the expression on his face, apologize to anyone for his wife's behavior. He did look for a long moment at Bronson Wells, and for a moment Mary thought he was about to say something to him. But he said nothing, and led his wife from the circle. In the aisle between the chairs and tables she walked erectly, with dignity. After a few steps, he released her arm.

That was the third incident. It broke up the cocktail hour. It broke the group into its components. And Mary Wister was surprised, walking between the long thin doctor and the solid policeman from New York, to discover that the three of them had, somehow, managed to become one of the components. It seemed entirely natural that she should join them at their table when they reached the dining room although, as far as location went, it was not so desirable a table as the one she had had the evening before.

It was not, indeed, at all a desirable table. It was near no window; it was near the front of the big room, where it amounted to a promontory, jutting forward toward the entrance and the rail which enclosed, but did not diminish, the musicians. Sitting so that she faced the entrance, Mary had an admirable view of the wiry headwaiter, tonight in even a greater frenzy than the night before—tonight gesturing with anger toward remiss waiters, slapping a hand sharply against a sheaf of menus to call wandering attentions to the business at hand, shaking his head in hopelessness. But he was deft and quick in finding tables for newcomers; in making those realignments which, even in a resort hotel where seating is theoretically stabilized, so often become necessary as guests shift alliances among themselves—as Mary had, in abandoning her table by the window to join the long drink of water and the solid Heimrich in this advanced outpost.

The three of them had gone directly to the dining room from the lounge; the rest of the group apparently had not. They were midway of jumbo shrimps in Coral Isles Sauce when the first of the others who had congregated in the lounge—around, was it, the nucleus of Bronson Wells?—entered the dining room.

Paul Shepard had taken time to change; perhaps the gaudiness of his earlier raiment had, in the end, frightened him. He had made the change complete; the neat blond man was now neater than ever in black trousers and white dinner jacket. He was also, Mary thought, somewhat more in character. He and his reasonably beautiful wife, graceful in her summery evening frock, did not hesitate at the entrance. They nodded to the headwaiter's bow and went down the center of the room toward, it was evident, an assigned table. Penny Shepard was smiling, carefree. Paul Shepard did not smile.

Oslen and the vivid Rachel Jones came next and presented a problem to the headwaiter, who looked around anxiously, slapped his sheaf of menus imploringly, finally brightened and led them the length of the dining room. Passing, Oslen and then the girl nodded and smiled at Mary and MacDonald, at Heimrich, who regarded them with blue eyes quite widely open.

'Now that—' he began, and then stopped when the others turned to him and waited. 'Nothing,' he said. 'Quite probably I'm mistaken.'

They waited longer, but he shook his head. He concentrated on vichyssoise.

The Sibleys came next, dignity wrapped about them. It was quite impossible, looking at the tall, gray-haired woman beside the taller, gray-haired man, to believe that, less than half an hour before, she had giggled outrageously, told Bronson Wells that he was a funny, funny, *funny* man. Like the Shepards before them, the Sibleys accepted the bow of the headwaiter and went their own way.

When Bronson Wells came he came alone. He gestured aside the headwaiter and looked around the room, saw Mary and nodded but did not smile, continued what appeared to be a search. Then he found what he sought and, after a word to the headwaiter, moved toward it—toward, as it turned out, them. Halfway down the room, at the side, he stopped beside the table at which the Sibleys sat. He said something and, after a moment, joined them at their table.

'Well,' Barclay MacDonald said, 'all is forgiven.' He turned back and looked, thoughtfully, at pompano on his plate. 'Do you know,' he said, to the pompano, 'I find it difficult to like Mr. Wells.' He looked at Heimrich. 'Have you any feeling others share my difficulty?'

'Now doctor,' Heimrich said. 'We're all on vacation, aren't we? Except Miss Wister, here. We don't even have to speculate, do we?'

'Nevertheless,' MacDonald said, 'you have, haven't you? About Oslen and this Miss Jones of his, for example?'

'Now doctor,' Heimrich said, and closed his eyes. 'Now doctor. Do you diagnose the people you meet?'

'Yes,' MacDonald said. 'Certainly. You are in excellent health, incidentally, barring the shoulder. Miss Wister has a sunburned neck and—' He stopped.

60

'And?' she said.

'Yesterday, a chip on the shoulder,' he said. 'It's fallen off, now.' He smiled.

She hesitated a moment. What business was it—? But then she felt herself smiling in return, and did not hinder the smile.

'It melted,' she said. 'Melted in the sun.'

'You are a very nice girl,' MacDonald said. 'Had I mentioned that? I can't remember that I had. Will you dance with me this evening?' He looked at the orchestra, busy in its enclosure. 'The orchestra is really an outdoor type,' he said.

'Yes,' Mary said. 'I'd like to.'

'She's a very nice girl, isn't she, captain?' Barclay MacDonald said.

But Heimrich had turned a little in his chair and was looking down the length of the room. Watching him, Mary decided he was looking again at William Oslen and the girl inadequately named Jones. They were at a table for two; they seemed to be talking with animation.

Heimrich turned back, rejoined them.

'Miss Wister?' Heimrich said. 'Why, naturally, doctor. Naturally.'

*　　　*　　　*

The moon had only just risen, but already the world was white with it. The palm trees threw long black shadows on the grass; the

61

graveled walks were white in moonlight. The sea sparkled peacefully. They walked down one of the paths to the parapet and turned there to look back at the sprawling hotel, at its lights, at the moonlight on its roof. The porch was a composition in black and white, dark shadows and bright tile. Mary Wister and Barclay MacDonald found low chairs on the lawn and lowered themselves into them, MacDonald very carefully, rueful at his care. He was not what he had been, he told Mary. Not at all what he had been.

'But you will be?' she asked.

'Oh yes,' he said. 'I think so, now. Talk about yourself.'

Oddly enough, she did; unexpectedly enough, she did. She did not talk about Lee. She talked about her work and only half realized how MacDonald's interest, evident in his face, evident in the little he said to prompt her, led her on. She had never, she thought (but the thought did not stop her) talked so much to anyone about what painting meant to her, or might some day mean to her. He was easy to talk to, quiet in the low chair, in the moonlight. It was after some time that she said he had asked for it, had got her started.

'No,' he said. 'You talk well. And I talked about cations, remember. A much dryer subject.'

'I didn't really understand much of it,' Mary said. 'Any of it, really.'

'No,' he said. 'I don't suppose you did. It was—' He ended the sentence there. 'I had a brother who was an artist,' he said. 'Among other things, an artist. He felt as you do, I imagine. He was doing quite good things, I think. But—he died.'

'I'm sorry,' she said.

'Yes,' he said. 'I'm sorry too.' He was silent for a moment. 'Very sorry,' he said. He spoke abstractedly, as if from memories, and was silent afterward. Mary said nothing. She lay back in the chair and looked at a palm, its high hanging coconuts sharp and strange in the moonlight. After a little she was conscious that Barclay MacDonald was looking at her. She did not turn, but was aware that she waited for him to come back out of the past—waited contentedly, sure that he would come. It did not seem, any longer, strange that she should have this confidence in, this expectation from, a man she had first met not much more than a day ago.

'It is a fine night,' he said. 'A striking night. It almost looks man-made.'

'People have got self-conscious about the moon,' she said. She continued to regard the palm tree.

'Because it rhymes too easily,' he told her. 'It is insufficiently esoteric.'

'It's all right,' she said. 'A palm tree is an improbable thing, when you really look at it.'

Then, from the area beyond the tennis

courts, the orchestra started a rhumba. There was no doubt that the orchestra was best in the open spaces.

'That,' he said, 'is laying it on almost too thick. However—'

She turned her head then, and found he was still watching her. His face was in shadow, and she could only guess at his expression.

'You want what?' she said. 'A note of contrast?'

'I suppose so,' he said. 'I suppose I'm suspicious of—serenity. That we all are. You find you're waiting for the incongruous irony. Or what they used to call the prat-fall.'

'You worry it,' she said. 'Why, Doctor MacDonald?'

'I don't know,' he said. 'Perhaps I've just lost the knack of not worrying things. It's a jumpy world.'

But at that moment, she thought, it was not actually a jumpy world, for her or, except in the abstract, for him. It was an improbable world of moonlight and vari-lighted palm trees and music floating across a lawn. He is, she thought, like so many men. He can't admit now, just as now; see what, at this second, there is to see, before the moon moves and the shadows change or—or the world does a prat-fall.

'You agreed to dance,' he said, and proved her point. She laughed, very lightly. She felt pleased with both of them, and did not try to decide why she was pleased.

'Of course,' she said. 'We'll go and dance.'

They walked across the lawn. As he walked beside her he cast a very long shadow in front of them. He was, certainly, a very long man.

There were tables grouped around the dance floor, which was partly—and that did seem to lay it on a little—in the shadow of a palm tree. The headwaiter was sharply black and white on the outskirts; he advanced toward them. He led them behind several tables to a table at the far end of the dance floor, close to the high hedge beyond which were the tennis courts. He pulled out their chairs; then he stood and looked anxiously around him. A boy in a white jacket came almost at once, and they ordered drinks.

There were half a dozen couples on the floor, dancing in more than half a dozen ways. The orchestra was involved now in a samba; one of the couples accepted this with grace. Another couple essayed it; the others did what occurred to them. In the case of Judge and Mrs. Sibley, this was to walk, to turn and circle, with dignity, to music which was, which had to be, playing only for their ears. The orchestra reached the end and flourished and the dancers applauded. The Sibleys walked off together, to a table in the shadows. The other couples remained, waiting. The orchestra began again, this time in simpler rhythm. Barclay MacDonald stood up and held a hand down to her—a long, slender, surprisingly muscular hand.

He danced well; better, Mary thought, than she did. He moved with unexpected lightness, and assurance, weaving among the others on the floor. William Oslen and the dark Rachel Jones danced near and Oslen smiled at them above his partner's black hair. 'Great night,' Oslen said, as they passed.

The music stopped and they went back to the table, and found drinks waiting, and sipped. It began again, and this time they did not dance, but sat watching. The Sibleys were on the floor again, and now Grogan, with a woman they had not seen before. Midway of the number, the Shepards came out of the shadows and danced superlatively well together.

Mary and MacDonald danced again and sat again and, when he indicated her glass enquiringly, she shook her head.

'I want to start early tomorrow,' she said. 'There was a certain light this morning.'

He nodded, and offered her a cigarette, and took one.

'One more,' he said, 'and I'll let you go.'

The orchestra had paused for cigarettes of their own. Waiters in white coats multiplied, more cigarette ends were red in the shadows, and now there were voices. After a time, the orchestra stepped on cigarette butts and arranged itself. The leader advanced in front with a cornet. He was a slender, dark man in a

66

white jacket. He gave a down beat with his cornet and the orchestra began. This time the rhythm was extremely intricate. MacDonald raised eyebrows, but Mary shook her head.

'It's beyond me,' she said. He nodded.

It was beyond a good many, apparently. At first, no one went to the floor. Then a young couple—the couple which had done well by the samba—went out and began to glide. Encouraged, another pair tried it, but their feet were worried. The leader, with the orchestra swinging behind him, raised the cornet. The other instruments quietened and the cornet spoke, high and clear.

Then Bronson Wells was on the floor with Penny Shepard in his arms. They danced well, although with this partner Mrs. Shepard was clearly the better. There was a grace, an assurance, in her dancing which was almost professional—which might well be professional. Nevertheless, it was clear that Wells was leading. They circled wide, near the edge of the floor; moved down the length of the floor, then, on the side nearest the orchestra. The cornet was clear and sweet in the night. As he played, the cornettist turned with the rhythm from side to side to side, seeming to play now for one of the dancing couples, now for another.

He turned toward Wells and Penny Shepard as they danced nearer and the music from the trumpet reached out toward them. But then, as

67

the sound rose it seemed for a second to falter and then, almost crazily, it broke. The note was shattered; the cornet wailed higher—wailed into harsh discord, until finally it seemed to shriek, angry, as if to burlesque the night, to howl down music.

The sound lasted for only a second, and then the other instruments swelled behind it and the cornet was silent. For a second its player held it still to his lips. Then he lowered it angrily and shook it, as if to shake the discord out of it. As he did this, he looked at Wells and the girl in his arms. They, and the others on the floor, had stopped when the music broke. Wells was facing the cornettist and looked over Penny Shepard's head at him or, to Mary, seemed to.

But then, the cornet was raised again, caught the rhythm again, was pure again in the moonlight, in the night's quiet. The dancers moved again.

That was the fourth incident.

'Well,' Mary said across the table. 'There's the prat-fall.'

Barclay MacDonald nodded, but he was not looking at her. He was looking at Bronson Wells. The muscles were hard in the physician's thin face.

CHAPTER FOUR

Mary Wister dreamed that someone was knocking, slowly, heavily, tirelessly. She heard herself saying, 'Yes?' before she awoke. Again, almost awake, she said, 'Yes? Who is it?' and then realized that the sound did not come from the door of her room, but from outside. She lay a moment trying to identify the slow, irregular thumping. Then she went to the open window.

Two men were working on the palm trees, harvesting coconuts. One of the men had a long pole with pruning shears at the end of it; he would snip with the shears and the coconut would fall, thump hollowly on the lawn, bounce and roll for a moment. The second man would pick it up. Both men wore singlets and khaki trousers; the man with the pole dodged coconuts as they fell, and the other laughed at him and he laughed in turn. They seemed to consider what they were doing as much a game as labor.

Mary got a robe and a sketch pad. Standing by the window, she sketched the two men and the tall palm tree, lengthening the men and the tree, trying to catch some of the amusement the two seemed to feel in their harvesting, trying to suggest the crazy rolling of the fallen nuts. The man who was picking them up shook each as he held it and, apparently by sound from within, differentiated among them, putting some in a burlap bag, leaving others in a pile. His face was intent as he listened to whatever sound the nuts made as they were shaken; possibly, Mary thought, a gurgle of stoppered milk.

She had what she wanted in minutes and left the men to their coconutting and put on a sleeveless white dress. It was, she found, only a little after seven, but she had slept long enough. As on the morning before, she went, carrying pencils and crayons and the drawing pad, through the deserted lounge and out into the morning.

She walked away from the hotel, looking back at it, considering flattering angles for portraiture. She walked to the railed, awninged enclosure by the tennis courts and then crossed the courts, keeping properly behind the base lines, off the playing surface. Beyond the courts she sat on a bench and sketched the hotel across them, the courts suggested in the foreground. As she sketched, she began to like the result—the pale green of the courts as a foreground, the trees beyond, beyond them the hotel itself, with the bougainvillaea climbing its façade in the slanting rays of the morning sun. This one, she thought, I'll do tomorrow in water color.

It was close to nine when she had what she wanted, and began, as she had the morning before, to realize a need of breakfast. The

70

tables on the lawn beyond the dancing floor were in light and shadow as they had been before, and tempting. She could circle the courts, cross the floor beyond the high hedge and so reach orange juice and coffee. She put the completed sketch with others in the case and went in the bright, warm sun toward the end of the tennis courts.

As she walked the length of the courts, a shuffleboard alley was on her left. Beyond it, there was what she at first took to be a concrete wall, high and blank. But then she saw a door in it, set some three feet up the side of the wall, and then she looked again at the wall, and saw that it was the side of a low, sloping-roofed building. It was a building so odd, at first glance so without meaning, that she postponed breakfast to investigate further. She crossed the shuffleboard court, and walked along the wall, which had no windows and only the single door, to the end.

It ended at a sidewalk outside the hotel. She was barred from the sidewalk by a metal fence, which had a padlocked mesh gate. But she could look along the wall which paralleled the sidewalk, and see that it, meeting the wall beside the shuffleboard court at a sharp angle, was, like the first wall, unpierced by windows. It lacked even a door. On this side, the building was protected from the street by a continuous fence, which was topped by double strands of barbed wire. It was all, Mary thought, very like a prison; it contrasted oddly with the expansive openness of all other areas within the hotel's enclosure.

She retraced her steps, recrossed the shuffleboard court and, standing with her back to the tennis courts, looked at the building more carefully. The wall was about twelve feet high; the roof sloped to broad gutters, and from the gutters heavy metal pipes led down to the ground and into it. The building, she saw, was triangular. The roof was of some silvery metal. The whole of it was without apparent purpose, was an anomaly. Mary shook her head over it, and gave it up, and walked on along the tennis court toward breakfast.

In grading for the courts, a retaining wall two or three feet high had proved necessary at their northern end, toward which she walked. Along the wall, but a few feet from it, the thick, high hedge had been planted. Why she glanced, in passing, into the narrow passage between hedge and wall Mary Wister did not know then, and could not afterward explain. It was not, she had to say a good many times over, because she expected to see anything—to see first merely something white, to know, in an instant, that it was the white dinner jacket of a man lying there, to all appearance quite peacefully, on his back.

She stopped, and her hand went involuntarily to her lips, although she had not thought to make any sound. She stood so for a moment, motionless in the sun. Then she crouched to see better, and realized at once that she could not, in that position, see much better than before.

The man was lying a dozen feet from the corner of the retaining wall, a dozen feet in the dark passage between wall and hedge. She went along the hedge until she was opposite the body, and crouched again, and this time forced the stiff hedge branches enough apart so that she could see through them. She was only a little way, then, from the white face of Bronson Wells. The black eyes were open; they stared up at the green bending above; they might have glimpsed a little of the sky's blue. But she did not need to touch Bronson Wells to know that the eyes saw nothing—nothing green or blue, saw not even blackness; could not see the dark stain on his white dinner jacket; would not see anything again.

Mary stood then, and then she ran. She ran across the slippery surface of the dance floor, her low-heeled shoes clattering. She ran across the lawn beyond, and the dozen or so people breakfasting at the tables in shade and sunlight turned toward her. She seemed to run toward the whiteness of faces, for all the faces seemed, somehow, as white as that of the dead man she fled. She saw Heimrich, first sitting alone at a table, then slowly rising from it. She ran to him, and for a moment could hardly speak. She looked into the wide-open blue eyes of the solid

73

man from New York and for an instant words did not come. Then they came, hurried out, gasped out.

'Back there,' she said. 'Wells. He's—he's lying there. He's—'

'Show me,' Heimrich said, and came around the table. He reached for her arm, awkwardly, with his right hand; let the arm fall slowly, stiffly, and reached toward her with his left hand. These motions seemed to her slow and unreal. He touched her arm.

'Now Miss Wister,' he said. 'You're all right. Come and show me.'

Strangely, she was all right, then. Reality came back. She saw Grogan walking toward them across the lawn; heard him say, his voice quick, worried, 'What is it?' when he was still some little distance away. But his voice was not raised; his tone suggested disaster was a secret among them. The others at the patio tables looked at them curiously, with uneasiness. Grogan smiled around, his smile weakly, not convincingly, denying unpleasantness. He looked at Mary Wister and the smile was weaker still; he shook his head, deprecatingly. There was a suggestion that she could have seen nothing actually to disturb her; that nothing disturbing could occur at The Coral Isles.

But by then Heimrich's touch on her arm directed Mary and she walked back with him to the thick hedge at the end of the tennis

74

courts. After a moment, Grogan came with them.

Heimrich crouched where Mary told him, as she had crouched. Awkwardly, using his left hand, patiently, he parted the heavy bushes so that he could see the white, upturned face of Bronson Wells. He did not touch the body, but he looked at it for a much longer time than Mary had. After a time, Captain Heimrich stood up. He said, mildly, that Grogan had better call the police.

Grogan, peering down through the hedge, had not seen much, but he had seen enough.

'It's Mr. Wells,' he told them. His tone said '*the* Mr. Wells.' He said, 'A doctor.'

'If you like, naturally,' Heimrich said. 'But the police too, Mr. Grogan. He's been dead for some time, I think. But a doctor by all means.'

'God!' Grogan said. 'It's—' He ran out of words, appeared to run out of belief. He tried again. 'His heart?' Grogan said, trying to get hope into his voice.

'A bullet,' Heimrich told him. 'Or a knife. In the back. They'll know more when they get him out. But I think a bullet or a knife. You'd better get the police, Mr. Grogan. We can't do anything until the police get here, you know.'

Grogan still hesitated. He shook his head unbelievingly; he looked around at the early sun on the lawns, at the partially shadowed green of the tennis courts. This couldn't, his florid, pleasant, worried face said, have

75

happened here. Not at—not to—The Coral Isles. Finally he went off, avoiding the patio and the men and women at the tables. He shook his head as he walked.

'Unpleasant for the hotel,' Captain Heimrich said. 'But then, unpleasant for Mr. Wells too, naturally. How did you happen to find him, Miss Wister?'

Mary told what she could, pointed to where she had sat sketching, showed how she had walked along the courts and, turning to walk behind them, seen the something white.

'Yes,' Heimrich said. 'Of course. How did you happen to look behind the hedge, Miss Wister?'

'I don't know,' she said. 'I just happened to.'

'He wasn't killed there,' Heimrich said. 'Awkward place. And what would he have been doing there, in the first place?'

He did not precisely ask Mary Wister this; he asked himself. He closed his eyes for a moment and opened them again.

'He'll be hard to photograph,' Heimrich said. 'Very inconvenient all around, this is going to be. However—' He looked at her. 'You'd better get something to eat,' he said. 'Before they get here.'

'No,' she said. 'I couldn't.'

'Now Miss Wister,' Heimrich said. 'Now Miss Wister. Coffee, anyway. It's all unpleasant, naturally. But you didn't know him, did you?' He waited a second. 'I assume you didn't,' he said. 'Before yesterday, I mean?'

'I'd heard of him,' Mary said. 'That's all.'

'Then get yourself some coffee,' Heimrich said. 'Some food. You'll just about have time, probably.' She started to shake her head again. 'Now Miss Wister,' Heimrich said, and took her arm. 'Now Miss Wister.' He led her back to the table at which he had been sitting, beckoned a waitress.

'How do you like your eggs, Miss Wister?' he asked Mary. She shook her head. 'Orange juice,' Heimrich told the waitress. 'Coffee. A boiled egg, I think.' He felt his own coffee pot. 'Two coffees, please,' he said. He sat so that he could look toward the place where Bronson Wells's body was hidden behind the vigorous green of the hedge. He looked at the tennis courts, and then up toward the slanting sun.

'I'd think,' he said, 'that the light would be bad for perhaps a couple of hours yet, wouldn't you, Miss Wister? Or an hour, anyway.'

'The light?' she repeated.

'For tennis,' Heimrich said. 'And even then, naturally, it might be some time before anybody happened to look down.'

'Oh,' Mary said. 'Yes, I suppose so.'

'So the boys may get here a couple of hours ahead of plan,' Heimrich said.

'Will that make a difference?' Mary asked. He looked at her. Then he closed his eyes.

'Now Miss Wister,' he said. 'How would I

77

know? Sometimes it does, naturally. Sometimes a schedule matters. Sometimes it doesn't. If the time—'

He broke off. Grogan was coming back from the hotel, and Dr. Barclay MacDonald was with him.

'A very hopeful man, Mr. Grogan,' Heimrich said. The waitress brought orange juice and coffee; toast in a napkin; the egg Mary was certain she would never eat.

Heimrich said, 'Now eat some breakfast, Miss Wister,' and got up and went off across the lawn to intercept Grogan and Barclay MacDonald. He joined them and the three went to the hedge; Heimrich crouched and pointed, then relinquished the place to MacDonald, who groped with the hedge. Mary watched them, and the others at the tables watched them. Mary found that, while she watched, she sipped orange juice; poured herself a cup of coffee. Abstractedly, she reached for the order pad to sign a check. Heimrich had not torn his own sheet from the pad and for a moment Mary stared at it, hardly knowing she saw it. Then she lifted the sheet and, on the next, signed her name and wrote her room number.

MacDonald stood up after only a minute and spoke for another minute or so with Heimrich and the hotel manager. Then MacDonald left the other two, still talking, and walked across the dance floor, across the lawn, to Mary's table. The few still at the other tables watched him. MacDonald pulled out a chair, sat in it—carefully—and poured coffee from Heimrich's pot into a fresh cup.

'Well,' MacDonald said, 'he's dead, all right. I never saw anyone deader. Poor Grogan kept hoping.'

'It's dreadful,' Mary said. She felt, unexpectedly, annoyance with Barclay MacDonald, although what he thought and said, what his attitude was, were not concerns of hers. She felt disappointment in him.

'Now Miss Wister,' MacDonald said. 'Drink your coffee. Of course it's dreadful. Violent death is. No death is pleasant. But drink your coffee.' He looked at her plate. 'And,' he said, 'eat your egg. *You're* alive, Mary.' He seemed surprised that he had used her name so casually. 'People call me Mac, generally,' he said. 'I suppose the alternative would be "Bark."' He considered. 'Or "Clay,"' he added. 'Eat your egg.'

She looked at him. He nodded.

'I know,' he said. 'All the same, eat your breakfast. Remember, you'd only met the man.'

'Does that make it better?' she asked, and then said, 'I suppose it does, really.'

'Naturally,' MacDonald said. Again he listened to himself, as he apparently had a habit of doing. 'Heimrich is infectious,' he said. He watched while she cracked her egg, scooped

79

it into the egg cup. 'Good girl,' he told her. He watched her eat, and himself drank coffee.

Hunger had come back, Mary found. She finished the egg, finished toast, filled her coffee cup again.

'Very good girl,' MacDonald told her, and opened his cigarette case for her, held a light for her. 'Heimrich says the police will want to talk to you. As a formality.'

She nodded. It was obvious.

'By the way,' he said, 'you didn't know Wells, did you? Away from here, I mean. Before yesterday?'

'No,' she said. After a moment she said, 'No, Mac.'

'Good,' he said. 'From all I've heard, you're fortunate. My brother—' he stopped suddenly. Then he shrugged. 'My brother knew him or, at any rate, he appears to have known my brother,' he said. He looked at her. 'I'd rather like to tell you,' he said. 'My brother was Ralph MacDonald.' He looked at her and waited. She shook her head. 'He jumped out of a window a year or so ago,' Barclay MacDonald said. 'In Chicago. He'd—he'd been having some trouble.' He looked at her and waited again, and this time it came back to her.

'Oh,' she said. 'I do remember.'

'Yes,' he said. 'A good many people will now, I'm afraid.' He paused and drew deeply on his cigarette. 'My brother was a very honest man,' he said. 'He was also a very loyal one.'

He nodded slowly. 'In all respects,' he said.

Then they heard sirens. At first the sirens were some distance away. The sound swelled, then faded a little, then swelled again. It was very loud and close, as the cars turned into the hotel drive. Then the sirens stopped and left a silence which was, for a moment, more forbidding even than the wail had been. Those still at the tables, Mary and Barclay MacDonald among them, turned their heads, first following the sound, then looking watchfully at the stairs leading down from the porch. Midway between the hotel and the beach, a man and a woman in bright robes stopped and turned and stood, immobilized, in the sun.

The first man down the stairs was short and broad, and wore a loosely fitting white suit—he looked, Mary found herself thinking, as if he were walking under a tent. The several men who followed him were in uniform. Grogan went across the lawn to them, leaving Heimrich standing by the hedge. 'What goes on here, John?' the man in the tent said, in an unexpectedly high pitched and carrying voice. Mary could see John Grogan shaking his head, could see him talking but could not hear what he said. 'Now that's something,' the short broad man said. 'That sure is.' He and Grogan went back to the hedge and now, for the first time, some of those at the tables got up and began to move toward the group at the hedge.

81

One or two moved with purpose; the others were elaborately indirect, suggesting that they had happened to remember business in that direction.

Grogan detached himself and went toward his guests, the smile returning to his pleasant face. There had, he began to explain, been a little accident. Everything was being taken care of. A little accident. Unfortunate, but being taken care of.

'Just run along,' the short broad man said from behind Grogan, in his carrying voice. 'Nothing to see.' He then crouched, with evident difficulty, and peered into the hedge. He got up, red faced from the exertion, and talked momentarily to the uniformed men, one of whom went off across the lawn toward the hotel. Everybody watched them. Then a third man detached himself from the uniformed group and, after Grogan pointed, came to Barclay MacDonald. He said, 'You the doctor?' and, when MacDonald nodded, said, 'You figure he's dead?'

'Very,' MacDonald said.

'O. K., doc,' the policeman said, and went back to the group. He nodded to the fat man and said something. 'Makes it official, sort of,' the fat man said, in his incongruously high voice. He left the others, then, and walked across the dance floor to the table at which Mary and MacDonald sat. Grogan came with him. Grogan brought with him an atmosphere of anxiety.

'This is Mr. Little, Miss Wister,' Grogan said, with the air of a man who hopes, without believing, that things will work out well.

'Justice of the Peace Little,' he added.

'And coroner,' Mr. Little said, in his high and carrying voice. 'And coroner, young lady. He's dead, seems like.' He gestured behind him, toward the uniformed policeman, toward what remained of Bronson Wells. 'Foul play,' he added. 'You found him, they tell me.'

'Yes,' Mary said. 'I saw—him.'

'What they tell me,' Justice of the Peace Little said. 'Lying the way he is now, was he?'

'Yes,' Mary said. 'Unless you've moved—unless—'

'Have to let the sheriff see him first,' Little said. 'Chief deputy, that is. Don't suppose Charlie's up yet.' The last was to Grogan; it was a jest. Grogan smiled, rather as if it hurt him to smile. 'Great man to sleep, Charlie,' the Justice of the Peace said, amplifying for the benefit of Mary, of Dr. MacDonald. 'You said he was dead, doc?' This did not, evidently, refer to Charlie, the great man to sleep.

'Yes,' MacDonald said. 'He's quite dead.'

'Foul play,' Little said. 'Looks like he was stabbed.'

'Yes,' MacDonald said. 'It does, coroner.'

'Have to have an inquest, all right,' Little said. 'Soon as—'

A siren interrupted him.

83

'That'll be Ronny,' Little said. 'Got here quick, didn't he? Nothing sleepy about Ronny. Bright as a button, Ronny is.' He paused. 'As a button,' he repeated.

The siren stopped. Mr. Little stood, looking at the steps from the porch, waited. After a few moments, a young man in a dark suit came down the steps—a darkly burned young man, his hair incongruously blond above mahogany. After him there came an even younger man, markedly untanned, carrying a camera case. 'Picked up the boy from the *Sentinel*,' Little said. 'Bright as a button, Ronny is.' He advanced to meet the tanned man. He brought him to the table; the man with the camera veered away, toward the group by the hedge.

'This lady found it, seems like,' Little said. 'Miss Wister, they tell me. This is the Chief Deputy, folks. Miss Wister. This one'—he indicated MacDonald—'is a doctor, Ronny. Confirms death, the doctor does.'

The chief deputy looked at MacDonald, who nodded.

'My name's Jefferson,' Ronny said. 'Ronald Jefferson. Chief Deputy Sheriff of Monroe County, as the justice here's probably told you. We investigate homicides. I'll have to ask you a few questions, Miss Wister.'

She nodded.

'So,' Jefferson said, 'if you'll just—'

'Leave it with you, Ronny,' Justice Little

84

interjected. 'Got to get back. Got a wedding coming up.'

'We'll take care of it, justice,' Ronald Jefferson promised. He was told to do that. Then Justice of the Peace and Coroner Little departed, his tent fluttering. Jefferson pulled up a chair and sat in it.

'Now just tell me about it,' he said to Mary, and turned pale gray eyes on her.

Mary told him.

'How did you happen to be looking in there, Miss Wister?' he asked when she had finished. 'Seems like you'd just have been looking ahead.'

'I don't know,' she said. 'It just happened. There was something white. I just happened to see it.'

The chief deputy appeared to think this over. He appeared doubtful. But he said, 'Could be, I guess. Then you looked and saw what it was and told somebody?'

'Yes,' she said. 'Captain Heimrich.'

'He a friend of yours?' Jefferson asked.

'I met him yesterday,' she said. 'He—he was sitting here. He was somebody I knew.'

'Know *him*?' Jefferson asked, and jerked a fat hand in the direction of the hedge.

'I met him yesterday,' Mary said. 'I'd heard of him, of course.'

'That right?' Ronald Jefferson said. 'Never had, myself. New Yorker, most likely.'

Mary did not know the answer to that, but

Jefferson seemed to expect no answer.

'Most likely,' he repeated, as if, so, he explained everything. He turned to MacDonald, then, and said, 'How long you figure, doc?'

MacDonald shrugged.

'Make a guess, doc,' Jefferson urged.

'I didn't examine him,' MacDonald said. 'Except to make sure he was dead. I'd guess, not for too long. A few hours. Your own man can make an estimate for you.'

'Our own man?' Jefferson said. 'Oh. This isn't New York, doctor. We haven't a police doctor. You have a look when we get him out, doc?'

'If you like,' MacDonald said.

'That's the ticket,' Jefferson told him. ''Preciate that, doc.'

He went back then and watched the photographer, who was shooting down from the tennis court, through the wire mesh. There were several shots from there, at such differing angles as the situation made possible. The photographer then crawled between hedge and retaining wall, and there were several flashes from within. He backed out again and said something to the sheriff's deputy.

'O. K., boys,' the deputy said, and two of the boys crawled behind the hedge. The hedge shook perceptibly with their efforts behind it.

'Mary,' MacDonald said, 'Why don't you go sit in the sun, or something? Some place else?'

She nodded and stood up.

'Be seeing you,' Barclay MacDonald said and got slowly out of his chair and walked, very tall, a little stiffly, toward the group at the hedge.

Mary went and sat in the sun. She did nothing else, and let the sun warm her. It was half an hour before Barclay MacDonald rejoined her. She looked up at him.

'He was stabbed,' MacDonald told her, and sat down on the grass. 'From behind, through the heart. Whoever did it was expert. Or lucky. Wells fell somewhere else, I imagine. Was carried, or dragged—the deputy sheriff thinks put on something, a piece of canvas, perhaps, and dragged—in there. Presumably to keep things hidden. He's been dead, at a very rough guess, for three to five hours.' He looked at his watch. 'Since between four and six o'clock this morning,' he said. 'One of the city policemen thinks he knows him.' He looked suddenly at Mary. 'Not as Bronson Wells, however,' MacDonald said. 'Thinks he had another name and—used to live here under it.'

'But,' Mary said, 'he was so well known. Surely—'

MacDonald shrugged.

'I don't know,' he said. 'Probably their man's wrong. They're checking, of course.' He pulled up a few blades of grass and examined them. 'Not much soil here,' he said, and threw

87

the grass away. He lay back on the grass and looked up at the sky. He was a very long man. He was not, Mary realized looking down at him, at all frail, as she had thought him at first. His shoulders were broad; his chest deep. He was merely very thin. She became conscious that, while she looked at him, he had turned his head and was watching her.

'It is,' he said, 'unlikely that I will fall apart.' Suddenly he grinned at her, and his face changed; the amusement was not, for that moment, detached. It was as if, from a distance, he joined her. 'I could even swim,' he said. 'In an angular fashion. Do you think we might try it?'

'I've work to do,' she said.

He sat up, and shook his head.

'You'd see the wrong things,' he told her. 'Take the advice of your—of a doctor.'

They did swim, briefly, after half an hour or so. In bathing trunks he was quite amazingly thin, but at the same time gave even less an impression of fragility. 'I'm a bony man,' he said, with detachment, regarding himself. After they had swum they lay in the sun, on adjacent sun chaises, talking very little. It was MacDonald who, after a time, said they had both had enough to start with. After they had dressed they met again, apparently by mutual decision—although Mary could not remember that the decision was ever expressed in words, given any shape—on the wide porch, where they lay back again in adjacent chairs and still talked little, and smoked, and let the sun soak into them. It was easy, lying so, not to think of murder; not to think of anything.

'We get along well,' MacDonald said, at one point. 'In almost complete silence, but well.'

She turned her head to smile, but said nothing. Nor, for several minutes, did he speak again. He lay back, half in the sun and half out of it, and looked across the wide lawn toward the sea. 'The Atlantic and the Gulf meet here,' he said, idly. 'Along somewhere there there's a line in the water. Gulf on one side, Atlantic on the other.' Again he was silent. 'It would be hard to draw the line,' he said, and again was silent. But this time the silence seemed to wait.

'You said you remembered about my brother,' he said, then. He did not look at her; he looked at the sea, where a line was drawn in water.

'Something,' she said.

'He was older than I am,' Barclay MacDonald said. 'Twelve years older. In his late forties. In some ways, he was of a different generation.'

Again he was momentarily silent.

'Did you ever read a book called *The Vital Center*?' he asked her then, and this time he turned to look at her. 'By Schlesinger?'

She shook her head.

'A good book,' he said. 'An interesting book. Maybe a valuable one. Schlesinger
89

makes it clearer than I can. About the difference in generations, I mean. My brother was born in 1905. I was a kid when things fell apart in the late twenties. You—' He looked at her again. 'You were just about getting born. My brother was in his twenties, of course. He—wondered why things were falling apart. Wondered if there weren't a better way to arrange things. It was in the air, then, he told me once—in the kind of air he breathed, at any rate. He was working for his doctorate. He was a sensitive person. He—joined things, along with a good many other men and women who were born about when he was, and thought things were falling apart. Maybe they thought things couldn't be put back together again, ever, in the old patterns.' He shook his head. 'That was before this was what Schlesinger calls "a New Deal country,"' he said. 'It's been that since I was fifteen. Since you were—about four—three or four?'

'Five,' she said.

'Five,' he repeated. 'Neither of us has ever known any other kind of country—a country where people were, at the least, asking the right questions. Or don't you agree?'

'Yes,' she said. 'I agree.'

'You and I weren't ever tempted,' he said. 'At least, not as a lot of people who're older now were tempted by—by what Schlesinger calls the "unearthly radiance" of communism. I don't think his term is very well chosen. It's too—exclamatory. At least, my brother wouldn't have thought of it as that. Of course, he wasn't a writer.'

'An artist, you said,' Mary told him. 'A painter.'

'That too,' MacDonald said. 'But, not professionally. He painted in his spare time. Like—Churchill. Like a lot of doctors. He was a professor. And a researcher in physics. Anyway, he thought of what was happening in Russia as an experiment in a new way of living. Thought perhaps the promise was there, or that something was there.'

He was silent again, for a longer time.

'It's hard for me to understand what he felt,' he said, then. 'That's why it's really a difference in generations, not merely a difference of a dozen years. I understand it academically, but just that. Schlesinger didn't do much more, it seems to me. He's just my age, Schlesinger is. He thinks people like my brother were just—oh, fuzzy minded. I suppose I do, too. It's easy for us to see there isn't any radiance there, unearthly or otherwise—that there is merely another darkness. A darkness deeper than any we've ever been threatened with. My brother saw as clearly as anybody before he— died. In his last letter he said, "You have to remember we were young and, I suppose, frightened. I still think there was a good deal to be frightened of." Anyway—'

He stopped. He looked at her.

91

'I won't ask whether this is boring you,' he said. 'I'd rather think it wasn't.'

'It isn't,' she said.

'I did ask, of course,' he admitted. 'Anyway—my brother left the university he was teaching at and went to Chicago, and got a room on the twentieth floor of a hotel and jumped. They had just decided to dismiss him from the faculty—as, since he was a physicist, a bad security risk. He had two children. He didn't have much money, but he had insurance, with no stipulation against suicide—or, I suppose, a stipulation that had run out. But I don't think it was only that. His letter to me wasn't very logical. He wrote it in the room, and then one to his wife, and then he jumped. I don't know actually what happened to him. I suppose that, in some way, the bottom just fell out.' He paused again. 'I told you he was a loyal man,' he said. 'In all things. Didn't I tell you that?'

'Yes,' she said. 'You told me that, Mac.'

'He'd been accused of being a member of the Communist Party,' MacDonald said. 'In his letter he said that that wasn't true—that he wasn't a member of the party, and never had been. He had told the university that, and they said they had proof he was lying. Finally, they told him they got the proof from Bronson Wells. They had a list of things he had joined, and some of them were border-line. Some had changed in twenty-odd years, so that they were

92

more than border-line. But what decided it was Wells's oath that Ralph MacDonald had been a party member. Wells said he didn't know whether he was one then—two years ago—but certainly didn't know he wasn't. Wells lied.'

He paused once more.

'Or say I believed my brother instead of Bronson Wells,' he said. 'Say Wells may have believed what he said; got my brother mixed up with someone else.'

Again he paused.

'I was very fond of my brother,' he said. 'I told you that. I couldn't tell anybody I'm heartbroken over Wells's death. It would be convenient if I could, perhaps.'

'You won't be asked,' she told him. 'Anyway it's all—ridiculous.'

'Oh,' he said, 'as for that—yes, it's ridiculous enough. To me. But to the sheriff and Mr. Little—who knows?'

'Anybody,' she said.

'It is,' he said, 'advisable for young women to think seriously about their associates.'

'I think it's time we had some lunch,' Mary Wister told the long, thin doctor, who blinked at her, and then said, 'I'll buy you a drink, first.'

They had a drink in the Penguin Bar, which opened off the patio, where lunchers were gathering. The Penguin Bar had a mural of penguins, parading gravely in procession around the walls. They were not, Mary thought, very animated penguins.

It was interesting, MacDonald said, when they had found a table under an umbrella and had ordered lunch, how quietly everyone seemed to be taking the violent demise of *the* Mr. Bronson Wells. It must be gratifying to Mr. Grogan. No one shunned the tennis courts because of their proximity to violent death; it was true that the dance floor was deserted, but that might be because the guests would rather eat than dance. The police had taken themselves off, along with Bronson Wells's body. Mr. Grogan moved undismayed among the tables, tending his sheep. It was as if nothing at all had happened, which was surprising.

'I don't know,' MacDonald said. 'I suppose that, in a place like this, we're all out of context. There aren't any patterns to be broken. Everything is shifting and unreal—a man named Wells was around, and now he isn't around. "Where are those nice Joneses we saw so much of yesterday?" "Oh, they left this morning." "Oh—there're the Smiths." Also, the authorities are co-operating, undoubtedly. Don't disturb the Northern geese. They're laying. However, I doubt if it will last.'

The calm lasted, at any rate, through lunch. Afterward, Mary Wister talked again about working, and this time she insisted; this time, indeed, MacDonald did not argue. As a matter of fact, he told her, he was trying to make himself sleep each afternoon. 'As a doctor, I order it,' he said. 'As a patient, I try to obey orders. I'm a fairly good patient.'

So, for three hours or so, Mary sketched and, working, forgot that she had found the body of a murdered man and forgot Dr. Barclay MacDonald, also. If a sub-knowledge that he was about somewhere persisted, and was somehow comforting, she was not specifically conscious of it.

CHAPTER FIVE

Mary Wister did not think particularly about Dr. Barclay MacDonald, but nevertheless, she took especial pains as she dressed that second evening at The Coral Isles. Soft brown hair was very thoroughly brushed; lipstick most carefully and artfully applied. In the enormous closet she hesitated a moment, and then took down a short dinner dress in muted green of which Sophie of Saks Fifth Avenue was, on the not to be questioned word of Mrs. Snodgrass of the Salon Moderne, very proud. She did not, Mary decided, need to wear black for the late Mr. Bronson Wells.

And for him, she found when she was again in the lounge, nobody found it necessary to wear black. The group which had gathered the evening before was in the process of gathering again, not needing a nucleus, if Wells had been

95

a nucleus. Judge and Mrs. Robert Sibley were there, the incident of the evening before forgotten, gracious dignity again wrapped about them. Paul Shepard was there, neat in white dinner jacket, with his reasonably beautiful wife. And Dr. Barclay MacDonald was there, talking to Shepard, but not so engrossed that he did not see a brown-haired girl in a dinner dress of muted green as she walked toward the corner. He saw her, and began to lift his length carefully out of a chair, and pursed his lips in a whistle which was soundless, which also was gratifying.

No one wore black for Bronson Wells. Nor did his passing seem to shadow the minds of those who, the evening before, had sat and watched him drink ginger ale, speak commandingly of the subversive perils from which he sought to protect an insufficiently aroused nation. He was not, however, forgotten. Mary's arrival reminded them.

It reminded Mrs. Robert Sibley, beside whom Mary found a place to sit, with Barclay MacDonald in front of them both, on an ottoman.

'Such a shocking thing about poor Mr. Wells,' Mrs. Sibley said. 'And so dreadful for you, my dear. To find him that way.'

'It was,' Mary said. 'I—'

And then the picture of Wells lying there, on his back, black eyes staring up at green and blue they could not see, was all at once horribly vivid in Mary's mind and she was moistening lips which suddenly were dry, holding the lower lip momentarily between her teeth.

'Forget it, Mary,' MacDonald said, his voice almost sharp, and at the same time Mrs. Sibley said, 'Oh, my dear, I'm so sorry. So thoughtless.'

'It's all right,' Mary said. 'I hadn't been thinking about it. I—I did, for a minute. But it's perfectly all right. I mean—I'm all right. Poor Mr. Wells—'

Mrs. Sibley shook her head, but the gesture was only an appropriate one; she deplored, but in the abstract.

'What a lovely dress,' she said, of Sophie's triumph, and then her interest was authentic. She enquired further about the dress, and was informed. 'We get to New York so infrequently,' she said. 'My poor husband has been so—so tied to Washington. But perhaps now—' She left the sentence incomplete, and lifted a glass and sipped from it.

Her attitude was, it seemed to Mary as the impromptu party continued, characteristic. Penny Shepard also considered Mr. Wells's abrupt departure from the scene a shocking thing, and Mary's ordeal of discovery hardly less so. Judge Sibley shook his head with gloomy dignity, but did not linger on the subject. He described, to Barclay MacDonald, the arrival that day of a cargo of sea turtles, whose destination was soup, and urged

MacDonald not to miss the next unloading. Oslen came, and the vivid Miss Rachel Jones was with him, and he had, he told them, not even heard—he'd spent the day on a fishing boat. When he did hear, he made a clicking sound with tongue and teeth, and shook his head in the familiar fashion, 'Who'd do a thing like that?' he wondered, and then all shook heads and expressed bafflement.

But nobody wore black for Mr. Wells. Paul Shepard came nearest—and became the first to admit past association with Bronson Wells. It was, Shepard told Oslen, but in a voice for anyone to hear, not only a shocking thing, and a damn strange one but also, for him, a damned annoying one.

'Just about got him signed up,' Shepard said. 'Going to do a fifteen minute commentary for us. Had a sponsor lined up. Now look.'

This time they all were interested.

'A commentary?' Oslen repeated.

'Paul's with the United Broadcasting Alliance,' Penny Shepard said. 'I'm afraid he's apt to think everybody knows.' Her tone was tolerant; she looked at Mary and offered amused, womanly appreciation of the self-assurance of the male—of, of course, the successful male, the outstanding male.

'Three times a week,' Paul Shepard said, letting this pass. 'And I've been working on it a month. Now—' He snapped his fingers.

It was, their faces said, tough luck. 'Tough,'

Oslen said, for them. 'He'd have done a good job.' He looked around at everybody. 'Damn good job,' he said, to cinch it. 'Kind of job that needs doing. Smoke out these reds.'

Nobody disagreed.

'Counteract some of this stuff we've been getting,' Oslen said, pursuing it, but not specifying. 'Pinkos. Hope you can get somebody else to do the job.' The last was to Paul Shepard, who shrugged. It would, he said, be difficult. They would, naturally, try. He shook his head. The United Broadcasting Alliance, the UBA, wore black for Bronson Wells, through its accredited representative.

'Some commie did it,' Oslen said. 'Poor guy knew his life was in danger.'

'You may be right,' Sibley agreed, with the dignity of a judge. 'I imagine the FBI will look into that.' He paused, still judicial. 'He was a great force,' Sibley said, with judicial finality.

'Well,' Shepard said, and shrugged again. 'How was fishing?' he asked William Oslen. 'Want to have a go at it while we're here. Even if it does mean getting up at six.'

Oslen told them all how fishing had been, starting with his very early rising. They spent the next ten minutes in a boat with Oslen, going over the day, it seemed to Mary Wister, fin by fin. Bronson Wells, being already dead as a man, died again as a topic.

After Oslen finished, they talked again by twos and threes, about matters of no importance—about the surprising warmth and the forecaster's assurance it would be warm again tomorrow; about the steak dinner, with broiling in the open over charcoal, which was the Saturday custom of The Coral Isles; about the Marine Museum, where one could see sharks—although small ones, to be sure— swimming contentedly over enormous turtles which did nothing with equal contentment; about the sponges to be bought outside the museum and the pile of coconuts which waited there, fresh from palms, for customers who liked coconuts.

The conversation was much as it had been the evening before, but this time there were no incidents. Mrs. Sibley did not drink too much; it was hardly possible, looking at her, to believe she ever had. Rachel Jones did not come surprisingly out of nowhere; she was merely there, and one of the group. No one, after the brief memorial service for Wells—and his never to be spoken commentary on the world today—talked at all of serious matters. No one admonished. And, as the hour passed, it seemed to Mary that there was a relaxation in the group which there had not been the evening before. By comparison, looking back, the other cocktail hour had been a little marred by tension, even before Mrs. Sibley marred it by losing her dignity. There was nothing like that this evening.

The time for cocktails was almost over when

Deputy Sheriff Jefferson came in through the main entrance and turned toward the desk. He spoke to the clerk there for a moment and then went around the desk and through a door which must, Mary thought, be that of the manager. She looked at Barclay MacDonald, who raised his eyebrows. The deputy came back through the door after a few minutes, and this time Grogan was with him. The two shook hands, with cordiality. As Jefferson turned to go, Grogan patted him on the shoulder, evidently with approval. The deputy sheriff went the way he had come. It seemed to Mary that there was a certain finality in their parting, as if something had been settled. Mary looked at MacDonald and, although she said nothing, he answered her without hesitation.

'Looks like it,' he said. 'Situation well in hand, which must be a relief to Grogan.'

'Relief?' she repeated. 'Yes, I suppose so.'

'I'd gather,' he said, 'that the sanctuary is not to be invaded, wouldn't you? That the guests will not be bothered?'

She nodded to that.

Then Captain Heimrich came through the entrance. Just inside, he paused and looked around for a moment; he looked toward the group and then walked across the lounge to it. He was, jovially, accused of being late. Room was made for him on a sofa; several helped him attract a waiter. Spurred by his example, they all ordered new drinks. Heimrich's square face,

101

in which the blue eyes were so unexpectedly alive, expressed nothing, except relaxation. After a moment, he relaxed further, and closed his eyes. But Mary had a feeling that he was, unhurriedly, with assurance, waiting for something.

'What do you hear about—?' Oslen said, and jerked a thumb in the general direction of the tennis courts to conclude the sentence.

'About Mr. Wells?' Heimrich said, without opening his eyes. 'Why, I believe they're making progress, Mr. Oslen. Quite good progress, I think. The sheriff's office seems quite satisfied.'

Heimrich opened his eyes, located his drink, picked it up and sipped, closed his eyes again. He seemed rather tired. He also seemed to feel that he had closed the subject. When Paul Shepard reopened it, Captain Heimrich appeared to be a little surprised.

'You mean,' Shepard asked, 'that they've got their man? Or woman?'

'Now, Mr. Shepard,' Heimrich said. 'I don't think they've arrested anyone. They hadn't an hour ago, anyway. They won't be precipitate, naturally. Peace officers seldom are, you know.'

'You've been working with them, captain?' MacDonald said. This time Heimrich opened his eyes.

'Now doctor,' he said. 'Observing. Professional interest, you know. As you might have in another man's operation.'

'I'm not a surgeon,' MacDonald said.

'No,' Heimrich said. 'Nevertheless. One is interested in technics, naturally. One likes to look on. Merely that, doctor. The—research is all theirs.' He paused, and closed his eyes. 'Particularly as they feel it's entirely a local case,' he added. 'It seems Mr. Wells used to live here and—may have made enemies.'

'They're crazy,' Oslen said. He did not speak with violence, but as one who merely selects an appropriate word. 'Small-town cops.'

'Now Mr. Oslen,' Heimrich said. 'Why do you say that? They're quite efficient, really. Why do you think they aren't?'

He opened his eyes and regarded Oslen. Oslen looked back at him for a moment, and then lifted his shoulders and let them fall.

'I spoke out of turn,' he said. 'You'd know better than I, of course. I merely thought—' He stopped.

'Oslen thought some commie killed Wells,' Paul Shepard said. 'To stop his spilling secrets, maybe. So did I.' He looked around. 'I'm not sure I still don't,' he added.

He looked rather sternly at Captain Heimrich.

'Don't they know who Wells was?' Oslen asked.

'Now Mr. Oslen,' Heimrich said. 'They do know, naturally. They are considering various possibilities. Do you suspect someone,

103

Mr. Oslen?'

'I?' Oslen said. 'My God, no. I merely—' He spread his hands in a gesture more fluid than one would have expected. Of course, Mary thought, he's a pianist, an artist. I should have remembered.

'Mr. Wells lived here for some time a few years ago,' Heimrich said. 'Under another name, it seems. The police are quite sure he did make at least one enemy, and not because of politics. You may be right, naturally. But then, so may they, Mr. Oslen.' He closed his eyes. 'It is their business,' he said. He paused. 'There was also a matter of a package of cigarettes,' he said. 'It does seem suggestive.'

They waited; it occurred to Mary that they were supposed to wait; were even supposed to ask.

'Cigarettes?' Robert Sibley repeated, asking.

'Wells was carrying part of a package of cigarettes,' Heimrich said. 'Not the kind you buy anywhere—Cuban cigarettes. Brown paper, Havana filler. Very strong and harsh. They aren't for sale here at the hotel, but they're very common in town, of course. Many of the Cubans smoke them.' He paused. 'There are a good many Cubans here, naturally.'

They waited again.

'Since they're not sold here at the hotel,' Heimrich said, 'the deputy sheriff thinks Wells picked them up in town. Last night. And that he may have met this enemy there, naturally.

Been followed back here and killed. He apparently was killed behind the orchestra shell, incidentally, and carried or dragged over to where Miss Wister found him.'

'Why?' Barclay MacDonald asked.

'Now doctor,' Heimrich said. 'Only one man really knows that. But the entrance to the staff dormitory is back of the orchestra shell. Some of the hotel people start work very early, naturally. They'd have seen the body if it had been left there.'

'So?' Shepard said.

'In general,' Heimrich told them, and now he spoke sleepily, 'it is much easier to estimate the time of death if the body is found soon. As time passes, it becomes progressively more difficult. The doctor here will tell you that.'

'Of course,' MacDonald said.

'Of course,' Heimrich repeated after him. 'The police feel the temporary concealment of the body fits in. Ordinarily, they think, it might have been almost noon before somebody—a tennis player, probably—happened to find it. Rigor might have set in by noon, don't you think, doctor?'

'Possibly,' MacDonald said. 'A good many factors are involved. It was beginning when I examined the body. It might have been complete by noon if death occurred around four in the morning.'

'And if it was complete,' Heimrich said, 'death might have occurred eight hours before, or twelve hours—or twenty or more. Isn't that right, doctor?'

'On the basis of rigor, generally yes,' MacDonald said. 'Of course, an autopsy—' But then he shrugged. 'It gets more difficult as time passes, certainly,' he said.

'I'm afraid,' Penny Shepard said, 'that I don't quite see what difference it makes.'

'Now Mrs. Shepard,' Heimrich said. 'The purpose of a killer is always to confuse, naturally. To create a fog and—hide in it.' He opened his eyes. 'Of course,' he said, 'a fog is impartial. It may hide the innocent as well.' He closed his eyes. Mary looked at Barclay MacDonald and slightly enlarged her own eyes. MacDonald raised his eyebrows and shook his head. He looked with speculation at Captain Heimrich.

'They've been questioning one of the musicians,' Heimrich said, without opening his eyes. 'They're not holding him—yet. A man named García. Mario García. He leads the orchestra, actually. He plays the cornet.'

(*The cornet's pure tone had broken, shattered; it had become a cry, not music. A slender dark man in a white jacket had held the cornet high, and it had screamed in the night.*)

'They think,' Heimrich said, 'that there was an involvement between García's sister and Mr. Wells when Mr. Wells lived here before. Not a very pleasant involvement. Something to do with drugs, they think.'

106

'Listen,' Oslen said, and spoke sharply. 'You're clear off the track. Wells wasn't like that. He was giving everything he had to wake this country up.'

'Giving?' Heimrich said. 'Well, no doubt he was, Mr. Oslen.' He opened his eyes and looked at Oslen; then looked around at the others. 'It isn't my track,' he said. 'I told you that. It's what the police think.' He paused. 'I thought you all might like to know,' he added, and closed his eyes again.

'I still think they're wrong,' Oslen said.

'Now Mr. Oslen,' Heimrich said. 'They may be, naturally.' He nodded slowly. 'They may very well be,' he said. 'In whole or in part. In whole or in part, Mr. Oslen.' He spoke slowly and then stopped speaking. It seemed to Mary Wister that he was uncertain whether to continue, perhaps to amplify. The others, she thought, had the same feeling. But if he planned to continue, Heimrich was not given the chance. An emissary in a red jacket came from the desk. New York was calling Captain Heimrich. 'Oh yes. Thanks,' Captain Heimrich said, and went with the messenger. For a moment, those in the group looked after him; even Rachel Jones, who of them all had seemed most detached, kept her eyes on Captain Heimrich until he reached the desk and walked around it to a telephone booth at the far end.

'I understand,' Judge Sibley said, after Heimrich was no longer in view, 'that Captain

Heimrich is a policeman. On vacation?'

The question floated, seeking a recipient. Dr. Barclay MacDonald accepted it. He said that Heimrich was, actually, on sick leave, recovering from an injury. Sibley nodded.

'Of course,' he said, 'he has no authority here, has he?'

The last was not really a question, although Sibley's judicial, controlled voice rose at the end.

'I suppose,' William Oslen said, 'that a homicide man can't help being interested in murder. Can't be expected to keep his fingers out of the pie, even if it isn't his pie.'

No one answered this, even indirectly. Barclay MacDonald touched Mary's arm. 'What d'you say we eat?' he said. ...

MacDonald assumed that they would dine together, and the headwaiter assumed it. After a moment, Mary found that she assumed it too. Being with MacDonald had come to seem in the nature of things, although how that had happened remained a little obscure. Call it a shipboard acquaintance, Mary thought, and in her mind called it that. Call it an association out of the context of both their lives, engendered by chance circumstance, nurtured by the relaxation which, in spite even of the circumstance of murder, was part of being south in the winter, of finding the days warm and the evenings barely cool, and white with moonlight. Say they were both in the drift of

108

summer in February.

It appeared, however, that Heimrich had drifted elsewhere. The table was set for three, but the square police captain, whose bright blue eyes needed so much resting (but was that really it?) did not appear for shrimps in Coral Isles Sauce, for green turtle soup, for thick slices of admirable roast beef. They were at coffee before he came, and by then they were, idly, discussing him. Was he, in a special sense, a homicide man, Mary asked and the answer MacDonald did not know.

'I met him in the car that brought us down,' MacDonald said. 'He was pleasant, but not particularly communicative. It did come out, I've forgotten precisely how, that he'd been shot by somebody he was arresting for murder. He killed the man who shot him, and that bothers him. He said something about having let it go too far—but you heard him say that, when you were being so haughty with us. Why were you?'

'I don't know,' she said. 'I—I thought I'd had enough of people for the time being. Didn't want to get—' She stopped, having almost said 'involved,' which would have been a foolish thing to say, even an embarrassing one. She was not 'involved' with this—this long drink of water. Thinking of him so, she smiled to herself, but not wholly to herself, since the smile was briefly on her lips.

'I do remember something about it,' she

said. 'I'd have thought a policeman would get used to things like that.'

MacDonald supposed most did, adding that he knew few. But there was, he said, no reason that an occupation, even that of policeman, should necessarily, and basically, change a man.

'Even a doctor,' he said, 'doesn't always get used to death.'

'He looks,' she said, 'like a matter-of-fact man. But somehow—'

He agreed with the implication of the unfinished sentence.

'I had,' Mary said, 'the feeling in there'—she indicated the lounge with a motion of her head—'that he was—waiting for something. For someone to do something, or say something. And—I was surprised he said so much. About Mr. Wells's death, I mean.'

He nodded to that, quickly.

'A sieve,' he agreed. Then he stopped suddenly and his face changed. 'Come to think of it,' he said, 'you use a sieve to sift things out, don't you? Say if you're sifting—oh, gravel. Top soil. The small stuff goes through; the big stuff doesn't. You separate and what you want, big stuff or small stuff, you keep. The rest you throw away.'

He was, she said, turning it upside down. What they had both meant was that Heimrich had the retention powers of—

'Now Miss Wister,' Heimrich said, from

110

behind her. 'Now Miss Wister.' He sat down. He did not seem perturbed; he smiled amiably enough. 'I thought all you people would be interested,' he said. 'How are the shrimps this evening?'

Mary flushed slightly.

'I didn't—' she began.

'You'll like the shrimps, captain,' Barclay MacDonald said, firmly. 'Don't embarrass the girl. What did you expect us to talk about?'

'Oh, the murder, naturally,' Heimrich said. 'It's uppermost in your minds, of course. Very interesting thing, murder.' The waitress came. She took the pad on which Heimrich had written his order and beamed on him and said it was a beautiful evening, wasn't it. She said, 'They tell me you're a detective.'

'Do they, Mae?' Heimrich said.

'From the FBI,' Mae said. 'That poor Mr. Wells was a G-man too and—'

'Now Mae,' Heimrich said. 'You tell them they're all wrong. After you bring me some shrimps, hm-m?'

'Oh, you!' Mae said, and went.

'To laymen, particularly,' Heimrich said, picking up without effort. 'Actually, it's very ugly.' He paused, and closed his eyes. 'I don't like murder,' he said, mildly. 'I don't like people who murder.'

It was, of course, an affirmation against sin, and outwardly as obvious. But there was something in the very mildness of Heimrich's tone, its studied quiet, which made the obvious almost impressive—and almost frightening. Heimrich opened his eyes.

'There is no reason good enough for murder,' he said. 'No provocation. You agree, doctor?'

'I suppose not,' MacDonald said. 'Some people seem to ask for it, you know.'

'Oh,' Heimrich said. 'People who are murdered are often regrettable people, naturally. You were thinking of Mr. Wells?'

'Not especially,' MacDonald said.

'Now doctor,' Heimrich said. 'Of Wells and—your brother, say?'

There was a rather long silence, a rather hard silence.

'I thought you said you weren't in this,' Barclay MacDonald said then, and there was an odd detachment in his voice. 'That it wasn't your track.'

'Did I?' Heimrich said. 'Yes, I suppose I did. However—'

'A busman's holiday,' MacDonald said.

'Now doctor,' Heimrich said. 'Not a holiday. A holiday should be gay, shouldn't it? About your brother?'

'Apparently you know,' MacDonald said.

'He blamed Wells?'

'He may have.'

'And you? You blamed Wells, naturally?'

'I believed he lied about my brother,' Dr. Barclay MacDonald said, his voice level. 'I believed he did it to further his own ends, aggrandize himself. In the end, through articles, books, lecture fees, to make money for himself. I think he was, as you say, a regrettable person. And, for a year or more, I hadn't thought about him. I had never met him, and he had never met me. Until here, at the hotel. And that was accidental.'

He paused.

'And,' he said, 'I've no more sympathy for communism than Wells had. I never worshipped God in the Kremlin. Wells did.'

Mae came, prosaically, with shrimps. Heimrich nodded at them, or in response to what MacDonald said. He speared a shrimp, ate it, and nodded.

'I do like the shrimps, doctor,' he said. He ate another.

'It's odd to see Miss Jones and Mr. Oslen together,' he said, and nodded down the room. MacDonald continued to watch Heimrich, obviously waiting. Mary looked down the room to the distant table at which the pianist and Rachel Jones were dining. She looked back at Heimrich.

'Different types,' Heimrich said. 'More different than you'd suppose, actually. There was a little disturbance up in my part of the country a while back. The Legion broke up a meeting, which was ill advised of it although, perhaps, understandable. Miss Jones and Mr. Oslen were both involved.' He paused and ate his last shrimp. 'On opposite sides,' he added, mildly. 'Mr. Oslen is active in the Legion.'

'I gather,' MacDonald said, slowly, 'that you have been checking up on us. I gather you don't agree that it was this musician. What's his name?'

'García,' Heimrich said. 'Mario García. It may very well have been García, naturally. The chief deputy seems to be efficient. It seems very likely that Mr. García had reason to hate Mr. Wells. Or thought he had. It seems likely that he saw Wells early this morning, although he denies it. A knife might be the weapon he would choose.'

'And,' MacDonald said, 'it isn't your case. You say it isn't.'

'Now doctor,' Heimrich said. 'I don't like murder.'

'So you check up on Oslen and Miss Jones,' MacDonald said. 'Apparently on me. On who else?'

Heimrich closed his eyes.

'I'm a curious man, doctor,' Heimrich said. 'It's my occupation. As yours is internal medicine, research on gastro-intestinal processes. You want to make the diagnosis fit the symptoms, naturally. I want to make the character fit the crime.'

'And García's doesn't fit?'

'Now doctor,' Heimrich said. 'I don't say that.'

'Do you mean,' Mary said, 'that this Miss
114

Jones was one of the—what were they? Rioters? That Mr. Oslen doesn't know it?'

'We took some pictures,' Heimrich said. 'She was in one of them, with some people we already knew. It's true, however, that her name doesn't show up on any of the lists that we've— that have come into our hands. It would be understandable if Mr. Oslen didn't know of her activities. It isn't even at all certain that there are any activities to know of. The picture isn't evidence, and as I say her name doesn't—' He broke off, to greet the arrival of roast beef. He began to eat it, with his eyes open.

Heimrich showed, even after he had eaten, no inclination to return to the subject of the murder. He concentrated on the menu; decided to experiment with lime pie. By then, Mary and MacDonald had finished the last of their coffee. MacDonald said, 'Well?' to Mary and she nodded. Heimrich, avuncular, advised them to have a good time.

'I'm restless,' MacDonald said as they stood in the lounge. 'Would you at all like to walk?'

She said, 'In these?' and looked at her high-heeled slippers. He appeared saddened. 'All right,' she said. 'Give me time to change. It will only be a minute.'

In her room it did not take long to change to walking shoes. But then the dress was wrong; Sophie would not have approved. Mary changed to green linen, which was better; was better still with a short, white summer coat. All

115

in all, it was more than a minute.

There had been time enough, she found as she and MacDonald started out of the hotel, for Heimrich to have finished his experiment with lime pie. He was sitting on the little-used porch at the front of the hotel, and Paul Shepard was sitting with him. They were talking; more precisely, Heimrich was listening while Shepard talked. He appeared to have his eyes closed, but nevertheless he managed to see Mary and the tall doctor. He waved at them casually with his left hand, in which a cigarette glowed. He told them they must try lime pie the next time. Shepard started to stand, but subsided when Mary shook her head. As they went down the steps to the drive, Mary heard Shepard's sharp, incisive voice resume behind them. '—we retain complete—' she heard him say, and the voice died out behind her.

They walked along a wide street, in and out of the black shadows of palm trees, in the warm night. They walked in the deep shadow of a high brick wall, and the shadow of the house behind the wall stretched out beyond the wall's shadow to the sidewalk across the street. They walked across Truman Avenue and down a narrower street, flanked by older houses, with here and there a new house uneasy among them. 'What do they call them?' Mary asked, and indicated one. 'Bungalows,' he told her. 'The progenitor of the ranch type.' She said, 'Really?' looking again, and he said he didn't

116

know, really.

'Does he make you uneasy?' he asked, after another block. 'Heimrich?'

'Is that why you're restless?' she asked. 'Because of your brother?'

He supposed so.

'Don't be,' she said. Then she added, 'I like the captain.'

'It seems to me,' MacDonald said, 'that he is quite capable of absorbing my mind. Your mind. Anybody's.' He looked down at her. 'Absorb somebody else's mind and use it to think with. Or—pervade it.'

'You *are* restless,' she said. 'He's just an ordinary man. Perhaps he listens more than most. That's all.'

He realized that, he told her. It was merely that—But he stopped there and they walked another block in silence along a black and white street. Then MacDonald said, 'I wouldn't want him after me, all the same.'

She said, 'Nobody's after you, Mac,' and then he put a hand, momentarily, on her shoulder. He removed it at once and said, 'You're a nice girl, Mary. Are you married or anything?'

She hesitated. Or anything? She said, 'No.'

'Good,' he said. They walked half a block. This time a high brick wall was across the street from them, the moonlight flooding it. 'That's a pleasant coincidence.'

There were lights ahead, then. They walked

another block and now, to their left, there was an area of weeds; now MacDonald had to reach up and hold aside the fronds of palm trees so they could pass under them. But beyond, in the next block, trailers were parked with only breathing space between; with chairs huddled in narrow passages between the coaches. 'It's a mixed-up town,' Mary said.

At the next corner they turned right, and were in Duval Street, which was not quite like any other street either had seen before. It had no unity, yet it had an odd kind of individuality. There were unpainted, one-story buildings on either side; then there was a minareted building of frame and stucco, announced as the Sociedad Cuba. It abutted on the Ideal Cleaners, which was bright with neon and beyond which Frigidaire was brighter still, with the greenish white of vapor tubes reflected by row after row of antiseptic white. But next to this, behind palm trees, was a square, two-story house, with porches at both levels and from each porch a species of wooden lace dripping. This house—although it offered rooms for rent—was aloof from the street and from neon; it receded in darkness and seemed to recede into the past. The 'San Carlos Palace' was beyond it, as they walked down the slowly busying street, and it was evident that the San Carlos had been an opera house before it was either a 'palace' or a cinema. But the cinema across the street, showing that evening the movie version of *Sailor Beware* was as modern as neon, and as popular.

And from there, where sailors clustered thick, waiting in line—and protesting the waiting—Duval Street was another street altogether. It was a street in which bars spilled onto sidewalks; barber shops were, like stages, open to the world; from both sides of which music blared into the night. The Cabana Cocktail Lounge spread its jam session under the moon; behind a low wall, an outdoor restaurant—'Italian and Spanish specialities'—offered couples the deep shadows of the palms. (But a block or so farther along, the B.P.O.E. was impressively fraternal and the Key West Women's Club offered culture. It also offered the Key West Players in *Kind Lady*.) La Concha, which was the downtown hotel, announced itself proudly to the sky; it had, and admitted having, the highest cocktail lounge in the southernmost city of the United States.

And sailors were everywhere. They walked in twos and in fours; they walked in summer whites, except where here and there a man, captured by summer in midwinter and a commanding officer addicted to the calendar, went hotly in blue. They walked with young faces, artfully hardened, and sought adventure where neon harshly flattened night. Sailors sat in bars, leaning on elbows, waiting without

119

hope—yet, being young, not really without hope—for some sudden strangeness. Men of the shore police, hunting in pairs, looked warily and with suspicion into the open-faced bars they passed, and the sailors—guiltless of any infraction of any rule—nevertheless stiffened over their drinks and did not lift them until authority had gone by.

'They're so dreadfully young,' Mary said. 'So—anxious.'

She was agreed with. She was told she was a good girl.

'All the same,' Mary Wister said, and MacDonald touched her shoulder lightly, and said he knew; of course he knew. A voice of metal spoke suddenly, over all other sounds; spoke so loudly that Mary jumped. 'Twenty beautiful girls under twenty at The Club,' the voice said. 'The most sensational entertainment in the southernmost city! Continuous from eight-thirty until four every night.' The metallic voice cleared itself. 'Never a dull moment. Every night in the week!' it reported, with a kind of pleased surprise. 'Don't miss the twenty most—'

The sound truck went on down Duval. A sailor looked hard at Mary, his eyes demanding response; his eyes saying that this, surely this, was the sudden strangeness of an unprecedented night. 'O.K., mac,' Barclay MacDonald said, his voice easy, and the sailor saluted, burlesquing it only a little, and his eyes

120

blanked, searched elsewhere. The sailor was reasonably drunk, but only reasonably. He turned into the next bar, which was the next door—which was, almost inevitably, the next door to any other door.

They were abreast The Club, then. Neon told them that; music through the open door told them that. MacDonald looked down at her. They stopped, and were jostled. A young voice, fresh, from the Middle West, said, 'Excuse me, miss,' and Mary said, 'Of course.'

'All right,' she said, then, and they crossed the street. A doorman made much of them.

CHAPTER SIX

At first the girl had worn a white dress—a chaste white dress, covering her fully, coming high at neck and long on arms, brushing the floor of the stage which was all apron, with room behind only for the thumping orchestra. The orchestra thumped in moderation at first and the girl, who was improbably blond, wriggled in moderation. She had, Dr. Barclay MacDonald said, admirable muscle tone. The abdominal musculature was particularly noteworthy.

The room was low ceilinged, full of smoke, of tables, of sailors drinking beer. The sailors made sounds at the girl, encouraging, raucous,

121

yet strangely (to Mary Wister) lacking in exuberance. They made sounds, said 'take it off,' as if sounds and injunction were expected of them; as if they were bored by what was expected of them. Only the stage was bright; the room itself was dim. The mass voice of the Navy was hoarse, dull in tone. The girl in white wriggled. She put fingers on a zipper under her left arm. 'Take it off,' the sailors told her, in a multiple voice of weariness. The girl pulled and the dress was off. She wore white silk pants under it and a white silk bra. The orchestra thumped more heavily; the girl's wriggling became more emphatic.

She could not dance; she did not try to sing. She wriggled, and the sailors made tired sounds at her. She turned as if to leave the stage and the sailors made further sounds. She turned back, as if surprised; she gestured toward the pants, indicating astonished disbelief. The music thumped; the audience told her to take it off.

She had a g-string covered with red sequins under the pants. She wriggled, half danced, in a circle on the stage. She made again as if to leave, and the stage lights darkened to a spot, with the blond girl in the middle of it. Her back to the audience, she reached up toward the fastening of the bra. She withdrew her hand; she turned, her face all the burlesque of astonishment. 'Oh,' a single voice said, 'take it off, sister.' She shook her head, and the

122

orchestra thumped more loudly, seemed to command. She turned away again, and again the hand teased at the fastening of the bra. Her fingers touched it, released the catch. But then she held the bra over her breasts with both hands, turning with it held so. 'Take it off,' the sailors told her.

She let the bra fall, and pretended to shield her face with modest hands. She had red rhinestone nipples. She stood, her face still covered, and, with the rest of her body almost motionless, rotated her rhinestone-pointed breasts.

'Now that,' MacDonald said, 'is quite unusual muscular control. Not one woman in a hundred can do that.' He turned to Mary Wister. 'This is really quite interesting,' he said. 'I'll wager—'

'No,' Mary Wister said. 'I wouldn't.'

'I'm afraid,' MacDonald said, 'that this doesn't amuse you terribly.'

'Well,' Mary said, 'I'm not a man.'

He nodded; he said that he had noticed. He looked around the dim room, at sailors drinking beer, watching the improbably blond girl perform her unlikely feat. The girl stopped abruptly, a drum banged; she turned and walked from the stage, her neat, small buttocks keeping time. The audience applauded. A few whistles followed her. A dark girl, wearing a red dress which was not chaste, came through the curtains, prancing heavily. She aroused

123

enthusiasm in the drum.

'What happens to these girls?' Mary asked. 'Where do they go from here? Anywhere?'

'I don't suppose so,' MacDonald said. 'Not onward and upward. They just—lose muscle tone.'

'Which is their talent,' she said. 'Even as it is—' She indicated the sailors. 'Do they like it?'

'They'd like to,' he said. 'They're all kinds, Mary. Some of them would rather hear a symphony. All of them would rather—' He shrugged. 'They're kids from everywhere,' he said. 'All kinds of kids. They haven't much choice here, you know.' Again he lifted his shoulders. 'I was in the Navy for awhile,' he said. 'At a hospital on Long Island—St. Albans.' He paused again. 'They get the diseases the rest of us get,' he said. 'In addition to everything else.' He paused and looked at her. 'I'm sure,' he said, 'I must be giving you a wonderful time. Do you want to get out of here? It's dreary, isn't it?'

She nodded. But when he moved as if to get up from the table, she shook her head; said to finish his drink, and then they'd go. There was a gritty fascination in the place. The dark girl was down to g-string and bra; she was being urged to take it off. She was heavier than the other girl. 'This one has less talent,' Mary said. 'By—by how many years, Mac?'

He looked at the dark girl.

'Ten,' he said. 'Perhaps more. The girls

124

worry you.'

'Yes,' she said. 'I suppose so.'

He waited for her to continue, but she watched the dark girl, who was bumping.

'You want to think everybody's going somewhere,' he said. 'Onward and upward. We all like to think that. It's a comforting thought.' He smiled at her. 'You've had a bad day,' he said. 'Violent death to—this dreary frolic.'

'When this one finishes,' she said. She sipped from her almost filled glass. 'It's just that I'm tired. And—the first girl was young, wasn't she? Almost pretty.'

The dark girl finally took it off. Her breasts were unsheathed. The sailors whistled with a semblance of approval.

'All right,' Mary said, 'let's—' But then she stopped. The blond girl, wearing the white dress again, came from behind the stage and down the side of the room. A solid man who had been sitting alone at a table against the wall stood up, and pink-stained light fell on his face from above. The girl sat down across from Captain Heimrich of the New York State police, and Heimrich, turning, sought a waiter. He looked at them and nodded across the room. Then a waiter intervened between them.

'Well,' MacDonald said, and his eyebrows went up slightly.

'A new aspect of the captain,' Mary said.

MacDonald seemed about to nod

agreement, but he checked the motion.

'You know,' he said, 'I wonder if it is?'

They started to leave, then. It took a little time to get their check; a little more to get their change. Heimrich and the blond girl were talking, by then. The girl was doing most of it. Heimrich moved his head occasionally, showing that he heard. Mary wondered whether, under these circumstances, he was managing to keep his eyes open.

When they finally started out, their departure was again delayed, this time briefly. Just coming into the night club were the Sibleys and Penny and Paul Shepard.

'More slummers,' Penny Shepard said.

'We go to slum no more,' MacDonald told her. 'But don't let us discourage you.'

'There's no dancing tonight,' Penny said. 'At the hotel, I mean. Out of respect, apparently. It's put us on the town.'

That did not, Mary thought, explain the Sibleys. But perhaps they were restless, too.

Mary and MacDonald went back by cab to The Coral Isles, and said little on the way; he was abstracted and seemed, for minutes at a time, to forget her presence. She thought of the dim night club, and the strip tease girls, who weren't beautiful, weren't under twenty and weren't going anywhere. She thought also of Captain Heimrich, his face colored by the pinkness of the shade through which light fell on it, and the blond girl (except that she probably wasn't) in the long white dress.

In the lighted hotel lobby—the light by no means pinkish—Mac's face was drawn and tired, although at the last moment, just when they parted, a quick smile changed it, so that weariness was momentarily wiped away.

'You're a good girl,' he told her. 'Some day I'll do something for you. Tomorrow? I'll think of something.'

She had to work tomorrow; she had to work sometime; she was there to work. But she looked up at him and did not say that. She said, 'Tomorrow, Mac.' He patted her shoulder again, as he had done earlier, and then went past the desk to the elevator, a very tall, thin man, moving carefully, moving wearily.

Mary stopped at the desk and found mail waiting her. She sat in a corner of the almost deserted lounge and looked at the mail, none of which mattered. When she had finished, she still sat for a time, postponing the moment of rising, of walking down the lounge and up the stairs to her room. And then, Rachel Jones, crossing the lounge from the french doors to the porch, stopped suddenly, hesitated a moment, and walked toward Mary Wister. She was a small girl on high heels, a black dress leaving pretty shoulders bare, her mouth painted vividly on a pale face. She looked like a sophisticated toy, but she walked with purpose.

'Miss Wister,' she said. 'Can I talk to you?'

She stood and looked down at Mary and waited.

'Of course,' Mary said.

'I have to talk to someone,' the girl said. 'Before—' She decided not to finish that. With a quick movement she sat beside Mary.

'It's complicated,' she said. 'Will you listen?'

'Yes,' Mary said. The girl seemed oddly tense. It was as if she drew purpose tight between slim hands.

'It's about Wells,' Rachel Jones said, and turned so that, sitting on the edge of the sofa, she could look at Mary. 'And—Bill Oslen. It's something I can't handle alone and can't—' She stopped and shook her head. 'It's very complicated,' she said, again. 'I want to tell you something, and then I want you to tell somebody—I think Captain Heimrich—but not that it came from me. Will you do that?'

'I guess—' Mary began, but then she thought, and shook her head. 'If it's about Mr. Wells's death, and something the police should know,' she said, 'I can't promise that. How could I? Why don't you just go to the sheriff? Or Captain Heimrich, if you'd rather?'

'There're several reasons,' the girl said. 'You won't just take my word for it?'

'No,' Mary said. 'I can't. I don't ask you to tell me anything.'

'You know Captain Heimrich,' the girl said. 'He'll listen to you. I want to stay out of it.'

Mary shook her head. Rachel looked at her

intently for a moment.

'Well,' she said, and now spoke slowly, 'will you do this? Will you listen to what I want to tell you and then pass it along, but not right away? Say I told you, if you have to, but give me—oh, until tomorrow? Say about noon? Then tell somebody—anybody you want to. By that time—' She stopped again. 'You see,' she said, 'I want to stay alive, like anybody else.'

She said this as if it were the most natural thing in the world to say; as if, from one civilized young woman to another, in the lobby of a resort hotel, the risk that one might fail to stay alive was a risk so obvious that to acknowledge it was mere formality.

'What do you mean?' Mary said. 'What are you talking about?'

'Just that,' Rachel Jones said. 'Not to be killed, like Wells. They wouldn't think twice about it, you know.'

It should have been preposterous; the girl's almost off-hand acceptance of a danger still undefined, emanating from a source not disclosed but taken for granted, should have been the more beyond credence because of the very casualness of its announcement. Mary looked at the vivid girl intently and Rachel waited. Only after almost a minute did she smile faintly.

'You're out of it, aren't you?' she said. 'Clear out of it. Or you think you are. You can't bring yourself to believe me. Poor Wells. He fought so hard to wake up people like you. To make them *see!*'

Now the matter-of-factness had disappeared. Now Rachel spoke with emphasis, and seemed to use words she had often used before, or often thought before.

'I just want you to listen,' she said. 'Tell somebody tomorrow. That isn't much, is it? *Is* it?'

Before it had been believable and, so, frightening. That, Mary thought, was because her mind was tired, and because of the girl's matter-of-factness. Now it was melodrama, and melodrama was—was a cliché. An impressionable young woman, excited by her brushing contact with murder, imagined herself centered in a swirl of mystery, threatened by conspirators, no doubt masked, who 'wouldn't think twice' about the most final violence.

'What do you mean by "they"?' Mary asked.

'Will you listen to me?' Rachel asked again, her voice strained. 'Do what I ask?'

'I'll listen,' Mary said. 'Of course I'll listen.' She hesitated. After all, tomorrow was only around the corner of a few hours' sleep; until tomorrow whatever she was to be told would keep safely. She would not have to bother to keep it. And, it wouldn't be important. 'I won't say anything until tomorrow,' she said. It wouldn't matter, one way or the other.

'Oslen killed Wells,' the girl said, after a further moment during which she scrutinized Mary's face. 'I don't know how—I mean, precisely how he managed it. I know why. Because Wells was going to tell people about him. About what he's doing.'

'Oslen?' Mary said, although of course the girl was talking about William Oslen, concert pianist and—what else? Oh yes—crusader against communism, leader in the breaking up of subversive meetings. What had Heimrich said of that? 'Ill advised, but understandable.' And—he had also said that Rachel Jones was, or appeared to be, on the other side.

'People like you won't let yourselves understand,' Rachel said. 'Won't *let* yourselves. Of course, Oslen. Who else?'

'What could Mr. Wells have to tell anybody about Mr. Oslen?' Mary asked. She made it very clear, for her own benefit as much as for Rachel Jones's. 'Mr. Wells was a former communist,' she said. 'That's right? He changed his mind and has been doing everything he can to expose people who were communists, or are communists now, and are trying to hide it. Isn't that true?'

'Of course,' Rachel said. She was impatient. 'That's what I'm—'

'Wait,' Mary said. 'Captain Heimrich told us—told Dr. MacDonald and me—something about Mr. Oslen. He's active in the American Legion somewhere. In New York somewhere?

131

There was some kind of meeting—a communist meeting, or a meeting arranged by communists—and Mr. Oslen was one of the leaders in breaking it up. What could Mr. Wells have said about Mr. Oslen?'

'That he was told to do that,' Rachel said. 'That it was part of their plan. That he's really working for them. They staged the whole thing—they *wanted* it broken up. So it would go all over the world—the violent Americans, the "cannibals." To make all we say about freedom, about free speech, sound like lying. To people who don't know any better. Don't you see?'

'No,' Mary said.

'The Grand Jury that investigated saw that much,' Rachel told her. 'That the communists wanted violence. For propaganda. To take in the liberals—in this country, in England, everywhere. The *liberals*!' She made the word an epithet. 'They announced the meeting. They challenged anybody to stop them. They baited the Legion people; dared them. They wanted an incident.' She shook her head. 'You're all asleep,' she said. 'You don't know what's going on—what the danger is.'

'Listen,' Mary said. 'You're excited. I know that things like that go on. I do remember the riot—and obviously they wanted it. What's that got to do with Mr. Oslen. What was he told to do? Who told him?'

'Did you think they'd leave it to chance?'

Rachel asked. 'They don't leave anything. Suppose the people they wanted to get excited didn't get excited? Suppose they just said, "Let them shoot their faces off. Nobody pays any attention to them." There'd be some who would argue that way, wouldn't there? People who would see through the whole thing?'

'Yes,' Mary said. 'Of course.'

'So,' Rachel said, 'they take care of that. They get somebody inside, under cover. Somebody who'll stir the other side up. Say, *"Come on. Let's go get the bastards! We'll show them whose country this is."* That way, they get their—incident. Their propaganda incident. Oslen's fine for that—good standing, public patriotism, all of it. Oh, they know the tricks.'

Rachel was violent enough, now, although her voice remained low. She leaned forward, stabbed words at Mary.

'*Understand!*' she said. '*Wake up!* This is a conspiracy we're talking about—a criminal conspiracy. It's not free speech—any of the nice, easy things. This is different. Can you see?'

'You mean,' Mary said, 'that Mr. Oslen was—is—an agent? An agent provocateur? Working for the communists inside the Legion? I suppose in other groups which are active against communism. Getting them to use violence—lawlessness? So that people— sane, middle-of-the-road people in other countries—will get to feeling, a plague on both

133

their houses? Feel there's not so much choice after all?'

'Of course,' Rachel said. 'What did you think I was saying?'

She believes it utterly, Mary thought, looking at the vivid girl. That it is all organized this way, plotted this way, this devious. That a man like Oslen—

'How do you know about this?' Mary said. 'Say something like that could happen. I don't know. Maybe it could. But you talk as if you know.'

'Of course I know,' Rachel said. 'I'm one of them—or they think I am. I'm a contact for Oslen. With the men who tell him what to do. He can't be seen with them. Can't go to meetings, of course. He has to be careful. I'm not known to be one of them. I'm not important. Nobody's ever heard of me. Oslen can know me—I'm a music student he's met somewhere. We're both interested in music. If they ever find out about me, he's still all right. All he knew about me, he can say, is that I'm a girl he met—a girl who wants to be a pianist. A protégée of his. If people don't believe it's that simple, they'll believe it's just as simple in another way. Man and pretty girl. That's why they chose me.'

'But if you're one of them—'

'I said, "They think I am,"' the girl said. 'I was, once, because—well, there was somebody I knew, I thought was wonderful. He made it all seem—well, not what it is. Not this vicious thing it really is.'

'But you've stayed in,' Mary said. 'That's what you say.'

'I can do something by staying in,' Rachel said. 'There are things I can find out and tell people. People like Wells. People like—' But then she shook her head. 'You'll have to guess the rest of it,' she said.

'Go on,' Mary said. 'You say that Oslen killed Mr. Wells. Why? Because Mr. Wells had found out about him?'

'Of course,' Rachel Jones said. 'I told Wells. You see—what he's doing, Oslen I mean, isn't against any law. It ought to be, but it isn't. So nobody can do anything—officially. But a man like Wells, who doesn't—didn't—have to be official could see that the right people found out. People in the Legion. In other groups. See that he got thrown out.'

'You told Wells,' Mary said. 'Then?'

'Wells has—had—to be careful,' Rachel said. 'He had to be sure, particularly with a man like Oslen, who isn't in the government or anything. He asked Mr. Oslen to come down and talk about these—charges. I came along. Oslen was surprised. But I convinced him it was a party contact. Actually, I came to answer the lies I knew he'd tell Wells. Only—I guess Wells found out some other way that it was all true. So—Oslen killed him so he couldn't talk.'

She paused.

'That's the way it had to be,' she said.

'Why don't you tell this yourself?' Mary asked. 'To the police. To Captain Heimrich.'

The girl shook her head impatiently.

'They'd find out,' she said. 'Then I'd be no use any more. They might even—well, I said I want to stay alive. I want time to—'

She stopped and shook her head again.

'Never mind,' she said. 'You tell Heimrich tomorrow. Tell him the whole thing, if you have to. By that time—' She shook her head again. Then, quickly, she stood up.

'You tell them,' she said. 'I can always say you made it up. But they'll look into it all the same. Maybe I can—'

She stopped again. Then, after a moment, she said, 'Good night,' and turned and went down the lounge on high heels, the sophisticated toy again, not looking back. Mary watched her go and tried to decide what she believed of what she had been told. It was hard to believe. And yet—Again the picture was in her mind, each line sharp, each color clear—the green of leaves, the white of a dinner jacket—and the red. As if he were there before her, Mary saw Bronson Wells on his back in a narrow tunnel, open eyes staring up and seeing nothing they stared at. Mary Wister shivered and then stood up. Once you believed in murder, you could believe, you had to believe, in anything. She had been wrong to promise the girl.

But she had. She carried that promise with her, heavy in her mind, across the lounge and upstairs to her room on the second floor. Moonlight poured through the open window, but she closed the venetian blinds against it and turned on a lamp. She lighted a cigarette and sat in the easier of the chairs, making no move to undress and go to bed. She had promised; she shouldn't have. If what Rachel said was true—Of course it isn't true, Mary told herself. It's all too—too utterly far-fetched. There isn't a conspiracy like that. The girl is hysterical. There's something wrong with her. She hates Oslen; she's made all this up so that—But Bronson Wells lay in a green tunnel between a wall and the thick hedge, and there was blood on his white dinner jacket and his eyes—That was real. She could not get away from that. With the rawness of that melodrama accepted, then—then what could she refuse to accept?

She sat there for an hour or more, and cigarettes filled the ash tray. Most of them were almost as long when she discarded them as when they had been lighted—long, broken tubes of white, twisting in the tray. Finally, she made up her mind. She could not palliate what she planned to do. She planned to break a promise; a promise reluctantly given, to be sure, but a promise nevertheless. She would have to tell Heimrich what she had been told; she could not take the responsibility of not telling him. Probably he would do nothing

137

until morning; she could tell him of the girl's fears and let him make what he could of them, act as he thought best.

She reached for the telephone and then stopped. She could, at least, avoid talking to him openly, calling him through the hotel switchboard. It would be better to go to his room. If only she knew which room—But then a picture formed again in her mind. This time it was of words written clearly, in a firm hand, on the top sheet of a pad. 'Orange juice. Scrambled eggs. Toast. Coffee.' Of a signature: 'M. L. Heimrich.' Finally, of a room number: '209.' It was all there in her mind, to be read again as, hardly knowing she did so, she had read it that morning and so filed a photograph which now could be taken out and studied.

She turned out the lamp and went to the door. A man and a woman were coming along the corridor, talking, and she waited until they passed. Then she went out, making no noise, and closed the door behind her. She looked at the number on the door—202. She went along the corridor, which was lighted dimly, but adequately. At the far end, a red exit light burned. There were room doors only on her right. She passed 204 and 206 before she realized that she was going wrong. There were only even numbers this way.

She turned back, walked past her own room and then, very quickly, through the more brightly lighted stair hall and into the corridor beyond. Here the room doors were on her left; here the first was numbered 201. She was right, now. She went down the corridor, still quickly but almost silently on the carpeted floor. 203, 205—

There were transoms over the doors, and through the transom of 209 light showed. She stopped in front of the door and looked up and down the corridor, listened for any sound. She saw no one, heard nothing. She knocked on the door, quickly, lightly. There was no response. But the door, which had not been latched, began to open inward. She knocked again, and the door swung a little more, away from the light touch of her knuckles.

'Captain Heimrich,' she said then, speaking softly, speaking almost in a whisper. 'Captain Heimrich!'

She heard a faint sound then, and thought it was that of breath exhaled in pain. She spoke Heimrich's name again and, when this time no sound answered her, she pushed open the door.

Heimrich was sitting in a chair facing the door. His eyes were closed; he seemed to be breathing heavily, with difficulty. And there was blood on the front of his linen jacket.

'Captain!' she said and her voice, still low, was urgent. She was in the room, then. The door was open behind her.

Then Heimrich opened his blue eyes. They were as clear as always, as alive.

'Close the door,' Heimrich said. His voice

was low, as hers had been. 'Hurry, Miss Wister.'

She closed the door. She closed it too quickly. The sound of the closing was sharp in the room, in the corridor outside. Heimrich made a quick, one-handed, gesture, as if he were the conductor of an orchestra, signaling for pianissimo. The gesture seemed involuntary; it was obviously too late. Heimrich sighed.

'You're hurt!' she said. Now her voice was low enough.

'Our friend with the knife,' Heimrich said. 'I was—but never mind that now. It's nothing serious, I think.' He moved, and winced as he moved. 'It would be the same shoulder, naturally,' he said. 'Now Miss Wister. What are you doing here?'

'I want to tell you something,' she said. 'But—you have to have a doctor. I'll call Mac. I'll—'

'Wait,' he said. 'I—' But then he stopped. 'All right,' he said, 'you may as well. No doubt you were seen, or heard. Unless—' He looked at her for a long moment. 'No,' he said, 'I doubt it very much. I was waiting for someone. However. See if you can get Doctor MacDonald, Miss Wister. He may as well have a look at this.' He indicated his right shoulder.

The switchboard operator was slow to answer; there was more time taken to find MacDonald's room number. But MacDonald

140

answered when the telephone had rung only twice. He listened, and was quick. He came quickly; it was not two minutes after she had recradled the telephone that she heard hurrying steps in the corridor. During those minutes, Heimrich sat with his eyes closed. He opened them when Barclay MacDonald came in, with the bag of his profession. 'Go in the closet or somewhere if you don't like blood, Miss Wister,' Heimrich told her, pleasantly. But she stayed. She got hot water on a clean towel when MacDonald asked for it. MacDonald's fingers were quick.

'Well, doctor?' Heimrich asked.

'You'll be all right,' MacDonald said. 'We'll get you to a hospital, get some penicillin on it. But it's nothing to worry about.'

'I fell away from it, naturally,' Heimrich said. 'We'll see about the hospital tomorrow. I tried to get you a few minutes before Miss Wister came, doctor. You didn't answer.'

'I couldn't sleep,' MacDonald said. 'I was outside. I'd just come in when Mary called.'

'Yes,' Heimrich said. 'It's a nice night. All moonlight and deep shadows. Were you down by the entrance, doctor? I mean, the entrance to the hotel drive?'

'No,' MacDonald said. 'I walked out on the pier.'

'Somebody was down by the entrance,' Heimrich said. 'I don't know who. Waiting in a deep shadow until I walked past. However.' He started to shrug, and grimaced. 'Very inept, whoever it was,' Heimrich said. 'Assuming he meant to kill me, naturally. I thought he might come along here to see how he made out. But— Miss Wister came.'

'You don't think—' Mary began.

'Now Miss Wister,' Heimrich said, and closed his eyes. 'Now Miss Wister.' He opened his eyes. 'I'll admit I was surprised,' he said. 'By all of it, naturally. Such a quick reaction—and more direct than I expected. However. What did you come to tell me, Miss Wister?'

She hesitated for a moment; looked involuntarily at MacDonald.

'I've finished,' MacDonald said. 'He ought to get some rest.' He turned to Heimrich. 'Take plenty of aspirin,' he said. 'Or do you want codeine?'

'Now doctor,' Heimrich said. 'You may as well hear what Miss Wister has to say. Don't you think so, Miss Wister?'

'I'm breaking a promise anyway,' she said. 'I don't suppose it matters if I—break it twice. I'd like Mac to hear.'

'Go ahead, Miss Wister,' Heimrich said.

She went ahead. Heimrich listened with his eyes closed. MacDonald's face was expressive. At the end, the expression was one of doubt.

'An hysteric,' he said, when Mary finished. 'She wants to get back at Oslen for something.' But then he paused. 'Of course—' he said, and uncertainly left it open.

142

'Now doctor,' Heimrich said, without opening his eyes. 'Why does it seem so improbable to you?' He opened his eyes then and looked at MacDonald and, after a moment, MacDonald shook his head. That seemed to answer Heimrich, who nodded and closed his eyes again.

'They can be quite as devious as Miss Jones says,' Heimrich told them. 'It's quite true that this riot was staged—was asked for. The Legion was baited into it. It was planned to happen. It's also true that Oslen was very active in—instigating to violence. It could have been for the reasons Miss Jones thinks.'

'I gather you investigated this riot?' MacDonald asked.

'No,' Heimrich said. 'I looked over some of the reports. I got a few more details this afternoon, naturally.'

'You're checking up on all of us, aren't you?' Mary asked.

'Now Miss Wister,' Heimrich said. 'The sheriff's office wants what information it can get, naturally. I try to be co-operative.'

'I thought,' MacDonald said, 'that Jefferson was willing to settle for this man García. Didn't you tell us that? All of us?'

'Now doctor,' Heimrich said. 'Perhaps I did. Perhaps he is.'

'Listen,' Mary said. 'Did what you heard this afternoon—does it bear out Rachel Jones's story?'

'Only to the extent I said,' Heimrich told her. He seemed about to continue, but in the end did not. Instead, he said that he might, possibly, take a few grains of codeine.

'Captain,' Mary said, 'what are you going to do?'

He opened his eyes.

'Now Miss Wister,' he said. 'Nothing tonight.' He smiled faintly. 'I've done enough tonight,' he said. He moved, and the movement obviously was painful. 'Conceivably too much,' he said. He smiled again. 'So your promise isn't really broken, Miss Wister,' he said. 'At any rate, the result is the same.'

'Aren't you taking a chance?' MacDonald asked him, and to this Heimrich nodded.

'Sometimes one has to,' he said. 'We have to give a little rope, naturally.'

'You did earlier tonight, didn't you?' Mary asked, but got only 'Now Miss Wister, now Miss Wister.' It appeared Heimrich did not, after all, tell everything.

CHAPTER SEVEN

Paul Shepard's first service was just over the line. Ted Silvermann, receiving, looked at it, made a face at it and at himself and said, 'Good as gold.' It wasn't, and Mary shook her head.

144

'Too long,' she said, and turned to Shepard, behind her at the baseline. He frowned for a moment, but then he nodded and told her it was whatever she said. 'Long,' she repeated. She looked at Betty Silvermann. 'It looked long to me,' the slim, blond girl on the other side of the net said. 'Looked all right to me,' her husband insisted. 'Take two, Mr Shepard.'

'If you say so,' Shepard said, which was not what Mary Wister, playing net in a mixed doubles round-robin in which—and now she could not easily understand how—she had involved herself, had expected him to say. Shepard served again, and this time caught the corner. Silvermann's backhand blooped high; Shepard, coming in, took it overhead and smashed at Betty Silvermann, who dodged and said, 'Wow!' 'Thirty-love,' Shepard said, with satisfaction. Shepard certainly played to win, Mary thought. There had been a hole between the Silvermanns. Shepard was good enough overhead to—

'Other side, partner,' Shepard said behind her. There was not quite impatience in his tone. Mary crossed to stand guard duty on their left-hand alley. That, so far as she could tell, was what she was on court for. What I am, she thought, is a girl who can't say 'no.' Betty Silvermann played deep; she shook her head at Mary, and laughed. 'All I want to do is save my life,' she said. The Silvermanns, as had now been evident for two games, played for fun.

Shepard's first service was in the alley. His second was to Betty's backhand corner; it bounced high and away. She got wood of her racket on it, and netted. 'Forty-love,' Shepard told them.

Just a girl who can't say 'no,' Mary Wister thought, going back to the other side, brief white skirt swirling around slender legs which were beginning to turn reddish brown.

But there had been no particular reason to say 'no' when Paul Shepard came seeking a partner. She had worked all morning, and worked satisfyingly, which was unexpected. She had thought her mind would go off on its own, so that concentration would be impossible. But it had been surprisingly easy to work; to forget everything but line and color, shadow and light. That was, presumably, because everybody else seemed to have forgotten murder, forgotten tall tales of improbable conspiracy. At any rate, nobody seemed to be doing anything about either. Heimrich was not to be seen—presumably he had gone to a hospital to have his shoulder taken care of. Mac was not to be seen—perhaps he had gone with Heimrich. Mary had not seen Rachel Jones and when she had, briefly, seen William Oslen he was reading the *New York Times* on the porch and lifted a carefree hand in greeting. All this made work easy, made it inevitable. All this also left things uncomfortably hanging. She had, she realized as she worked, expected that she and Mac would meet, perhaps at breakfast, and try together to work out some meaning for what was happening. She had, and this she realized with some surprise and a little reluctance, looked forward to it.

She was calling it a morning, at a little after noon, putting pad and sketches in their folder, when Paul Shepard came across the lawn toward her. He was dressed in tennis slacks and shirt, and had a sweater over his shoulders. He was neat still; his hair was smoothly in place. He was still by no means a large man, nor physically impressive. But he had been put together very precisely, according to plan. He somehow made her feel that the plan had been his.

'You play tennis,' he had said. It was more statement than question.

'A little,' she said.

'I thought so,' he told her. 'You look like it. I'm looking for a partner. This afternoon. There's a mixed doubles round-robin set up. Give us some exercise.' He paused. 'Take our minds off things,' he added.

Then she should have said 'no.' Instead, she had said, hesitantly, 'Well—'

'My wife's no good at it,' he said. 'No good at it and knows it. What do you say, Miss Wister? You've got the clothes and things?'

She had the clothes. She had no racket. That he brushed aside. The pro had rackets; she

147

needn't worry about that.

'Be good for you,' he said, and she said, again, 'Well,' and this time capitulated. Perhaps it would be fun.

It was not really being, she thought again as she waited, guarding their right-hand alley, the score forty-love, two games to love, against the engaging Silvermanns, who played gayly, willing to win—or otherwise there was no point at all to it—but not caring much. (Not caring nearly enough, as things were working out.) The Silvermanns were weighted down by no—what was it? No feeling of responsibility. They were driven by no compulsion. They merely wanted to hit some tennis balls, if possible back across the net. When Betty Silvermann had said, 'Wow!' and dodged Paul Shepard's smash, she had ended laughing and her husband had laughed with her, had said, 'That's showing them, baby!'

'Watch your alley,' Paul Shepard said behind her. 'Watch your alley, partner.'

He served, and this time his first service was good—down the center, a foot short of the service line. Silvermann took it on his forehand, hitting a little ahead of the ball, so that he hooked toward Mary's alley. The ball went high, but was within reach. He had, she knew—while she jumped for the ball—planned a cross-court at the feet of Paul Shepard, who would be charging in. As it was, Shepard was not charging in. She heard him running behind

148

her. 'I'll take,' she heard him say, just as her racket met the ball. Her racket met the ball squarely; the ball went back, cross court, between the Silvermanns. Betty lunged for it, got only wood on it, and sent it out of court.

'Three love,' Shepard said. 'We change.'

'Better let me get those,' Shepard told her, as they went around the end of the net. 'I was right behind you.'

It was, so far as she could remember, the first ball she had hit since her own service.

'Well,' she said, 'you wanted me to watch the alley. And we made the point.'

'Oh,' he said, 'it was nice going, as it turned out.' He smiled quickly. 'We're too good for them,' he said, with satisfaction. 'Look out for the twist. I've been watching him.'

There were half a dozen couples in the tournament; they played around, until all teams had met; they played four games a match and in the end counted games won. It was midafternoon and Shepard and Mary had played two previous matches, in each winning three of the four games, losing only against the service of the opposing man. When they were not playing Shepard had, it was evident, been watching carefully.

Now he walked back to the baseline with her. He said, 'I'd stand about here,' and showed her. He watched her stand about there. 'It kicks high,' he said. 'Better take it on the drop. I'd move back a couple of feet and a little more this way.'

She had played tennis, on and off, since she was twelve. Not so much lately, to be sure— but still. But it didn't matter; she moved to stand where he told her.

'Remember,' he said, 'I'll go in. You stay back.'

And so, Mary Wister thought, we win the Davis Cup. But she nodded understanding.

Ted Silvermann served. The ball landed almost on the center line, but just in her court; it bounced high and to her backhand. She drove, but, because of the angle, almost down the middle. Betty Silvermann met the ball and volleyed it to the feet of Paul Shepard, who was coming in. Shepard tried a half volley and netted. He walked back, shaking his head. 'Right to her,' he told Mary, who said she was sorry. 'I told you about the bounce,' Shepard said. 'Come on. Let's take him!' The last was a command.

Shepard returned service deep to Ted Silvermann's backhand and went in. When Silvermann answered down the line, Shepard leaped for the ball, cutting it off—and leaving his side of the court uncovered. He gestured frantically behind his back to Mary, who dutifully crossed. But for the return, from Betty Silvermann, Shepard was back again to the center line, cutting off again. He continued on across, and Mary crossed again behind him. Again it was her duty, but it seemed a little silly.

If Shepard could manage it, he would get them all. Her participation was technical; in mixed doubles, four people must be on court. Nothing in the rules requires further participation, except the serving of one game in four, and reception of service at specified intervals.

Shepard won the point, *his* point, on the next volley, and it was fifteen-all. Waiting to receive, Mary remembered a tennis story she had heard sometime, or read somewhere—the story of a girl situated as she was in a mixed doubles match, partnered as she was, waiting to receive service, as she was. As the service came to her, the girl had called out, in a voice which rang through a stadium (Forest Hills, was it?), '*Mine!*' Mary resisted temptation, and was rewarded. Silvermann double faulted. But then Shepard overdrove and it was thirty-all. Shepard accepted the call against him with a moment's hesitation, followed by slightly overemphatic agreement. The ball, Mary thought, had been long by a foot.

She lost her next point, netting, and Shepard shook his head at her. He made his, taking a service which failed to break, and driving it, with all his wiry strength, at Betty Silvermann, playing net. She said, 'Wow!' again, and managed to deflect the ball from her face. Silvermann, Mary noticed, did not smile this time. He looked for a moment at Shepard, who was walking back to the baseline. He moved to serve to Mary, and grinned at her. She answered service with a lob over Betty's head and Silvermann took it in the air, with a furious backhand smash at Shepard, who was coming in. Shepard dodged and the ball went out. Silvermann's pleasant face had, momentarily, an expression of disappointment.

'One more to go,' Shepard told Mary, and prepared to make it. It was longer than the other points had been; once in the exchange, Mary was allowed—had to be, since Shepard had got himself hopelessly out of position—to keep the ball in play. Shepard crowded the net on the last return, playing so close he almost brushed it. Betty Silvermann's drive came to him, and he flicked it away, almost parallel to the net, for a placement. That was game. It was also, Mary thought, at least possibly a case of reaching illegally over the net. So, she thought, did Ted Silvermann. He waited for a moment where he had stopped as the ball angled away for the point. He looked at Paul Shepard. Shepard, who alone could have something to say, said nothing.

'Well,' Silvermann said, 'they sure ruined us, baby,' and patted his wife on the back. 'Nice going,' he told Shepard, who said, 'Oh, we got the breaks,' in a tone notable for its lack of conviction. The four of them walked off court together, clustered together around the table where they had piled sweaters and jackets, where the women had left their purses. They were pleasantly warm; it was Shepard who said, 'Drinks on the winner.' Silvermann seemed to hesitate a moment; he looked quickly at his wife, who nodded. 'Sure,' Silvermann said, and they cleared the table and sat around it. A boy came through the sun, across the lawn. The Silvermanns ordered Tom collinses; Shepard said a Coke would do him. 'You'd better stick to that too, partner,' he said to Mary.

'I think,' Mary Wister said, 'that I'll have a Collins.' She smiled, disarmingly, at Shepard. 'It'll be enough if you stay in shape, Mr. Shepard,' she told him. Shepard frowned, momentarily; Silvermann looked at him, and then at Mary. For her, briefly, he grinned.

Half an hour later, Mary and Shepard played again, winning three of the four, which gave them thirteen won to three lost, with one more match to go. Mary's collins did not seem to have affected her, although her timing was seldom put to the test. Paul Shepard was everywhere, his will to win flying like a pennant. During the last game of that match, Heimrich and Barclay MacDonald appeared in the tennis enclosure, found a table, and sat there, drinks in front of them, watching. MacDonald caught Mary's eye, and smiled and nodded to her. Heimrich did not catch her eye; he concentrated on the play. His right arm was in a sling.

They started to leave the court after the

fourth game, but their final opponents were waiting and there was, Shepard pointed out, no reason to get cooled off. So they stayed on and played again, and this time won all four. This time Mary Wister kept count. She served her game and won it from fifteen, thanks—oh, certainly, thanks—to Shepard's daring and determined interceptions. In that game, she hit the ball nine times in serving and once off the ground. With Shepard serving, she did not touch the ball. From the opposing woman she accepted service three times, netting once; from the man five, outing once. In four games, she had eighteen times the agreeable, or depressing, feeling of a tennis ball against the gut of a swinging racket. But they won—all told they had won seventeen games of the twenty played and their nearest competition— oddly enough the Silvermanns, who played for fun—had a won total of thirteen. 'Nice going,' Shepard assured her as they walked to the pavilion. 'Knew we could do it.'

'The Davis Cup safely home again,' she said, not having intended to say it.

He looked at her for a moment and then laughed.

'All right,' he said. 'I like to win. Don't you?' He smiled. 'You think I take it pretty seriously?'

'Oh,' Mary said, 'no. Everybody likes to win.'

MacDonald and Heimrich got up as they

approached.   MacDonald   extended congratulations and Heimrich, his eyes open, nodded to second them. Shepard stared at the black sling across Heimrich's linen jacket. 'What,' Shepard said, 'happened to you, captain?'

'Nothing serious,' Heimrich said. 'Nothing at all serious, Mr. Shepard. You play a good game.' He paused. 'Aggressive,' he added.

'Had a good partner,' Shepard said. He pulled on a sweater. He looked, now that he was no longer running, hot and a little tired. He zipped a case over his racket; clamped it into a press. He said he was for a shower; he said he would be seeing them; he said, 'Thanks a lot, partner,' to Mary Wister. He went. Mary supposed she'd better do the same. She put on a white tennis jacket.

'I wonder,' Heimrich said, 'if you could put it off for—oh, say half an hour, Miss Wister? If you're not too tired, naturally.'

'Why yes,' she said.

'To talk to Mr. Oslen,' Heimrich said. 'Tell him what you told us.'

'Of course,' Mary said. 'If—if you want it that way.'

'He does,' Heimrich said. 'I gave him an outline. He wants to hear it from you.'

'I suppose he denies it,' Mary said. 'But, all right. I can't vouch for any of it, of course. Why not—'

'Now Miss Wister,' Heimrich said. 'He does
155

deny it, naturally. But I'd like to do it this way. If you're not too tired.'

She wasn't. Ten minutes later, in the Penguin Bar—which, at a corner table, gave more than the expected amount of privacy—she told William Oslen what Rachel Jones had told her. The situation was curiously informal for the story; it was incongruous to sit at a corner table, with a long drink at hand, and tell this unlikely story of intrigue to an open-faced man with a brush haircut, make these utterly improbable accusations. As she talked, as she watched bewilderment and disbelief spread on Oslen's face, the story she had been told, and now retold, seemed entirely preposterous.

And when she finished, William Oslen called it that. He shook his head over it. He said, 'But I barely know the girl,' in the accents of a good Eastern school. He spread agile hands in a gesture of bafflement. 'Why would she tell this story? This idiotic lie?'

He looked at Heimrich, at Mary, at Barclay MacDonald. He shook his head hopelessly. 'She must be crazy,' he said. 'Or—after notoriety?' The last was half a question. None of the three he spoke to offered him an answer. He shook his head again.

'I barely know her,' he repeated. 'She's studying at a place in New York—studying piano. I'm on the board—sometimes I listen to the piano students. Give them advice. I met her that way and—well, she's a pretty girl. I took her to dinner once or twice; to a concert or two. I hadn't any idea I'd meet her here. That she'd tell this crazy story—' Words appeared to fail Oslen. He spread his hands, which were so much more expressive than his face, than his voice.

'Did you expect to meet Mr. Wells here?' Heimrich asked.

'Wells?' Oslen repeated. 'I didn't know him, captain. I knew of him, of course. Knew the swell job he was doing to smoke out the commies. I'd never met him. I didn't expect to meet anybody here I knew. Just to spend a couple of weeks loafing around in the sun before the spring tour.'

That was, Heimrich told him, very natural. 'Now Mr. Oslen,' he began, but Oslen leaned toward him suddenly.

'Listen,' he said, 'why don't you get the girl here? Have her repeat this—this yarn of hers? To my face?'

He turned quickly to Mary Wister.

'I don't mean—' he said.

'I understand,' Mary said. 'I wondered that myself, captain.'

'Naturally,' Heimrich said. 'The trouble is, Miss Jones doesn't seem to be around. They've been trying to find her. That is, the deputy sheriff has, since I told him the story about noon. She's not around.'

They waited.

'Hasn't checked out,' Heimrich said. 'Her

things are in her room. She hasn't had breakfast here, or lunch. They haven't been able to pick her up in town.'

Mary looked at him.

'Now Miss Wister,' Heimrich said, 'I don't know, naturally.'

'Something's happened to her,' Mary said. 'I broke my promise and—'

'Now Miss Wister,' Heimrich said. 'Now Miss Wister. I did nothing until around noon, when I couldn't find her myself. What did you think she wanted the time for, Miss Wister?'

Mary hesitated.

'You mean,' she said, 'she wanted time to—to run away.' She looked at Oslen, who shook his head, who offered a blank face. 'You mean that, captain?'

'That would seem most likely, wouldn't it?' Heimrich said. 'If, as Mr. Oslen tells us, her story is preposterous, her disappearance might make it appear more creditable. Or she might think it would. Also, makes it harder to disprove, naturally, since she can't be cross-examined. And, of course, if there were any truth in her story—I don't say there is, Mr. Oslen—she might feel she was—safer—away from here.'

'There is,' Barclay MacDonald said slowly, 'another possibility, of course.'

He looked at Oslen.

'I tell you—' Oslen began, hotly.

'Now doctor,' Heimrich said. 'Now Mr.

Oslen. Of course there is another possibility—perhaps several possibilities. Mr. Oslen, not knowing she had already talked to Miss Wister, thinking she might talk to someone, may have made it impossible for her to talk. There are other possibilities, naturally.' He closed his eyes. 'There always are,' he said. 'There always are.' His voice sounded tired.

'I can't stop your thinking what you damn well please,' Oslen said.

Heimrich did not open his eyes. He said, 'Now Mr. Oslen. You can't, can you?' Then he opened his eyes. 'At about twenty minutes to one this morning,' he said, 'somebody jabbed me with a knife. From behind. He'd waited in a shadow by the entrance and after I'd walked past him, used this knife. I heard his movements and had time to fall away from it. So he only scratched my shoulder. That wasn't, probably, what he'd planned. He didn't wait to make sure.' Heimrich paused. He opened his eyes.

'Doctor MacDonald was out on the pier about that time, he tells me,' Heimrich said. 'Miss Wister was—I suppose in your room, Miss Wister?' She nodded. 'And you, Mr. Oslen?' Heimrich said.

'The hell with this,' Oslen said.

'Now Mr. Oslen,' Heimrich said, and closed his eyes again. 'If you like, naturally. But somebody's going to ask you. One time or another, you're going to answer. Where were

159

you, Mr. Oslen?'

'In my room,' Oslen said. 'Asleep.' He paused. 'Alone,' he said. He looked hard at Heimrich.

'Where was Sibley?' he asked, and his voice was hard, insistent. 'That idealistic wife of his, who thought Wells was such a funny, funny man?' He mimicked, not particularly well. 'You've thought about Sibley, haven't you?'

'About Judge Sibley?' Heimrich said. 'Now Mr. Oslen. What is there to think about Judge Sibley?'

'*I* don't know,' Oslen said. 'All I know is what everybody knows—that he's up for confirmation to this post, whatever it is. That there's some doubt about him, as a risk. Or seems to be. That the committee's digging into his—associations. That Wells had been asked to appear before the committee. Next week, I think. But he can't now, can he?' He waited. 'Can he?' he repeated.

'No,' Heimrich said. 'No, he can't appear, Mr. Oslen.' He opened his eyes. 'Yes,' he said, 'I've thought about Judge Sibley, naturally. I've thought about several people. Judge and Mrs. Sibley were in their room. They'd just gone to bed, or were getting ready to go.'

'So they tell you,' Oslen said.

'Naturally,' Heimrich said. 'So they tell me. You weren't in town yesterday evening, Mr. Oslen?'

'No,' Oslen said. 'I had a drink or two in the

lounge. Played a little on the piano. It needs tuning.' He shuddered, seeming to hear discordant sounds. 'Keeps my fingers loosened up, is about all.'

Heimrich said, 'Umm-h.' He said that he had been wondering about that; about Mr. Oslen's opportunity to practice.

'You hadn't made any special arrangements to have a piano available?' Heimrich asked. 'To keep in practice?'

'No,' Oslen said. 'I don't need all that.'

Heimrich said he saw. He opened his eyes.

'By the way,' he said, 'when does your tour begin, Mr. Oslen?'

Oslen thought a moment. 'A week from tomorrow,' he said.

Heimrich nodded, abstractedly.

'Well,' he said, 'I guess—' But then he stopped. He shrugged and, from the expression on his face, wished he had not.

'Probably,' he said, 'all this is needless—a blind alley. Probably our man's García, after all.' He nodded, as if to himself, as if affirming an idea. 'That was his sister I was talking to last night,' he said to MacDonald, to Mary. 'At a night club in town,' he added, including Oslen. 'She calls herself Rita Abelard.' He shook his head. 'They think up remarkable names,' he said. 'She's a strip tease girl at this club,' he told Oslen. 'A rather pretty girl, in a fashion. Blond.' He paused. 'Blond on purpose, naturally,' he added. 'She's Cuban, and

161

actually rather dark. She takes drugs; has for several years. She says Wells started her.'

'Of all the crazy—' Oslen began.

'Now Mr. Oslen,' Heimrich said. 'Now Mr. Oslen. I'm afraid that it's only quite recently that Mr. Wells—put on his armor. Started his crusade. Before that—' He spread his hard, square hands, so different from the expressive hands of William Oslen. 'Before that he had a somewhat varied career,' Heimrich told them. He closed his eyes.

Heimrich, Mary Wister decided, was about to be a sieve again. She looked quickly at MacDonald, who nodded just perceptibly.

'They,' Heimrich told them, had been checking up on Bronson Wells. Naturally. Some they got from New York, some from Washington, part in Key West. He did not argue they had it all, or would ever have it. They had aspects of a man, possibly not the man himself, almost certainly not all of the man. But that was usually the way. Heimrich nodded his head; he kept his eyes closed, but appeared to be thinking aloud. When he spoke of making the character fit the crime, he told them, he meant both sides of the crime, the active and the passive. A certain man might commit a certain kind of crime, or the crime of, say, murder, in a certain way, responding to a certain provocation, using a certain weapon. It would for example—and for the simplest example, naturally—be more likely that
162

García would use a knife if he wanted to kill than that, say, the doctor here would. Certain motives might be adequate for one man and not for another. The character of the murderer would determine the texture of the crime—in part. The character of the victim was equally a factor. Both had to be considered.

'So,' Captain Heimrich said. 'To get back to Mr. Wells.'

They had, he said, got quite a distance back into the life of Mr. Wells, who had been born in Chicago, very poor, in 1905 and who, still very poor, had joined the Communist Party in the early twenties. He had been in New York, then, trying to get on the stage. He had not been particularly successful.

'He may have blamed what they call the "system,"' Heimrich said. 'He may have been what other people call an "idealist." It's one of the things we don't know.'

'What the hell difference does it make?' Oslen asked. 'He was a commie.' The big pianist shook his head. 'Who wasn't poor once?' he asked. 'Who liked it?'

'Now Mr. Oslen,' Heimrich said. 'Nobody, naturally. I'm merely trying to give you a picture.'

But, Mary wondered, why? What a strange kind of policeman! But then, she thought, I don't know much about policemen; not really enough to tell whether this one is a strange kind.

At any rate, Heimrich said, Wells had joined the Communist Party. For some years, apparently, he had made his living at whatever came to hand. 'Probably,' Heimrich said, 'some odd things came to hand. It's one of the things we don't know too much about. He seems to have had a few small parts on the stage.' But Wells's main interest was in work for the party. In the early thirties, he went on the party payroll as a professional organizer. 'At, I imagine, barely enough to live on,' Heimrich said. 'It isn't a lucrative profession.' He looked at Oslen, he seemed about to speak. 'Now Mr. Oslen,' he said, 'it isn't, you know.'

'How the hell would I know?' Oslen asked. 'They get plenty from Moscow, if you ask me. But I don't know anything about it. I keep telling you that.'

'Now Mr. Oslen,' Heimrich said. 'Now Mr. Oslen.'

'A crazy little halfwit tells you a story,' Oslen said. 'A story crazy on the face of it! You believe—'

'Now Mr. Oslen,' Heimrich said, 'you don't know what I believe, do you? I was talking about Mr. Wells.' He waited, but Oslen merely glared at him, without speaking. 'So—' Heimrich said, and got back to it.

Bronson Wells had worked in the party for ten years or more, as a paid agitator. There was no secret about that. He had an office at the party's headquarters off Union Square. He

164

was, in a minor way, one of—Heimrich hesitated—call it the front men for the party. Then, in 1945, something happened. Quite suddenly, so far as could be determined, he dropped out of the party's councils.

'That sort of thing often happened,' Heimrich said. 'He got thrown out. Maybe the line zigged and he zagged; I don't know. Somebody decided he was a deviationist. The next year, he turned up here, in Key West. He went back to making his living as he could.'

One of his ways, and perhaps the most legitimate, Heimrich told them, was as a master of ceremonies at one of the honky-tonks. He introduced the girls; he invited big hands for them. He told jokes between numbers; now and then even sang a little. He had done similar work in New York from time to time.

'A leerer in chief,' Barclay MacDonald said.

He was told, by Heimrich, that that put it very neatly. Bronson Wells, although he was pretty old for it, was a leer leader. He was also, apparently, engaged in other activities, in several of which the police were interested; in one of which, the Federal Government was interested. He was, at the least, on the fringes of the narcotics racket.

Oslen shook his head at that; shook it with the air of a man listening to the flagrantly improbable, finding it too improbable even to deny.

'Oh,' Heimrich said, 'it wasn't proved, naturally. Otherwise, he'd have been picked up. But the sheriff says there isn't much doubt about it.'

Oslen spread his hands.

'García's sister is an addict,' Heimrich said. 'She denies she is now; admits she was; says she got started by Wells. She's still an addict, whatever she says. Heroin, now. She says she started on marijuana, which is probably true. She had been going to business college. Her brother—their parents are dead—was very proud of her. Now she's a strip tease girl. García blames Wells; she admits her brother's threatened Wells, in the past. I talked to her last night. She wanted to talk to me.'

She was, Heimrich told them, afraid for her brother—naturally. García denied to the deputy sheriff that he had seen Wells, or thought about him, for years until he saw him on the dance floor of The Coral Isles. He admitted he had been surprised at seeing Wells—violently surprised. But he denied that he had seen Wells afterward. The authorities were sure he had, partly because of the cigarettes Wells had in his pocket—a brand García smoked, as did many other Key Westers. The authorities were sure they could, given time, prove it.

'Which,' Heimrich said, 'they can, the girl thinks. Because it's true. She says Wells looked them up and offered to help—to see that she

166

got out of the club, and out of Key West, and went back to business school or whatever she wanted. She says that, after some talking, her brother was convinced Wells really wanted to help, although he told Wells they didn't need help. "We don't," she told me. "I'm all right, now. I'm going north in the spring and get out of all this."'

The three of them had talked for an hour or so, Rita García, who called herself Abelard, had told Heimrich the night before, sitting at a table in the night club, pinkish light from a shaded bulb falling on her face. It had ended amicably; the three had had a drink together and then coffee—Cuban coffee. Wells had left them and taken a cab back to the hotel.

'She wants me to see her brother, get him to admit this,' Heimrich said. 'If it's the truth, she's right, naturally.'

'If,' Oslen repeated. He shook his head again, pitying credulity. 'You say yourself she's still an addict,' he said. 'You think her brother doesn't know it? Doesn't know it's— hopeless? What are you people waiting for?'

'Now Mr. Oslen,' Heimrich said. 'Evidence, I suppose. However—'

'Look,' Oslen said, and leaned forward, 'García knows you talked to the girl. Knows she spilled the story. Knows nobody's going to believe everything was sweetness and light, as she says. He sees he's got to stick to his story— that he didn't see Wells at all. He can handle her, from now on. But, he's got to stop you from passing on what she said. So—' He shook his head again. 'I don't get it,' he said. 'I don't get what you're waiting for. Going down every blind alley—' He spread his hands. 'You say yourself García would use a knife,' he pointed out.

Heimrich nodded.

'It could be the way you think, naturally,' he said. 'They picked García up this afternoon. They didn't hold him yesterday.'

'And?' Mary asked.

'He's not talking,' Heimrich said. 'Denies killing Wells. Denies trying to kill me. That's all. He's got a lawyer.'

'And,' Oslen said, and got up suddenly, 'you've got a murderer.' He looked down at the others. His gaze was challenging. 'You don't want me any more,' he told them. He looked specifically at Mary Wister. 'You,' he said, 'had better learn not to believe anything a commie tells you. Not a goddamn thing.'

And then, red of face, his movements emphatic, William Oslen departed the Penguin Bar.

'Well,' Mary Wister said.

Heimrich's eyes were open; he looked after Oslen. Then, faintly, he smiled.

'A forthright man, Mr. Oslen,' he said. 'Violent in his views—which is very proper, naturally. He's quite right about party members, as a matter of fact. It isn't wise to

168

believe them. The end justifies any thing, naturally.'

'And,' Barclay MacDonald said, 'the means become the end, don't they?'

'Why yes, doctor,' Heimrich said. 'I think they do. I think they almost always do.'

'You hadn't finished about Mr. Wells,' Mary told him, after a moment. He nodded to that; he shut his eyes. He had, he said, almost finished.

Early in 1949, when American nerves had tightened under what seemed a constant threat, when real (and purported) communists were being discovered everywhere, Bronson Wells had left Key West. He had got in touch first with a senator who, perhaps sincerely, believed that the protection of the United States from communization was a task which devolved uniquely upon him. Wells had, it appeared, been helpful. Within a few months, he had outgrown the senator, or, at any rate, the senator's payroll, and had embarked on his own career as a defender of the American way of life. He apparently, Heimrich said, had found it lucrative.

'Look,' Mary said. 'You don't mean it was only that, do you? Most of us hate communism; are afraid of it. Wasn't Mr. Wells? Wasn't he honest, I mean?'

'Now Miss Wister,' Heimrich said. 'I said at the start we never know all about a man. We'd have to guess, wouldn't we? But—for what it's worth—I'd say he was honest. I'd say he believed all he said and remembered most of what he said he remembered. His methods—well, he'd been a party member. Perhaps one thing he remembered was the theory that the end justifies the means. About your brother, doctor, I'd say he was wrong and that that sort of wrongness is—dangerous. But probably he was honest—or mostly honest.'

He looked at Barclay MacDonald.

'The methods could ruin the country,' MacDonald said, slowly. 'They—killed my brother.'

'The individual,' Heimrich said, 'doesn't mean much to a great many people. That's one way, one important way, the communists differ from us. And—Wells had been a communist. He'd changed his beliefs, no doubt. But perhaps a habit of thought wasn't changed.' He closed his eyes. 'I don't extenuate,' he added. 'And I don't deny, naturally, that Mr. Wells profited from his crusade. But—'

Heimrich seemed to have finished.

'I wonder,' Mary said, 'why Mr. Oslen didn't wait to hear the rest about Mr. Wells?'

'Now Miss Wister,' Heimrich said, his eyes still closed. 'Because he knew it, naturally. Wouldn't you think so?' He opened his eyes. 'Just as he knows Miss Jones is a member of the Communist Party,' he added, 'although he says all the rest of her story is invented.'

'Where is she?' Mary asked. 'What's—has something happened to her?'

'Now Miss Wister,' Heimrich said. 'I shouldn't think so. I hope not, naturally.'

Heimrich closed his eyes again.

CHAPTER EIGHT

Captain Heimrich thought Oslen was lying. Of that, Mary Wister was certain; that beat in her mind as, with the tall, thin doctor beside her, she walked from the Penguin Bar through the deserted dining room toward the main lounge of the The Coral Isles. But if Oslen was lying, Mary thought, then Rachel Jones had been telling the truth. And then—

'It's my fault,' she said to MacDonald, as if she were continuing a conversation between them. 'It's my fault, Mac. I broke—'

'Nonsense,' MacDonald told her, looking down, shaking his head and smiling. 'Heimrich didn't do anything until today. That was all she asked. Anyway—' It was his turn not to complete a sentence. She waited.

'I'm not sure she was in any danger,' he said. 'Or is—or has been. Whatever truth there was in what she told you.'

'It was true,' Mary said. 'I'm sure it was. So is the captain.'

To that MacDonald nodded, after a hesitant moment.

171

'But,' he said, 'I don't think Heimrich is worried about her. I don't quite know why he isn't.' MacDonald paused. His eyes narrowed a little. 'Unless—' he began.

But he was interrupted by a red-jacketed bellboy, who was repeating, in accents of cooing affection, Mary Wister's name. 'Miss Wister,' he was saying, in the tone of a lover. 'Miss Wister, please.'

'Here,' Mary said, and took a telegram which he offered on a tray. She started to open her purse and the bellboy said 'Thank you' for MacDonald's coin. She opened the telegram. She said, 'That crazy Bernie' and handed it to MacDonald.

'Too much red in your palette,' Mac read. 'Am sending one lawyer postpaid.' It was signed, 'Bernie.' Mac smiled politely.

'Isaac Bernstein,' she said. 'A very swell guy. He's an agency man, handling the account I'm working on. He sent me down, really.'

'Oh,' MacDonald said.

'Advertising agency,' Mary explained, answering the blankness of his tone. 'There's this group of hotels—' She told him in some detail about 'this thing' she was working on, for Bernstein's agency. Mac said 'oh' again, this time in accents of enlightenment. He said she must remember he was a country doctor, unused to the ways of commerce.

'Bernie handles all sorts of advertising,' Mary said, talking more than she needed, more

172

than she intended; running back to safe things, and ordinary things. 'Radio programs. Space in magazines. Gets out things like this brochure and coordinates them with space. He has three floors of offices on Madison Avenue and—'

She stopped, because two youngish men and a youngish woman, dressed in Northern clothes, brisk in woolens in spite of summer warmth, converged.

'Miss Wister,' the shorter of the two men said, 'heard them paging you. Was going to have you paged myself.' He looked with disfavor upon the other man and the woman. 'The little foxes caught up,' he said. 'I'm from the U.P. The United—'

'I know,' Mary said. 'I don't know anything about anything.'

'You wouldn't be Doctor Barclay MacDonald, would you?' the woman said. 'I'm Ruth Osgood. *New York Times.* I've heard of you.'

'Good,' MacDonald said. 'Excellent, Miss Osgood. I have heard of the *New York Times.*'

'You're MacDonald, all right,' Miss Osgood said. 'The cation man. And your brother—'

'Yes,' Mac said. 'I'm MacDonald. I'm afraid I haven't anything to tell you.'

'For my money,' Ruth Osgood said, 'your brother got a bad deal. The *Times* thinks so, too.'

173

Barclay MacDonald said he was very glad. His tone was, however, non-committal.

'Nevertheless,' Miss Osgood said, 'it's a coincidence. We can't get away from that, can we?'

'It is,' MacDonald said, 'entirely. But I presume we can't.'

'Look,' the taller of the two men said, 'this is an unsatisfactory place to talk.' It was. They stood in front of the desk; between it and the case of Key West shirts, presided over by a delicate young man, wearing one of the shirts. 'I'm Franklin, Associated Press.' He paused momentarily. 'May as well get it over with,' he said. 'Ben Franklin. Now that we've had our laugh, isn't there some better place?'

'I don't—' Mary began, but MacDonald took her arm, gently.

'As Mr. Franklin says, we may as well get it over with,' he said. He looked around. He nodded toward a corner of the lounge. They went to it, sat in it.

'We've talked to—' the United Press man began, and then looked up. 'Oh, hello captain. Hope we're not tampering with witnesses.'

'Now Mr. Burns,' Heimrich said. 'Now Mr. Burns. Go right ahead, of course. Hello, Ruth, Ben.' He turned toward Mary. 'They'll want to know how you found the body, naturally,' he told her. 'What it looked like and that sort of thing. I've told them about the disappearance of Miss Jones, after she had told you she was

174

afraid. That she wouldn't tell you who she was afraid of.'

'Now Merton,' Ruth Osgood said. 'Now Merton. Don't fill the lady's head with ideas, will you not?'

Captain Heimrich closed his eyes, as if in pain.

'They call him Merton of the Mounties,' Ruth Osgood told Mary and MacDonald. 'He doesn't care for it.'

Captain Heimrich opened his eyes.

'You're quite a girl, Ruth,' he said, mildly. 'Quite a girl. Go ahead.'

'You're staying, I gather,' the United Press man said.

'Now Mr. Burns,' Heimrich said. 'I'm staying, naturally. But go right ahead. And start with Miss Wister. She's been playing tennis, wants to change.'

Mary herself had forgotten that. It was nevertheless true.

MacDonald slapped the pockets of his jacket suddenly.

'No cigarettes,' he said. 'I thought—' He stood up, although cigarettes were offered. 'Have to get some anyway,' he said. 'I'll be back, of course.'

They let him go. They turned to Mary. While she was answering the questions they asked, keeping in mind Heimrich's veiled caution, she happened to look toward the desk—looked in that direction when she sought a word. Dr.

Barclay MacDonald was standing at the desk. He was not buying cigarettes. He was writing a telegram on a yellow form—apparently a long telegram.

*   *   *

It was after five when Mary finally reached her room. She had left Barclay MacDonald in the lounge, still undergoing interview—a detached, apparently confident man; now and then, she thought, an oblique one. He had said nothing about the telegram. He had returned with cigarettes. The reporters, keyed, she thought, by Ruth Osgood, treated him with that courtesy many reporters reserve for people of some importance. Well, Mary thought, I never believed this country doctor business.

She showered and changed, not letting herself think of Rachel Jones, or trying not to. What Mac said was true. Her breaking of the promise was only technical, and without demonstrable result. If she had waited until that day, as she had promised to wait, it would have made no difference, since Heimrich had—or said he had—done nothing until that day. (And then, so far as the girl herself was concerned, apparently not much.)

It was not until Mary had dressed again—in green linen, with some feeling of repetition—that she saw the envelope, addressed 'Miss

Wister,' in a sprawling hand, propped against the telephone on its table by the bed. She opened the envelope. She read, in the same unformed hand:

'Miss Wister Miss Jones says not to wory tell you shes alright. Dont try to fine her.'

At first, Mary's feeling was one of great relief. But that lasted only a moment. She realized, then, that this scrawled, semiliterate communication carried no real reassurance. It was not from Rachel Jones; it was about her. It might merely be—All the things it might be swirled in Mary Wister's mind. She stood holding the letter when someone knocked at the door. She turned toward the door too quickly, and spoke in a voice too high.

'Yes?' she said. 'Who is it?'

'It's Florence Sibley, dear,' a voice said. 'Could I talk to you for a minute?'

*　　*　　*

The United Press had gone. The Associated Press had gone. They were to use Heimrich's name at the jail; there was no doubt that they could talk to Mario García, assuming him to be still in the jail. 'I don't know how good his lawyer is, naturally,' Heimrich said at that point, and the United Press said, 'Oh, it's that way?' Heimrich closed his eyes. 'I suppose I'd better see this Rita,' Ruth Osgood said. '"Abelard," for God's sake!' She looked hopefully at Heimrich, at Dr. Barclay MacDonald. 'I hate the woman's angle,' she said. 'You still say your being here is pure coincidence, doctor?'

'Yes,' MacDonald said.

'It's a pity, in a way,' Ruth Osgood said. 'I hope you don't mind my saying so, doctor?'

'Not at all,' MacDonald said. 'I appreciate your point.'

'If it's García, where are we?' Ruth Osgood said. 'You do see my point? Front page today; maybe tomorrow, since they flew me down. Then the split page. Then, God knows where. If it's really García.'

She was almost wistful.

'I'm sorry I can't help you,' MacDonald said, with great politeness. 'I can see García would rather flatten it out. Nevertheless, I'm afraid I didn't kill Mr. Wells.'

'All right,' Ruth Osgood said. 'One thing you learn in this business. You can't have everything.'

'At any rate,' MacDonald said, 'you can't have me.'

The tall thin doctor and the square, solid man with an arm in a sling stood politely. Miss Osgood sighed once more; she shook her head in regret; she left them.

'You're a disappointment to the lady, doctor,' Heimrich said, when they sat again.

'I hope not to you,' MacDonald said, and got, 'Now doctor, now doctor.'

'Since,' MacDonald said, 'you feel the same way about García. Although not, I suppose, for the same reasons.'

'Now doctor,' Heimrich said. 'Have I said that?'

'In effect,' MacDonald told him. 'At any rate, I think you have.'

'No,' Heimrich said. 'It's very simple, naturally. I've said that the deputy sheriff probably is right. The thing nearest to hand, the obvious thing, is usually the thing you want. Usually, the person you want. But the deputy is taking care of that—as I would, in his place. Ten to one, he's right. However—'

'Not ten to one,' MacDonald said. 'Three to one. Or, if you like, four to one. Aren't those the odds?'

'Now doctor,' Heimrich said. 'What makes you think that?'

'Oslen,' MacDonald said. 'Judge Sibley—or his wife. Paul Shepard.' He counted on his fingers, letting one finger stand for two Sibleys. 'Me. Four to one. I turn it upside down, of course.'

'You do,' Heimrich admitted. 'You sent a telegram, doctor. Would you like to tell me about it?'

'Why should—' MacDonald began, and stopped. 'On the other hand,' he said, 'why not? I sent a telegram to a man named Bernstein. He runs an advertising agency in New York. He sent Miss Wister here.

I asked—'

He stopped because Heimrich, eyes open, was nodding, seemed pleased.

'Isaac Bernstein,' Heimrich said. 'The agency's on Madison Avenue.' He gave the number. 'It was astute of you to think of that, doctor. Did Miss Wister suggest it?'

'No,' MacDonald said. 'You saw the telegram, apparently. Why ask me?'

'Now doctor,' Heimrich said. 'I didn't, as it happens.' He closed his eyes. 'I've thought there's a similarity between your job and mine, doctor,' he said. 'Research, mine into human actions, yours into—what should I say? Physiological reactions? Finding out what we can, trying to discover the meaning of what we find out.' He opened his eyes. 'I hope you don't mind the comparison,' he said.

MacDonald shook his head. He waited.

'If you phrased your question to Mr. Bernstein as you probably did, I think the answer will be "No,"' Heimrich said. 'He'll say, at any rate, not that he's heard.'

'Look,' MacDonald said, 'I gather you're ahead of me? That you've already got the answer?' Heimrich nodded. 'Was the question that obvious?' MacDonald asked.

'No,' Heimrich said. 'But you see, we try to ask all the possible questions. We waste a lot of time. Your question was a very good one, doctor. You thought of asking it—when?'

'This afternoon,' MacDonald said.

Heimrich nodded. He closed his eyes. He said, 'Naturally.'

'So?' MacDonald asked.

'Now doctor,' Heimrich said. 'It's early days. It's interesting, naturally. You must remember, though, that there may be a perfectly simple explanation.'

'You'll ask?'

'Now doctor,' Heimrich said. 'I always ask, naturally. How else do you find things out? You ask all the questions you can think of, of all the people who—might have answers. You try—'

'To make the character fit the crime,' MacDonald finished. 'You told us.'

'I talk a great deal,' Heimrich said. 'Foolish of me, I've been told. Of course, there are other things which have to fit, too. Practical things— where people were, for example.'

'My being out of the hotel when you were attacked,' MacDonald said.

'Why yes,' Heimrich said. 'That sort of thing, naturally.'

'But still,' MacDonald said, 'the character has to fit in the end.'

'Now doctor,' Heimrich said, 'it does. It has to, as you say. Once you find out what it is, of course.'

'I think Oslen was lying,' MacDonald said. 'Mary thinks so too. We think you do.'

'Oh yes,' Heimrich said. 'I think he probably was. About certain things, at any rate. He

181

would, naturally.'

'With Wells dead.'

'Oh, as for that,' Heimrich said. 'With Wells alive too, I'd think. Whenever it was necessary to his purpose. To his—ends.'

'Their ends,' MacDonald corrected.

Heimrich opened his eyes, then. He nodded again as he had earlier, seemed pleased again. His attitude patted Dr. Barclay MacDonald paternally on the back.

'He wouldn't diverge,' MacDonald said. 'Wouldn't take things into his own hands. You agree?'

'Well,' Heimrich said, 'we can't be sure, of course. Not from their ends, probably. But—means vary, don't they, doctor? One thing here, other things somewhere else. However, I do see what you mean, doctor. It's a nice point, I think.' He closed his eyes. 'A very nice point,' he said. 'I've asked Mr. Shepard to meet me here, doctor. Do you mind?'

'Why should—oh,' MacDonald said. He stood up.

'Good hunting,' he said.

'Now doctor,' Heimrich said. 'And you—you'll be careful, naturally?' He paused. 'Within reason,' he added.

Barclay MacDonald walked down the long lounge toward the elevator. He discovered that he was thinking of Mary Wister. He hoped she would be careful, too.

182

Florence Sibley's manner retained poise; she held her tall body with dignity; she was a distinguished woman in her late fifties. There was no strain in her voice when, standing in the door of Mary Wister's room, she expressed the correct hope that her intrusion was not unpardonable. But there was strain in her eyes. There was uncertainty in her eyes. At first, Mary was too unaccountably relieved to notice this. It was Mrs. Sibley. Not—But Mary could not imagine who she had been afraid it might be, or why she had any cause to fear. Nevertheless, she said, 'Oh,' in relief, before she said, 'Of course not, Mrs. Sibley,' and asked the gray-haired woman to come in.

'You have a very pleasant room, my dear,' Florence Sibley said. 'Pleasanter than ours, I think.' She went to the window and looked out at the lawn and the trees, lighted obliquely by the setting sun. 'It is so restful here,' she said. 'It could be.' She stood for a moment looking out and then she turned and spoke quickly, as if she finally had nerved herself to speak.

'I have to talk to someone,' she said. 'And— try to find out what's happening. I know I haven't any right but—will you be generous with a very—a worried woman. Because I'm terribly worried, my dear.'

'Of course,' Mary said. She sat on the edge of the bed, and motioned toward a chair and said,

'Please, Mrs. Sibley.'

Mrs. Sibley looked at the chair for a moment, and seemed uncertain. But then she sat in it.

'I don't know why I—come to you with my worries,' she said. 'But I think the policeman, Captain Heimrich I mean, talks to you. He does, doesn't he?'

'He talks to everyone,' Mary said.

But Florence Sibley shook her head. She said she did not mean that.

'You and the doctor,' she said. 'Such a charming man, my dear. You're both in his confidence. Isn't that true? Because you're both in all this and still, not in it.'

'I don't know that anybody's really in the captain's confidence,' Mary said. 'I can't tell. Neither Mac nor I knew him until a few days ago.'

Florence Sibley nodded, but she seemed hardly to listen.

'I'm terribly afraid about the judge,' she said. 'What does Captain Heimrich say about the judge?' She looked at Mary, and her eyes now were frightened. 'I know I shouldn't ask you,' she said. 'You must believe I realize that. I just—can't help myself.'

'The judge?' Mary repeated. 'Judge Sibley? I don't think the captain has said much about him. Not to me.'

'The judge won't tell me anything,' Mrs. Sibley said. 'He—he never likes to worry me.

When I try to talk he just says, "There's nothing to worry about, Flo. Don't worry your pretty head."' She lifted her hands to her ordered, gray hair. 'My pretty head,' she said, and her smile was oddly embarrassing in its deprecation. 'I'm afraid he hasn't really—really looked at me for years,' she said.

There was nothing to say to that. Mary could only shake her head slightly, and wait.

'I'm sorry, my dear,' she said. 'That's always so embarrassing for everyone, isn't it? So gauche, really. Forgive me. I'm almost an old woman, my dear.'

That could be answered. 'No,' Mary Wister said.

'I don't feel old,' Florence Sibley said. 'They say people never do, or most people never do. It isn't fair, somehow. Is it?' She did not give Mary time to answer. 'But you won't have to think of that for years, of course. Years and years.' She paused again. 'I'm trying to avoid it, aren't I?' she said then. 'I break in on you to ask—to ask you something, and I chatter about growing old.' She paused again.

'Miss Wister,' she said, 'does Captain Heimrich think the judge killed Mr. Wells?'

'Think the judge—' Mary said. 'Why should he?' There was incredulity in her voice, and in her mind. But then she remembered. It was strange she had forgotten. That she remembered showed in her face.

'He does,' Florence Sibley said. 'Oh, he

does!'

'I remember now,' Mary said. 'Mr. Oslen said something about the judge. About a hearing at which Mr. Wells was going to testify. And Captain Heimrich said, yes, he had thought of the judge—of the judge and you, Mrs. Sibley. But I felt he meant, just as he'd thought of everybody. Of Doctor MacDonald. I suppose of me. Of everybody. I didn't feel he—well, that he thought very seriously about the judge.'

'He will,' Florence Sibley said. 'Everybody will.' She lowered her head into her hands for a moment. She lifted it. 'And it's all because of me,' she said. 'Because—oh, years ago—I was foolish. Idealistic.'

('That idealistic wife of his,' Oslen had said.)

'Things are so dreadfully mixed up now,' Florence Sibley said, and she seemed to be talking to herself more than to the slim young woman in green linen, who sat erect on the edge of the bed, who listened. 'So dreadfully mixed up. Things that were innocent, that seemed like good things, are all mixed up with something else. Like what we do to the nigras.' Instantly she corrected her pronunciation. 'Negroes,' she said. 'I'm from the South, you know, and I felt—guilty. Many of us do, my dear. About their schools and—oh, everything. And this organization—it seemed to be for all the things I thought were true. And then there was Spain—so many of us thought

186

Franco, with Hitler and Mussolini—' She broke off. She looked at Mary. 'You're so young, my dear,' she said. 'Can you understand any of this—really understand it?'

Mary remembered what MacDonald had said about a difference in generations. Perhaps she couldn't.

'I'm not that young,' she said. 'Yes.' She remembered something else; something she had heard a lecturer read in a course on contemporary drama. '"If you want a clean, Armageddon battle, all the beasts of hell against the angels of light, you won't get that, not in this world,"' she quoted. 'Maxwell Anderson said that. In a play called *Key Largo*. But still you have to take sides. That was what the play meant, I think.'

Mrs. Sibley nodded.

'I thought that,' she said. 'Oh, I knew there were communists on the Loyalist side—that Stalin was in it, along with Hitler and Mussolini. But I thought—well, one thing at a time, and that I weighed where the greatest right was. But now, you see, it comes out that I associated with—with devils. Joined with devils. With communists.'

'Do you mean,' Mary asked, 'that you actually joined the Communist Party?'

Mrs. Sibley looked at her with utter astonishment, with some outrage.

'My dear Miss Wister!' Mrs. Sibley said. 'Whatever made you think that? Of *course* not!' She shook her head. 'You don't understand at all,' she said. 'You're like—like so many others.'

This is a statement which all resent; Mary Wister resented it. Also, in so far as she could tell from Mrs. Sibley's rather indirect approach—probably, Mary thought, to everything—she was not in this case like the 'others' to whom Mrs. Sibley referred.

'I'm not,' Mary said. 'I see perfectly how a person, an idealistic person, could be for things that even the communists are for, or say they're for. And not be any part of a communist.'

'That's it,' Mrs. Sibley said. 'I think perhaps you do, my dear. But—so many nowadays don't. That's why I said everything's so mixed up now. And Mr. Wells saw everything so black and white, you know. What he might have said, before the committee—well, the judge and I both didn't know what he might have said. Dreadful things that weren't really true, but could be made to sound true, particularly when people *wanted* them to sound true.' She shook her head. 'The judge is such a wonderful man,' she said. 'He can do so many things if they'll let him. For the country. For everybody. And he's been so *set* on it.'

It did come out. Not clearly; perhaps Mrs. Sibley did not want it to come out clearly; did not want to think of it clearly.

'You mean,' Mary said, 'that because you joined certain organizations, which perhaps

188

the communists had taken over as fronts, or have taken over since, your husband won't get this appointment?'

'Of course,' Mrs. Sibley said. 'His whole career—' Momentarily, she clenched well-cared-for hands into fists. 'Because of things I did. And, Miss Wister, innocently. *Innocently!*'

'I don't—' Mary started to say. But then she realized she did believe it; that it was the sort of thing which, that winter in their country, could happen.

'Did your husband know about these—these activities of yours?' she asked. The very word 'activities' had unpleasant connotations in her own mind.

'Oh yes,' Mrs. Sibley said. 'He didn't think much about them. But he didn't try to stop me or anything. After all, how could he know things would be—the way they are now? How could anybody know?'

There was no answer to that, or Mary could think of none. One had to believe what he believed in his time, not what, ten years later, it would be found proper, and safe, to have believed.

'And, of course,' Mrs. Sibley said, 'I can see that all this might make Captain Heimrich think—think—' She put her head in her hands. Mary waited, but Mrs. Sibley did not lift her face from her hands. Now, Mary saw, her shoulders were shaking. *She's not sure herself*, Mary thought. That's what it is, that's why

189

she's this way—so uncertain, so almost vague. She's not really thinking about what she's saying. *Because she's not sure herself!*

Mary waited. After a few moments, she said, 'You mustn't. You mustn't, Mrs. Sibley.'

For a moment, Florence Sibley sat as she had been sitting. Then she lifted her head. She looked at Mary. She seemed to find in the younger woman's eyes more than had been in her words. She managed something like a smile.

'You think I have little faith,' she said. The formality of the words was unexpected, yet was appropriate. 'I haven't, really. I know that the judge couldn't have had anything—*anything* to do with another person's death. But—you're so young, my dear. One can know something and yet, at the same time, or sometimes, not be sure—be afraid. One gets less—less sure as one gets older. Little fears come in. Sometimes you feel that things, important things are—slipping out of your hands.' She nodded. 'But it doesn't last,' she said. 'It doesn't really last.' She paused again and this time managed a somewhat better smile. 'It's gone now,' she said. 'You're a sweet child to listen.'

She moved as if to get up, but then did not. After a little she spoke again, and this time her voice was entirely steady, almost dispassionate.

'You see,' she said, 'the judge has been under strain recently. He feels that there are so many

190

things that need to be done, by this country in the world, in the United Nations, and he—he's *driven* to do what he thinks is his part of it. But there's always this—snarling, these attacks which have to be met. It drains so much time, so much energy and—so much confidence. He's been very tense in the last few months, sometimes not like himself. And, of course, being afraid that Mr. Wells would hit at him through me—would make me ridiculous, make me seem like a silly, irresponsible woman—all that upset the judge.' She smiled, and this time as if at something she remembered.

'It may be,' she said, 'that I *am* silly and irresponsible. But the judge doesn't think so. He's—he's proud of me, my dear.'

Mary nodded.

'You're very sweet,' Florence Sibley said. 'I'm not so worried now.' But as she said this, the worry came back into her eyes.

'Listen,' Mary said, 'there are simple things. Mr. Wells was killed early in the morning, they think. Before you and the judge were up, surely. You must know he couldn't—'

'Of course,' Florence Sibley said. 'Of course I know, dear. It's just that—'

But then she stopped and looked at Mary Wister; she looked at her intently, as if forcing belief on her.

'Of course I know,' she repeated. 'And last night when Captain Heimrich was attacked.

191

We were together then. Of *course* I know.'

'But then—' Mary started to say, and stopped herself before the words were spoken. 'But then, what are you afraid of?' she had started to say. But she did not need to ask the question; there was no point to asking the question. The whole sudden, uncharacteristic directness in the older woman's assertion was the answer to a question unasked. Because, Mary thought, her husband *wasn't* with her, either time. *She doesn't know where he was.*

Something of what she thought apparently was revealed in her face.

'The judge didn't leave the room that morning,' Florence Sibley said. 'Last night we were together all evening and were in our room when the captain was—hurt. I've told them that. I'll—tell anybody that.'

'Then it's all right,' Mary said. 'Then you shouldn't worry.'

But the knowledge that there was need to worry, because Mrs. Sibley was saying that she had lied, and would lie again—was saying that she did not know her husband not to be a murderer—was exposed between them. Knowledge was in Mary Wister's voice; acceptance of that knowledge in Florence Sibley's eyes.

'You're kind, my dear,' the older woman said, after a long pause. Then she went.

CHAPTER NINE

Paul Shepard was, he assured Captain Heimrich, anxious to do anything to help. He did not know what he could do. He awaited suggestions. He could listen, if he didn't mind, Heimrich said, and told him about the charge Rachel Jones had made against Oslen. Shepard's eyebrows went up as he listened; at the crux of the accusation he whistled softly. At the end, he said, 'Hm-m,' and his eyes narrowed in thought.

'You're in charge of the news staff of your network,' Heimrich said. 'That's right, isn't it?'

'That's right,' Shepard agreed. 'UBA News.'

'And you haven't ever heard anything to substantiate this—this story of Miss Jones's?'

'I was trying to think,' Shepard said. 'No—it sounds damned unlikely to me. From all I've ever heard, Oslen is just a pretty good pianist. Does concerts in this country and I think he's toured in Europe to a certain extent. Not newsworthy, as they say. I can only give you my opinion, captain.'

'Do that,' Heimrich said. 'Do that, Mr. Shepard.'

'It sounds to me,' Shepard said, 'like one of those stories people make up now and then to attract attention, to get notoriety. That sort of thing isn't uncommon. But you know that as well as I do, probably better.'

Heimrich closed his eyes; he nodded.

'Of course,' Shepard said, 'I wouldn't want to say that that sort of thing couldn't happen. I mean, the use of someone like Oslen, someone publicly known as an anti-communist, as an agent provocateur. There've been one or two cases in the past few years that people have wondered about. I wouldn't put it beyond the commies. I don't know what I would put beyond them. But I've never heard any rumors about Oslen. Never heard much about him in any connection, when you come to that.' He paused for a moment. 'Of course,' he said, 'secrecy would be of the essence, wouldn't it? Even rumors would queer any pitch like that.'

'Particularly,' Heimrich said, 'if a man like Mr. Wells, a man of his standing, spread them.'

'As apparently he planned to,' Shepard said. But to that Heimrich shook his head a little doubtfully, said, 'Now Mr. Shepard.'

'We don't know what Mr. Wells planned to do, naturally,' Heimrich said. 'We know what Rachel Jones says she hoped he would do. She might not have convinced him.'

'Wells wasn't particularly hard to convince on things like that,' Shepard said. 'Remember, he knew them. Things which might seem to us—well, too devious for reality, wouldn't to him. That was one of his arguments, you know—that people like you and me simply can't grasp that a conspiracy is really that—a

194

conspiracy. Complete with—well, with all kinds of deviousness.'

'You knew him,' Heimrich said. 'At least, I gather you did.'

Paul Shepard shook his head.

'Say, I knew about him,' he said. 'I've had correspondence with him. Met him a couple of times.' He looked at Heimrich with shrewdness in his eyes. 'Probably you thought he was something of a fanatic,' he said. 'A good many people did. Perhaps even that he wasn't too scrupulous?'

'I talked a little to him one evening, Mr. Shepard,' Heimrich said. 'I'd heard of him, of course. But in one evening—' Heimrich closed his eyes.

'Nevertheless,' Shepard said, 'you thought he was a fanatic.'

'Now Mr. Shepard,' Heimrich said. 'I thought he was a very zealous man. A man with a great ability to believe.'

Shepard appeared to consider that. Then he nodded. He said that that put it well enough. Beyond that, however, was an ability to act on his beliefs.

'Whoever was hurt,' Shepard said. 'One has to give him that. Of course, that made him dangerous to—to some people—I suppose.'

'Apparently,' Heimrich said, and opened his eyes. 'You planned to employ him, you said. To broadcast a commentary, wasn't it? Wouldn't there have been some risk?'

Shepard repeated the word.

'Now Mr. Shepard,' Heimrich said. 'Risk, naturally. He might have said things he thought true, but which he couldn't actually prove. And—what he said wouldn't have been privileged, of course. He's not a senator. It's libelous to, say, call a man a communist if you can't prove it—at least it is in New York.'

'We planned to watch him, of course,' Shepard said. 'He'd agreed to that. And, as a practical matter, people don't get very far with suits like that nowadays, you know. It's difficult to prove you're not a communist if somebody like Wells says you are—difficult to convince a jury. Whatever the truth is, you end up worse off than you started, nine times out of ten.'

'So,' Heimrich said, 'you figured you'd be reasonably safe—in a practical sense, naturally.'

There was no inflection in his voice. Nonetheless, Shepard looked at him sharply. Heimrich, after a moment, closed his eyes.

'That's about it, I suppose,' Shepard said then. 'We figured we could handle it. Go over his copy carefully. Warn him about ad-libbing. And, of course, put a clause in his contract binding him to hold us harmless of all claims growing out of anything he said we hadn't approved. We figured we'd be safe.' He looked at Heimrich intently, but his gaze was wasted. Heimrich's eyes remained closed. 'We considered it a public service,' Shepard said. Heimrich did open his eyes at that.

'Oh,' he said, 'I realize that, Mr. Shepard. I'm sure it would have been. Although there might have been private disservices, naturally.'

Shepard said the expected about the preparation of an omelet. He repeated that they had planned to be careful.

'And,' he said, 'the good would outweigh the harm.'

'The end and the means,' Heimrich said. 'All's fair, and so forth. No doubt you're right, Mr. Shepard.'

'You don't think so?' Shepard said.

'Now Mr. Shepard,' Heimrich said. 'Does it matter what I think? The innocent often suffer with the guilty. No one who has ever looked into a murder doubts that. Innocent lives are opened up, sometimes damaged. Something like that might have occurred in connection with the broadcasts, naturally. Particularly to the lives of people in—well, your line of work, for example.'

Shepard looked hard at him.

'Only for example,' Heimrich said, mildly. 'You know what I mean, Mr. Shepard. People in the motion picture industry—'

'Don't think there aren't plenty of commies there,' Shepard interrupted. 'Wells had the goods on plenty.'

'Now Mr. Shepard,' Heimrich said. 'I've no doubt there are, or were. Again, I merely use an example. People in radio. People in public life. They're most susceptible of all, naturally. Actors. Writers. Suspicion, allegations which can't be proved—they can be very hard on a good many people. Suppose, for example—only for example, Mr. Shepard—you had joined one or two of the wrong organizations when you were much younger, and now it came out. I'm sure you haven't any communist leanings. Still—you'd—well, you'd lose your job, wouldn't you?'

'I didn't,' Shepard said. 'So what are we talking about?'

He spoke with some violence, great emphasis.

'Oh,' Heimrich said, 'the breaking of eggs, naturally.'

'You can't coddle people,' Shepard said. 'People have to look out for themselves. If they let themselves be pushed around it's their own fault, isn't it?'

'Now Mr. Shepard,' Heimrich said. 'That depends on a number of things, doesn't it? The characters of those involved.'

'So?' Shepard said.

Heimrich opened his eyes.

'You're quite right, Mr. Shepard,' he said. 'This is all beside the point. To get back to Mr. Wells. I understand you had a sponsor for his commentary?'

Shepard hesitated a moment.

'Well,' he said then, 'nothing was actually

198

signed.'

'But you had a sponsor lined up,' Heimrich said. 'You said that, as I recall it.'

'All but the signing,' Shepard said.

'Do you mind telling me who?'

Shepard thought a moment. Then he said he did mind. For one thing, he said, he could not see what importance that had. For another, he felt that, without the approval of people higher up in UBA, he couldn't take any chance of jeopardizing negotiations still being carried on.

'Now Mr. Shepard,' Heimrich said. 'I'm a policeman.'

'Now captain,' Shepard said, 'a policeman out of his jurisdiction, aren't you? If you were a local man—But the local men haven't asked, you know.'

Heimrich responded by opening his eyes. Shepard looked at him, smiled and shook his head.

'Very well,' Heimrich said. 'Probably it doesn't matter.' He closed his eyes again. When he spoke next it was as if he made conversation. 'They've had to let García go again,' he said. 'It seems a couple of his friends joined him a little after Wells left him that evening and stayed with him for some time. It seems they were rehearsing a number.'

A bellboy went through the lounge, carrying a yellow envelope on a tray, calling Dr. Barclay MacDonald in soft, affectionate tones.

199

'Doctor MacDonald please. Doctor MacDonald please.' Heimrich opened his eyes to watch the boy.

'I'd think—' Shepard began, and Heimrich returned, apparently from a distance. He seemed a little surprised to see Paul Shepard still sitting beside him on the corner sofa.

'Oh,' Heimrich said. 'Yes, Mr. Shepard?'

'I thought García denied seeing Wells except for a moment on the dance floor,' Shepard said. 'That's the way the local paper has it. The *Miami Herald*, too.'

'Apparently he changed his story,' Heimrich said. 'After he'd—thought it over.'

'After these two friends came up with their story,' Shepard suggested. 'Good friends, I imagine?'

'Now Mr. Shepard,' Heimrich said. 'Now Mr. Shepard. The authorities have to use the evidence they have, naturally. The evidence they have appears to clear Mr. García. And, of course, he has a lawyer.'

'You believe this—' Shepard began, but Heimrich was shaking his head, saying 'Now Mr. Shepard.'

'As you pointed out,' he said, 'I'm out of my jurisdiction.'

Paul Shepard hesitated. He appeared to be puzzled. He said that, all along, he'd assumed it would turn out to be García. He hoped the local men weren't being fooled. He said of García that 'people like that' often seemed to

200

have conveniently devoted friends.

'Now Mr. Shepard,' Heimrich said. 'People like what? García is a musician; apparently a good one. Also, he was a former friend of your Mr. Wells.'

'Mine?' Shepard said. He added he had nothing against García; that what he had said was only a manner of speaking.

'Who then?' Shepard said. He nodded to himself. 'Oslen, I suppose,' he said. 'I suppose it holds together well enough. If the girl's right, he's got a motive. He would be sufficiently ruthless, I suppose. And commies don't care much about other people's lives.'

'No,' Heimrich said.

Paul Shepard's eyes narrowed.

'You say this girl is missing?' he said. 'This Rachel Jones? That she can't be found?'

'She hasn't been,' Heimrich agreed. 'She's apparently not in the hotel. They haven't found her in town, and they can't discover she's left town—at any rate not by bus or plane or hired car. Of course—'

'You think she's alive?' Shepard said.

'Now Mr. Shepard,' Heimrich said. 'I hope so, naturally.'

'You're an optimist, then,' Shepard told him. 'From Oslen's point of view, assuming she told the truth, she's an informer. And—she'll tell somebody else. If it comes to that, she can testify against Oslen. If she's alive.'

'Now Mr. Shepard,' Heimrich said.

'You're damned calm about it,' Shepard said. 'You're willing just to sit here. Talk about—for God's sake, about who was going to sponsor Wells, who's dead and can't be sponsored by anyone.'

It was not, Heimrich again pointed out mildly, his jurisdiction. Mr. Shepard had said that. The people whose jurisdiction was involved were doing what they could. About everything, he assumed. For example, they had found out that Oslen could only say that, first when Wells was killed, again when Heimrich himself was attacked, he had been in his hotel room, and been in it alone. They had found out that the Sibleys were, on both occasions, in their hotel room together—or that both said they were. That Mary Wister was in her room, but alone. That Dr. MacDonald had been out when Heimrich was attacked but said he was in his room asleep—and also alone—at the time Wells was murdered. Having said so much, Heimrich looked at the wiry, neatly made man beside him.

'Mr. Shepard,' Heimrich said, 'the evening before Mr. Wells was killed, in the lounge here, he said something to you. Do you remember?'

'He said several things,' Shepard said, and appeared to try to remember.

'He advised you to think about something again,' Heimrich told him. 'Words to that effect. Do you mind telling me what he meant?'

Momentarily, Shepard's face showed

202

puzzlement. Then it cleared.

'Oh, that,' he said. 'It was about the time of his broadcast. We'd fixed it for seven-thirty in the evening. He thought that was too early; wanted it around nine or ten-thirty for the East. I'd told him we couldn't clear that time—actually, we didn't want him then. He wanted me to think it over. That's all there was to that.'

Heimrich nodded. He asked whether Wells's commentary was to have been carried on radio or television; learned that, at any rate for the first thirteen weeks, the plan had been for a radio broadcast only, with television to depend on response to the radio version. Shepard couldn't, he said, see what difference it made, under the circumstances. Heimrich half apologized; said that he was a curious man by nature, as well as by profession.

'For example,' he said, 'I have an impression Mrs. Shepard sometimes uses sleeping pills. I'm curious about that.'

The effect on Shepard was marked. He leaned toward Heimrich with a sudden movement; he flushed.

'What the hell business is it of yours?' he demanded. He waited a moment. 'I've had about enough of your damned interference,' he said. 'Just about enough. Stay off my wife!'

'Now Mr. Shepard,' Heimrich said. 'Now Mr. Shepard. A harmless thing. A good many people use preparations of one kind or another when they have difficulty sleeping—want a

203

long, deep sleep.'

Shepard continued for a long moment to stare at Heimrich. Then, abruptly, he said, 'I get it.'

'Do you, Mr. Shepard?' Heimrich said. 'Then you know why I asked, naturally.'

'D'you know, captain,' Shepard said, and his voice was hard. 'D'you know, I don't like to be pushed around. You haven't any authority here. Also, I don't give a damn what crazy idea you think you have. I—'

'You're very violent, Mr. Shepard,' Heimrich told him. 'But don't answer if you don't want to.'

'I'll tell you this,' Shepard said. 'I didn't kill Wells. I had no reason to. I'll tell you that much. You haven't got a prayer.'

'Now Mr. Shepard,' Heimrich said. 'Everybody's got a prayer, naturally. I didn't say you killed Mr. Wells, did I?'

He was told he hadn't needed to.

'Now Mr. Shepard,' Heimrich said. 'I have quite an open mind.' He closed his eyes. 'At the moment,' he added.

'You'll be surprised,' Shepard said. 'I don't give a damn.'

Heimrich merely nodded, his eyes closed.

'I didn't kill Wells,' Shepard said. 'I was in bed, asleep. My wife was in the other bed, also asleep. She'll testify I couldn't have left the room without wakening her. The same thing was true last night when you say somebody attacked you.'

'Oh,' Heimrich said, 'somebody did, Mr. Shepard. The night Mr. Wells was killed you played bridge—you and Mrs. Shepard and Judge and Mrs. Sibley—until after two in the morning. You told the police that.'

'So?' Shepard said. He stood up. 'I'm damned tired of this,' he said, and looked down at Heimrich. 'Wells wasn't killed at that time. I don't argue he was.'

'No,' Heimrich said. 'You can't, can you? As things turned out. Neither you nor the Sibleys.'

Shepard looked at him. Then, without speaking, he turned away. He walked down the lounge. Heimrich sat and looked after him. Halfway down the lounge, Shepard met Mary Wister and the tall doctor. He stopped and for the moment the three talked. Then Shepard jerked a thumb toward Heimrich and said something further; then he went on. Mary, from whose right shoulder swayed a big straw purse, and MacDonald came up the lounge toward Heimrich who, as they reached him, stood up. (Standing, he saw Judge Sibley start to get up from a chair a little distance down the room and then, apparently changing his mind, relax into it.)

'Mr. Shepard doesn't like you, captain,' MacDonald said. 'He doesn't like you at all. He warned us against you.'

'No,' Heimrich said. 'I'm afraid he doesn't. He finds me—interfering.'

'At least,' MacDonald said, and watched Mary sit on the sofa beside Heimrich. 'He doesn't like interference, does he.' He smiled, faintly. 'Mary found that out,' he said. 'He's—' MacDonald paused. 'His own man,' he finished. 'But, is it more than that, captain?'

'Now doctor,' Heimrich said. 'It could be. On the other hand, he may merely resent being pushed around. As he told me he did. People like that can be difficult. Sometimes merely being asked questions irritates them. Which is a complication, naturally.'

MacDonald lowered himself carefully to the sofa beside Mary Wister, so that she sat between him and Heimrich. MacDonald said, then, that he had got an answer. He produced the yellow sheet of a telegram, and held it out.

'Not that I've heard,' the telegram read. 'Probably would have but will check tomorrow. Give Mary love.' It was signed, 'Isaac Bernstein.'

'As you thought,' MacDonald said, when Heimrich had finished reading, held the telegram back toward him. 'Of course, it's not conclusive. Except at the end, of course.' He took the telegram and re-read it. 'I do,' he said. 'I do indeed.' He held the telegram out to Mary, who read it, shook her head; read it again and looked suddenly at Dr. MacDonald.

'What do you?' she asked.

'Now Mary,' MacDonald said. 'What your friend Mr. Bernstein says to do, of course.

However—' He took the telegram from her. 'I asked Mr. Bernstein whether he had heard that Bronson Wells was to do a sponsored commentary on the news,' MacDonald said. 'I took the liberty of identifying myself as a friend of yours.'

Mary Wister said, 'Oh.' She said, 'But then—' She paused. 'Bernie would be likely to know,' she said. 'Only—what does it prove?'

She asked the question of both of them. MacDonald smiled and shrugged; Heimrich said, 'Now Miss Wister.' He closed his eyes.

'Nothing, actually,' Heimrich said. 'As the doctor says, it's not conclusive.' He sighed faintly. 'It does raise another question, naturally,' he said.

They waited, but he did not add to this. Then Mary opened the straw purse she had put on the sofa beside her. She reached into it with confidence and then reached again, her confidence ebbing. Of all the times, she thought, to play the woman-rummaging-purse game. She opened the purse with anger, and began to remove things from it, while the two men, united in male superiority, watched with contented approval. It was impossible that the envelope she sought, which she had put in last on top of all other things, could, in a journey down from the floor above, have hidden itself under—! It had; she came up with it. She was slightly red. With a certain indignation of manner, she handed it to Heimrich. She handled it with care, by the edges; Heimrich followed her example, although he smiled faintly. When the sheet of paper was out of its envelope, Heimrich read aloud:

'"Miss Wister Miss Jones says not to wory tell you shes alright. Dont try to fine her".'

He read the note again to himself; he turned the sheet over and looked on the back of it, finding blankness.

'On the table in my room when I went up this afternoon,' Mary told him. She waited.

'Apparently,' Heimrich said, 'this is thoughtful of Miss Jones.'

'Do you believe that?' Mary asked him. 'Really believe it?'

'Now Miss Wister,' Heimrich said, 'why not? She thought you might feel—some responsibility for her. She wanted to tell you she's all right. She sent a message by—' he looked again at the penciled scrawl—'someone who spells as she pronounces.'

'She?' Mary said.

Heimrich said he thought so.

'Don't you see,' Mary asked, and she pushed the question at the square, solid man, 'don't you see, it may not come from her at all? That it may be a—a fake? That she may be dead? Or may be a prisoner?'

'Now Miss Wister,' Heimrich said. 'Now Miss Wister. What would be the point, do you think?'

'To stop people from looking for her,'

Mary said.

But to that Heimrich closed his eyes, and shook his head. She underestimated people. If she meant that anyone would hope the police would be diverted so easily, she was confusing bad spelling with stupidity, which would be a mistake. Naturally.

'Look,' Mary said, '*are* the police looking for her?'

'Now Miss Wister,' Heimrich said. 'Of course.' He opened his eyes. 'You worry too much,' he said. He paused. 'Or,' he said, 'too soon.'

'I don't know what you mean,' Mary said. 'You're very calm about it, captain. Very—unconcerned.'

'No,' Heimrich said. 'I don't deny Miss Jones may be in danger or, may get into danger. I don't think she's been harmed as yet. I think she's hiding—and that she sent you this message.'

'You think,' Mary said. She repeated it. 'You don't *know*.' But then she looked with greater intensity at the relaxed policeman from New York. 'Or,' she asked, 'do you know?'

'Now Miss Wister,' Heimrich said. 'No more than you do, or the doctor here. Or—not much more. Nothing you couldn't find out, or guess at.'

'Why would she hide?' MacDonald asked, and spoke slowly. 'Because she's really frightened? Or to—what? Support the story she told Mary? Call attention to it. In a sense, act it out?'

'Now doctor,' Heimrich said. 'Suppose her story is true. Or she believes it is. Then she could have both reasons, couldn't she?' He closed his eyes. 'We always imagine that people have only one reason for things they do,' he said. 'So often, you know, they have several. Sometimes they even have reasons which seem to contradict one another.'

'If she were hiding,' Mary said, 'why wouldn't she be found. Surely the police could find her. If she's—alive.'

'Now Miss Wister,' Heimrich said. He opened his eyes. 'Actually,' he said, 'it's easier to find someone who isn't alive.' He smiled, faintly. 'They move around less,' he said. 'You, for example, Miss Wister, shouldn't have any great difficulty in hiding yourself for—oh, several days at least—if you wanted to.'

Mary Wister shook her head. She said she wouldn't know where to start.

'Oh,' Heimrich said, 'you'd start with money, I think. You'd spend money to get help. At least, if I were a young woman in a hotel like this, I'd start there.' He nodded. 'Think about it, Miss Wister,' he advised her. He closed his eyes. 'In a sense,' he said, 'there are always perhaps a hundred people hidden in a hotel this size.'

They both looked at him. Then Barclay MacDonald slowly nodded. Mary looked from one of the men to the other. She still was annoyed with both of them because they had seen her annoyed with herself at so trivial a thing as an envelope lost in a too-capacious purse.

'You're both very superior,' she said. She stood up. Then she wished she had not. What on earth is the matter with me? Mary Wister asked herself, and got no answer. Then she got an answer, which surprised her, and pushed it into a distant corner of her mind, where it shone with stubborn brightness. But by then, Mac was standing too, standing beside her; he was actually patting her shoulder. She started to draw away from his hand, and was surprised to discover that she did not.

'Come on, lady,' Mac said. 'Buy you a drink.'

He looked down at Heimrich, still sitting, but Heimrich shook his head. Mary found that she was being taken to the Penguin Bar where, after the lounge had opened for cocktails, few people went.

Heimrich watched them go. Then he waited. He did not have long to wait. Judge Robert Sibley again got up from the chair in which he had been sitting, and this time he did not change his mind. Coming toward Heimrich he was a tall and dignified man of sixty, gray haired, and with worry plain in his face— worry and, with it, resolution. He advanced toward Heimrich with the air of a man who has steeled himself, who wants to get something over with. He stopped and Heimrich stood up. Judge Sibley asked whether Heimrich could spare him a moment, and Heimrich said, 'Naturally, judge.'

'Where we won't be interrupted,' Judge Sibley suggested, and again Heimrich said, 'Naturally.' They went to the porch, to an enclosed section seldom used and now deserted. They found chairs in a corner; Heimrich refused a proffered cigar and watched while Judge Sibley cut the tip from one with the blade of a silver pocket knife, while the judge lighted his cigar with care. He was unhurried; Heimrich thought he was forcing himself to be unhurried.

'I presumed you would want to talk to me,' Judge Sibley said, when the cigar was going. 'My wife has told me.' He looked at Heimrich and waited.

'Has she, judge?' Heimrich said. 'About?'

'Please, captain,' Judge Sibley said. 'It is quite unnecessary to beat around the bush. About her conversation with Miss Wister. She was impulsive, of course—my wife is rather often impulsive, captain. She has a generous spirit, generous emotions. She—'

'Miss Wister hasn't said anything about a conversation with your wife,' Heimrich told him.

Judge Sibley looked blank. He said, 'But—'

'No, judge,' Heimrich said. 'Nothing at all.'

'But she was just talking to you,' Judge Sibley said. 'Surely—'

'About another matter,' Heimrich said. 'She's received a message purporting to be from, or to be about, Miss Jones. Who has disappeared, you know.'

Judge Sibley nodded his dignified head. The movement was abstracted; it at once accepted knowledge of Miss Rachel Jones's disappearance and relegated it to the area of the irrelevant. Judge Sibley looked puzzled and, to some extent, taken aback, as a man might who has put his shoulder to a door presumed recalcitrant and had it swing open at the touch.

'This,' Judge Sibley said, 'makes it slightly difficult. I assumed, naturally, that Miss Wister would go at once to you. I assumed she had.'

'No,' Heimrich said. He closed his eyes. He waited. He waited for almost a minute before Judge Sibley spoke again.

'It does not really matter,' Judge Sibley said then. 'If I had not come to you under this—this misapprehension, you would of course have come to me. I realize that.'

'Yes, judge?' Heimrich said. 'Why?'

'It is unnecessary to be tactful,' Judge Sibley said. 'Although I presume that is not precisely your purpose, captain. It is inevitable that you should consider me as a possible—murderer.' He hesitated over the word, spoke it with reluctance, seemingly with a kind of disbelief. 'It is difficult for me to imagine myself in that position,' he said. 'Very difficult.' He waited a moment, but Heimrich said nothing. 'I'm not wrong in thinking that,' Judge Sibley told the policeman from New York. Heimrich opened his eyes.

'Now judge,' he said. 'As you know, it isn't my case. I am a good many miles from my jurisdiction.'

'Captain Heimrich,' Judge Sibley said, and spoke as if from an imaginary bench, 'I am being frank with you. I propose to volunteer information. I expect reciprocal frankness.'

He phrased his sentences as if he spoke from the bench; as if what he said would be taken down.

'My wife went to Miss Wister to discover, to attempt to discover, at second-hand, what your views are as regards me,' the judge said. 'It was ill advised. At the best she could have got only hearsay. But—she is worried. And a woman. It was natural, probably, that she should go to another woman.' He paused again, and again waited.

'Very well,' Heimrich said. 'You are being investigated, by a congressional committee. Wells was supposed to appear before that committee. I've wondered, naturally, what he would have said.' He closed his eyes. 'You offer to be frank, judge.'

'Yes,' Judge Sibley said. 'Mr. Wells would

have testified that my wife was, some years ago, associated with several organizations which are now on the Attorney General's list as subversive. I presume he would have said, as people so often say, that she showed a predilection for communist causes. I presume that, as things presently are, his testimony would have resulted in an adverse report by the committee. I presume it would have made headlines in the newspapers—that my usefulness as a public servant would have been damaged, probably destroyed.' He paused once more. When he spoke again it was only partly to Heimrich. 'I have been a public servant for many years,' he said. 'I hope an effective one. I know a loyal one.'

Heimrich waited a moment. Then he said, 'Go on, judge.'

'My wife is not a careful person, captain,' Sibley said. He spoke slowly, seemed to seek accuracy. 'She is not a calculating person. She is easily moved by—by human problems. Perhaps she is too quick to think that solutions have been found to certain problems. She is warm hearted and, as I said, impulsive. At one time she did join certain organizations which have, since, been found to be—or at any rate said to be—communist controlled. About that she knew nothing.' He looked very carefully at Heimrich, as if he tried to read in the square, impassive face what was in the mind. 'She has no sympathy whatever with communism,'

Judge Sibley said, spacing the words. 'None whatever. She has never had.'

Heimrich still waited for him to continue.

'If, through what she had innocently done, years ago, my work would be interfered with, my wife's heart would be broken, captain,' Sibley said. 'In a very real sense, her life would be destroyed.' He waited for almost a minute before he spoke again, and then he did not look at Captain Heimrich. 'So would mine,' Judge Sibley said. Then he looked at Heimrich. 'That is quite simply true,' he added.

'It was about this Mrs. Sibley spoke to Miss Wister?' Heimrich asked him. 'In an effort to determine what importance I, that is the police, attach to this—situation?'

'Yes,' Sibley said. He hesitated. 'I am afraid,' he said, 'that there is another point. You may think it more significant. Mrs. Sibley and I have both said that, when Mr. Wells was killed, and again when you were attacked, we were together. In our room.' He hesitated. He drew in his breath. 'That is not true,' he said. 'On both occasions, I was out of the room. My wife has only my word for what I was doing.'

'Now judge,' Heimrich said. 'What were you doing?'

'I was not killing Mr. Wells,' Sibley said. 'I was not attacking you with—was it with a knife?'

'Yes,' Heimrich said. 'Go on, judge.'

'I have been worried lately,' Sibley said.

'You can understand that, whatever credence you give to what I have told you. It has made it difficult to sleep. I've fallen into the habit of getting up when I am sleepless and reading for a time. Macaulay's *History of England*. I find it very soothing. Are you familiar with Macaulay, captain?'

Heimrich shook his head.

'It has the effect of nembutal,' Judge Sibley said. 'With no after-effects or, at any rate, very few. I have a quite old set; quite small books. I carry a couple with me. When Mr. Wells was killed I was reading about the vagaries of James II. I had dressed and come downstairs to the lounge, which was entirely deserted.'

'What time was this?' Heimrich asked.

'I came down a little before four o'clock,' Sibley said. 'About three forty-five, I think. I was out of the room until—well, until almost seven.' He smiled faintly. 'Macaulay was unusually effective,' he said. 'I went to sleep in my chair.'

'You came down, I suppose, so as not to waken your wife?'

Sibley nodded. He told Heimrich he knew the rooms of The Coral Isles. Comfortable, certainly. But not commodious. 'My wife is wakened by light,' Sibley said. 'Of course, she woke when I got up. I told her I was going to read for a time. She was used to that. She tells me she went back to sleep almost at once.'

'You both said you were together,' Heimrich

pointed out.

'We did,' Judge Sibley said. 'I regret to say that that was not true. We—well, I'm afraid we both took what seemed the easier way. Or—'

'Mrs. Sibley was asked first,' Heimrich said. 'By one of the sheriff's men. You backed her up. Wasn't that what happened?'

'The responsibility is entirely mine,' Judge Sibley said. 'I hope you will believe that.'

'Very well,' Heimrich said. 'Go on, judge.'

'False testimony is always a mistake,' the judge said. 'As well as being immoral. And—well, my wife is worried, captain.' He paused. 'Deeply worried,' he said.

Heimrich did not reply for a moment. Then he nodded.

'I see, judge,' Heimrich said then. 'You're wise to tell me this, now. At least—'

'I did not kill Wells,' Judge Sibley said. 'If that were not true, this would be obviously unwise.'

'Now judge,' Heimrich said. 'Now judge. Perhaps it wouldn't, you know. However—'

'There are two more things,' Judge Sibley said. 'First, I came to Key West to——to talk to Mr. Wells. I believed him to be a sincere man. I hoped to make him understand the situation. I felt that, if I could persuade him of my wife's innocence of any—any subversive intention, he might—' He shrugged instead of finishing.

'Not testify,' Heimrich said. 'Naturally. Well, were you successful, judge?'

Judge Sibley hesitated for a moment.

'Would you believe me if I said I was?' he asked. 'Since that would, of course, eliminate any motive I might have had?'

'Now judge,' Heimrich said. 'Now judge.'

'Very well, then,' Judge Sibley said. 'I was not successful, as it happened. Mr. Wells did not believe in my wife's—innocence. Or, it did not matter to him. He said the facts would have to speak for themselves. He said it was his duty to give the facts. No, I was not successful, captain. I have a motive. I had opportunity. And—I probably was the last person to see Mr. Wells alive. With, of course, one exception.'

Heimrich opened his eyes; he opened them wide.

'At about four, perhaps five or ten minutes after, Mr. Wells came through the lounge,' Judge Sibley said. 'He walked toward the stairs at the far end—the easterly end, I believe. He was alone. I assumed he was going up to his room. The stairs are there.'

'You didn't speak to him?'

'No.' The judge paused. 'I had done the talking I had to do,' he said. 'With the results I gave you.'

'You saw no one else?'

'A woman was cleaning in the lounge, at the other end,' Judge Sibley said. 'No one else.'

'You didn't see Wells come down again? Because he did, naturally.'

'No. If he came back through the lounge, it

may have been when I was asleep.' Judge Sibley looked puzzled. 'Why would he go out again?' he asked.

'Perhaps somebody wanted to talk to him,' Heimrich said. 'Wanted to talk confidentially. The room wasn't a good place—'

'Of course,' Judge Sibley said. 'The walls are thin. We can hear the couple next to us very plainly. And do, at all hours.'

'Yes,' Heimrich said. 'That was probably the reason.' He closed his eyes. 'Judge Sibley,' he said, 'have you ever heard rumors connecting Mr. Oslen with communist activities?'

'Oslen?' Judge Sibley said. 'The pianist?'

'Now judge,' Heimrich said. 'Musicians can have other activities, naturally. They can have political views.'

'Yes,' Judge Sibley said. 'A pity. No, I never heard anything of the kind about Oslen. He was just a name to me until I met him here.'

'Miss Jones says he's a party member,' Heimrich said. 'Acting under-cover—what they call a "sleeper," I believe. And, she says, an agent provocateur.' He told the rest of it. Sibley listened in surprise; he looked at Heimrich with puzzlement, but if Heimrich noticed this, he paid it no attention.

'Why are you telling me this, captain?' the judge asked, when Heimrich had finished.

Heimrich opened his eyes. He smiled slightly.

'Well,' he said, 'Doctor MacDonald would
220

say, because I'm a sieve.'

Sibley waited.

'However,' Heimrich said, and left it there. 'Miss Jones has disappeared, as I said,' he added. 'We haven't been able to find her. Miss Wister is worried.'

'And you aren't?' Sibley was silent a moment. 'If you came to court, her testimony would be quite essential, captain. To establish motive, since what she's told Miss Wister isn't evidence, of course—isn't admissible evidence. And since, if what she said is true, others who knew the truth wouldn't be likely to come forward.'

'Yes,' Heimrich said. 'There is that.' He waited. Sibley did not speak. 'Well,' Heimrich said, 'what you've told me has been interesting, judge. Very interesting, naturally.'

CHAPTER TEN

For some time after Judge Sibley left him, Captain Heimrich sat in the corner of the covered porch. He smoked several cigarettes. When he was alone, he kept his eyes open, although he did not appear to be looking at anything.

It was, he decided, as clear as it was going to be until something happened. It was clear enough, but not for practical purposes. He considered what he knew, and reconsidered it. He nodded to himself. There was really no doubt, or very little. But—

It was often this way. After a certain time, the truth became obvious, while at the same time remaining inconveniently subjective. The law required more, and of this Captain Heimrich whole-heartedly approved, being a man who whole-heartedly served the law. Academically, Heimrich was willing to assume, being also a speculative man, there was what people sometimes called a 'higher law.' But Captain Heimrich had not, to his knowledge, yet encountered a situation to which the higher law, if it existed, was applicable. Further, the higher law was most commonly a 'law' invented by an individual for his own purposes, or by a group of individuals for their own advancement.

It came down, Heimrich thought with some amusement, to being scrupulous of the shell of the most inconspicuous egg—and this whether the egg was good or bad. It was not lawful, and hence not right, to break eleven good, or good enough, eggs in a search for the bad one in the dozen. It was equally not lawful to destroy the bad egg until it had been candled, no matter how convinced one might be of its badness. Of course, the progress of the law was frequently not rapid.

In this case, the law would require—and most properly—more than Heimrich at the

222

moment had; more, that was, than a conviction deeply rooted in observation of a number of people. The law would prefer an eyewitness, or several. This the law was not likely to get; this it seldom got. Failing such witnesses, the law would like opportunity and means, preferably exclusive. It did not appear that, in connection with the murder of Bronson Wells, the law was going to get anything so precise. At least— Heimrich mentally checked off names—at least four persons, and more than that if one cared to go a little afield, had had opportunity, in the sense that they were not probably elsewhere, and otherwise engaged, when Wells was stabbed. The means—about which the coroner's physician was less specific than Heimrich would have liked, except that a long knife had been used—were available, or at least not demonstrably unavailable, to any number of people. As for motive—

Heimrich sighed. Except in one case the motive was evident. In that case, it could be presumed.

It was not tidy; not at all tidy. But then, murder so seldom was. It was open at both ends, and not too tight in the middle. But that was often the case. The significant clue was so seldom left to be stumbled over; the most careful investigation so often accounted for everything except what was significant.

Well, Heimrich thought, it is time to prod. It was time to arrange a happening.

Captain Heimrich got up, being careful not to jiggle his right arm—which was a nuisance, as was the absence of his alter ego, Sergeant Forniss; as was, for that matter, his lack of authority and expert technical aid. (The vagueness about the knife now—that was really an irritation.) However—

Heimrich walked through the enclosed porch and through a door which led into the lounge. A young man in a red jacket was cooing his name. The young man led him, with proper deference, to a telephone. Heimrich identified himself and heard the voice of Chief Deputy Sheriff Jefferson. Heimrich listened. After a time he said that he wasn't surprised, naturally. He listened further. He said that it was, of course, up to the sheriff.

'However,' Heimrich said, 'I think it would be a mistake.' He listened again. 'Oh,' he said, 'because I don't really think he's your man. Even if you can prove his friends lied for him. And—I don't want others to.' He listened again. 'One other, if you prefer,' Heimrich said, and listened once more. 'Tonight, I think,' he said. 'If you take him in now, and word gets around, I don't think anything will happen. Why should it?' Once more he listened.

'I don't want to go into it here,' Heimrich said. 'Of course, it's your case. You don't want to make a mistake on it. I think that arresting García would be a mistake. Tonight, at any rate.' He listened. 'I think he'll be around in the morning,' Heimrich said. 'You can make sure of that, naturally.' He listened once more, this time for longer. He said he was not trying to be mysterious; he pointed out that he was talking through the hotel switchboard.

He said, 'Why not play it my way, for tonight at least? If you can come here, I'll explain why.' He listened briefly. 'I don't want to leave now,' he said. 'Otherwise I would.' He waited. 'Call it on a silver platter, if you like,' he said. 'Naturally, I may be wrong. I think the chance is good.' He listened.

'Now sheriff,' he said. 'Now sheriff. I'll give things a push.'

He listened once more to the voice on the telephone and said that that would be fine. He told Deputy Sheriff Jefferson that they would be seeing each other, and hung up. Then he went around the hotel desk to the door of the manager's office and knocked and was admitted. A few minutes later he came out and walked down the lounge.

The Shepards and Judge and Mrs. Sibley were drinking together. Mrs. Shepard smiled, and beckoned to Heimrich, but Heimrich shook his head and went on. The four of them looked at him, and Heimrich thought he could feel their uneasiness. At any rate, Heimrich hoped he could. He met Oslen just before he reached the stairs to the floors above and Oslen said, 'Hi,' with unexpected amiability.

225

Heimrich said, 'Good evening, Mr. Oslen,' and started to go on.

'Listen, captain,' Oslen said. 'I flew off the handle this afternoon. It's not your fault if Rachel made up this crazy story. I realize that. And, sure, you had to ask me about it.'

'Now Mr. Oslen,' Heimrich said. 'That's all right. Perfectly natural.'

'Haven't you found her yet?' Oslen asked.

Heimrich for a moment appeared to hesitate. Then he said, 'I think I know where she is, Mr. Oslen. I'm quite sure I do, in fact.'

'She's all right?' Oslen said. 'Crazy little fool or not, she's—well, hell, I hope she's all right.'

'Naturally,' Heimrich said.

'What the hell?' Oslen said. 'If I get a chance to talk to her, she'll crawl out of the whole thing. You can bet on that.'

He waited. Heimrich looked at him.

'Now Mr. Oslen,' he said. 'Now Mr. Oslen. You wouldn't really want to bet, would you?' He looked at the taller man, looked into a guileless, open face; straightforward eyes. 'Not bet your life on it, surely?' Then, before Oslen could say anything, Captain Heimrich walked on. He thought Oslen would join the Sibleys and the Shepards; he hoped he would. He wondered with interest what the five would make of one another now, how they would talk, how uneasy they would be and how suspicious. He hoped he could guess, and climbed the stairs to the second floor.

226

It took him some minutes to find the middle-aged woman in the blue uniform. He found her coming out of a room, with towels over her arm. He said, 'You're Ella, aren't you,' and noticed something like fear in her eyes.

'It's all right,' he said. 'It was a perfectly natural thing to do. There'll be no trouble if you do what I ask.'

'I don't know—' the maid began.

'Now Ella,' Heimrich said. 'Of course you do.' He told her what he wanted her to do.

'Please, sir,' she said. 'I can't do that. I—I promised. Anyway, if they see me with a guest, they'll fire me. It's a rule.'

'Now Ella,' Heimrich said. 'I'm not exactly a guest, you know. I'm a policeman. We'll go now, Ella.'

It was then a few minutes after seven.

*   *   *

'Over beyond the tennis courts,' Mary Wister said. 'A very strange building—like a prison, really.'

They were beside an open window in the Penguin Bar; they were sipping long drinks, slowly. Outside the vari-colored lights which lay cupped at the bases of palm trees had been turned on; the light of the moon softened them, so that they seemed, improbably, aspects of the moonlight. In the patio, waitresses in white blouses and Guatemalan skirts of many mixtures, were setting tables; white-jacketed boys carried chairs to them down the stairs from the main dining room. In the semi-cylinders of two bisected tanks, mounted on iron trestles, charcoal was flickering in blue flame.

'—one little door,' Mary said. 'The whole thing seems to be triangular.' She looked across the table, answered MacDonald's half smile, and its implication. 'It doesn't matter, Mac,' she said. 'I'm just—just talking.'

'No,' MacDonald said. 'As a matter of fact, I saw it too. I asked.' He nodded to himself and to her. 'I'm learning from the captain,' he told her. 'When I want to know something, I ask. It's the water shed.' She looked puzzled. 'It's full of water,' he said. 'Not of prisoners. Just of water.' She shook her head to that.

It was, he told her, reasonably simple. Key West one thought of as part of the mainland, as—so much any Key Wester would tell you, without being asked—the southernmost tip of the mainland. This was true, but only technically—only by the grace of the causeway which linked it with the rest of Florida. It was nevertheless an island, and a coral island at that. As coral an island, he told her, as one could find in the southernmost seas. And, being the kind of island it was, it had no indigenous fresh water.

Mary looked doubtful. She said, 'But—'

'Oh,' MacDonald said, 'it has fresh water,

228

now. Some years ago, the Navy built a pipeline, a conduit. You can see it, here and there, as you drive down.'

Through the conduit, by grace of the United States Navy, Key West enjoyed water, but not in quantity. There had been enough and to spare when the line was first constructed, but the city had continued to grow. It had grown as a place for tourists—for people who wanted summer in winter, without the decorations of Miami Beach; for people who wanted houses and apartments for the colder months; for the fewer who were willing to endure Key West's unrelenting summer for the lazy peace which came to the little city in the hottest days. The water supply had not grown with the community.

Before the conduit was built, the people who lived on the little island had trusted to rainfall. They had gathered it from roofs, hoarded it in cisterns, used it sparingly. To some extent, for some purposes, those who wished to be sure of their supply—who wanted to squander water, as The Coral Isles squandered it on hedges, and on bougainvillaea, on thirsty lawns—held to the old fashion, and saved the water as it fell, draining it into storage. The triangular building, with the spreading silvery roof, was in fact a considerable cistern. If one could look into it, one would be looking into a covered lake.

'You mean,' Mary asked, 'that we've been

drinking it?'

To that, Barclay MacDonald shook his head. They drank, he told her, water from the mainland, by courtesy of the Navy. The grass and the trees drank water more immediately provided by God.

'Oh,' Mary Wister said, relieved. He grinned at her, and motioned to the bar waitress. Mary hesitated; was told that it was her doctor's order.

'My doctor?' Mary said, before she thought, and was looked at with amusement.

'Entirely,' Barclay MacDonald said. 'Hadn't you noticed?'

He looked at her, and waited. She was conscious of his waiting, and conscious, for the first time in many years, of an uncertainty more than superficial. So she pretended; so she said, 'All right, doctor,' limiting acquiescence to the matter of a second drink. This seemed, on the whole, to amuse him, but he ordered the drinks. They sat over them, looking out through the window, watching the hurrying waitresses, the busy boys in white jackets; watching the blue flames which leaped higher, now, under the steak broilers.

'To change the subject,' MacDonald said, after a long moment of silence, 'I think our captain is arranging for something to happen.'

'Arranging?' she repeated.

MacDonald suspected, he told her, that that was the way Heimrich worked—his way out of the two most probable ways. He was, he said, assuming that there was a kinship between the search for a truth in, say, medicine, and for another, say, in criminal investigation. If so, he would say there were two ways.

'I am changing the subject,' he said, carefully. 'For now. It will come up again, you know.'

'Go on,' she said. 'What two most probable ways?'

'Accumulation,' he said. 'Postulation. Getting together everything you can find, hoping that a pattern will emerge from multiplicity. Postulating a pattern, seeking support from the observed. You decide the world is round; you discover support in the appearance first of the superstructure of ships. You view the physical world, presume a pattern of roundness, arrange experiments to prove your theory.' He considered. 'In science,' he said. 'In criminal investigation. But neither method is often used exclusively.'

She waited again. He smiled at her across the small table.

'I change the subject,' he said. 'You wanted it changed?'

'I don't know, Mac,' Mary said. 'Go on.'

'Neither excludes the other,' he said. 'Both methods are used together. Heimrich, I imagine, collects facts until he can guess at a pattern, but not until he can prove a pattern. Until he has a hunch. We all do that. Then, in my field, we conduct experiments intended to prove the hunch. Controlled experiments, we call them. Say we assume that the incidence of cancer of the stomach varies inversely with the presence of free hydrochloric acid. We get a hunch that is true on the basis of general observation. Then we accumulate more information, controlled, channeled, to the end of proving our theory. Or of disproving it, but with a provisional bias in its favor.' He paused. 'It's not a particularly good example,' he said. 'But no matter. I've fallen in love with you, you know.'

'I—' she said, and stopped.

'You know,' he said. 'But there's no hurry. I suspect that Captain Heimrich arranges experiments. I suspect that talking to García's sister, in public as he did, was an experiment. He wanted to make something happen.'

'But nothing—' Mary began, and stopped again.

'Yes,' MacDonald said. 'He got himself stabbed. Not fatally. Quite superficially, really. I wouldn't be surprised if a fatality wasn't intended.' He considered his phrasing and shook his head over it.

Mary didn't, she said, see what Heimrich had proved, except that steel will penetrate flesh.

MacDonald was not sure. One could, he pointed out, guess. If the stabbing was connected with the interview Heimrich had

had with García's sister, then the first thought would be that she had said something which incriminated García; that, hearing of it, García had taken steps. The second thought would be that that was too easy; that someone had taken advantage of the situation to make it appear that García had acted so, on such provocation. That the wound was superficial rather bore this out. Of course, Heimrich must have hoped to trap his man—and hadn't.

'You're oblique,' Mary told him. MacDonald shook his head to that.

'Not I,' he said. 'The circumstances. Perhaps the murderer. Perhaps the captain. He is—'

But then Barclay MacDonald stopped.

'What do you see?' he asked Mary. 'You've gone—'

'Wait!' she said, and looked fixedly out the window. Her head moved slightly as her gaze followed someone, or something. Then, quickly, she looked back.

'The girl,' she said. 'I'm almost certain. Rachel Jones. Only—she's dressed as a waitress. She's putting glasses on tables. But I'm certain—' She looked out of the window again. 'I'm almost certain.'

'Yes,' MacDonald said. 'I think that's what Heimrich meant. A place like this takes a big staff. They are housed in the dormitory, you know—near where—where you found Wells. I imagine they come and go. That if you were willing to pay, you could make it worth someone's while—a chambermaid's, say—to hide you in the dormitory.'

Mary was looking out the window again. She started to speak without turning her head. 'But you wouldn't—' she began, and broke off.

Barclay MacDonald watched her profile and, although he waited her words with interest, he waited also without impatience, pleased with what he saw.

'Captain Heimrich,' Mary said. 'He's coming this way. And—he passed right by the girl I'm sure is Rachel Jones and didn't see her. He—'

She turned, now, and looked toward the door which, from the patio, opened into the Penguin Bar. MacDonald turned in his chair and looked with her. After a longer interval than either had expected, Captain Heimrich came through the door, the black sling in which his right arm rested sharply outlined against a white jacket. He saw them at once, and appeared surprised to see them. He seemed about to pass on through the bar, acknowledging their presence only abstractedly. But Mary Wister said, 'Captain Heimrich,' and he stopped and then came to their table. He was offered a drink; he hesitated; he decided to accept a drink. MacDonald beckoned to the pretty girl who served in the bar. Heimrich decided on rye and plain water.

'Captain,' Mary said. 'Wasn't that Rachel

Jones out there?'

'Out there?' Heimrich repeated. Mary indicated the part of the patio visible through the window. Heimrich looked through the window, mild interest in his face.

'Dressed as a waitress,' Mary said. 'You passed a few feet from her. Didn't you see her?'

'Now Miss Wister,' Heimrich said. For a moment he continued to look through the window. 'You have good eyes,' he said then, and turned from the window. He appeared to hesitate. 'Yes,' he said then. 'I saw her, naturally.'

His tone was casual, oddly casual it seemed to Mary Wister. She looked at him, her eyes opening a little more widely. After a moment, Heimrich nodded. But then he closed his own eyes.

'But—' Mary said, and her voice was puzzled. 'Aren't you going to do anything? You were looking for her.'

'Now Miss Wister,' Heimrich said, and his eyes remained closed. 'What do you expect me to do? Arrest her?'

Mary made a quick gesture, dismissing that, labeling that subterfuge.

'She's in danger from Oslen,' Mary said. 'You know that. You've said as much.'

'Have I?' Heimrich asked. He opened blue eyes. 'Did I say that, Miss Wister?'

'Of course she is,' Mary said. 'Anybody can see that.'

Heimrich said, 'Now Miss Wister.' He regarded her. 'We haven't any proof, you know,' he said. 'No evidence.' He paused again. 'However,' he said, 'we'll pick Miss Jones up, naturally. In time.'

Mary merely looked at him. She continued to look at him while the pretty girl brought his drink; while, a little absently, he lifted the glass and drank.

'I don't—' she began then, but at the same time Barclay MacDonald spoke.

'You knew where she was, didn't you?' he asked Heimrich. 'You've known for some time now, haven't you, captain?'

'Now doctor,' Heimrich said. He looked for a moment at the glass in his hand. 'Perhaps I guessed,' he admitted.

'And did nothing?' MacDonald asked the question; it had been sharp in Mary's mind.

'Now doctor,' Heimrich said. 'She hasn't been harmed, has she? Or done harm?'

'You're very casual,' Mary Wister said. 'Unbearably casual.'

Heimrich looked at her thoughtfully. He shook his head.

'No,' he said. 'I'm not casual at all, Miss Wister. I'm never casual about murder. Never at all casual.'

'About a girl's life,' Mary said. 'You don't deny she's in danger? That you're letting her stay in danger?'

'She may be, naturally,' Heimrich said.

236

'She's been leading a rather risky life. If what she says is true.'

'It is,' Mary said. 'I'm certain it is.' She looked from Heimrich to MacDonald, and on him her eyes stayed longest. 'You know it, Mac,' she said. She sought the knowledge in his face, and did no find it—did not find certainty, response to her feeling of urgency. She looked back to Heimrich. 'Don't you *see*?' she demanded. 'What are you waiting for?'

'You still feel guilt,' MacDonald said then. 'Don't *you* see that, Mary?'

She shook her head.

'No,' she said. 'Not that. That doesn't matter. I heard her. She was telling the truth. I've been thinking about it. I know she was telling the truth. About Oslen. And—that makes her dangerous to him.' Again she looked from one to the other of the men at the table. 'What's the matter with both of you?' she demanded, and her voice was strained. 'Do you *want* her hurt? Killed? He's already killed once.'

'Now Miss Wister,' Heimrich said. 'You're—'

But Mary stood up, suddenly. She had felt that she was hammering with both fists at something without resilience, without response. She felt she could no longer endure this. Antagonism which was almost rage surged in her.

'I'm not going to sit here,' she was saying,

237

heard herself saying, her voice not raised but tight with the intensity of her decision. 'I'm going to find her. I'm going to—'

But both of Barclay MacDonald's slender, strong hands were on her shoulders, and the pressure of them—the sureness of them—stopped her words.

'Sit down, my dear,' MacDonald said. 'Sit down, Mary.'

For an instant she felt herself twisting against the hands; felt her mind twisting, fighting, against the unhurried command of the tall doctor's voice.

'Good girl,' MacDonald said. He smiled suddenly. 'Sit down, lady,' he said.

She looked at him, and now there was in her mind, and mirrored in her eyes, a kind of incredulity. And now MacDonald, who seemed to know precisely what she was thinking, nodded again, still without removing his hands.

'Yes,' he said, 'that's the way it is. You've had it, my dear. Didn't you know?' He smiled then, easily. 'And,' he said, 'don't try to change the subject.'

For a moment she said nothing. Then, without any intent of saying what she said, Mary Wister said, 'All right, Mac. All right.' She listened to her own words, and now was without surprise. 'I'll go quietly,' she said, and looked up at the thin, mobile face which was, all at once, almost unbelievably familiar.

Then she sat down. His dear face, she thought.

'A little something we had to get straightened out,' Barclay MacDonald said to Captain Heimrich, objectionably—but she did not really object—as one man to another.

'Oh,' Heimrich said, 'naturally, doctor.'

'You two,' Mary said. But then the moment passed, since the business of the moment, which had nothing to do with a girl named Rachel Jones, or the death of a man named Bronson Wells, was completed. 'All the same,' Mary Wister said, firmly, 'I'm not going to sit still and—'

'Now Miss Wister,' Heimrich said. 'Nobody is going to sit still, naturally.'

He finished his drink, then, and stood up. Both of them waited for him to speak again. He stood looking down at them.

'If anyone asks about Miss Jones,' Heimrich said, slowly, 'you might tell them where you saw her.' He nodded. 'Or,' he said, 'even if they don't ask.'

And then he turned, walked across the Penguin Bar, up a flight of stairs, into the still-deserted dining room. He left them to look at each other, and it was as if they were for the first time alone. After a moment, Mary spoke, and then started quickly. 'He is going—' she began, but Barclay MacDonald leaned toward her across the small table and said, 'Not yet. We don't change the subject now. Don't run

239

from it.'

And then he was, to the girl across from him, no longer a quiet force before which her own decision melted (although he would be that again) but merely a man who wanted things in words, as men did want them. Because he was that, she felt a tenderness toward him she had not felt before, and certainly not felt during the moment when his slender hands were so strong, and so reassuring, on her shoulders. She smiled at him, with gentleness.

'Dear Mac,' she said. 'I'm not running. We're there. Didn't you notice? No place else to run.'

'So long as you know,' he said. He looked around the bar, which did not provide seclusion. 'When I think of all the moonlight,' he said. 'All the space we had.' He gestured at the surroundings. He indicated the table between them. And Mary Wister laughed softly. 'To say nothing of—' MacDonald said, and stopped.

'Dear Mac,' she said. And then, 'I'll have to find another name for you, won't I? I don't like to hear women call their husbands by their last names, or even part of their last names.' She shook her head. 'Barclay,' she said. She shook her head again. She reached out and touched, just touched, one of the long, strong hands; the one in which he held his drink. She withdrew her fingers instantly. 'We'll have to make up something,' she said. She looked into his face.

'It doesn't need talking about,' she said, in a different tone.

'I know,' he said. 'It's hard to remember, just at first.' His long face lighted with a smile which involved all of it. 'Will you marry me, Miss Wister?'

'Now doctor,' she said, 'I'll be delighted.'

Then they both laughed, or almost laughed, and he took one of her hands, which was very conveniently placed for taking, and looked at it carefully. 'Nice muscle tone,' he said, and gave it back. For a moment she looked at the hand thus approved. Then, gravely, she nodded at it. But even as she did so, her face changed.

'The girl,' she said. 'We can't just sit here and—and not change the subject. The girl and Captain Heimrich—and Oslen.'

'And,' he said, 'the others.'

She shook her head at that. 'Oslen,' she said. 'What is he waiting for?'

'I suppose to be sure,' MacDonald said. 'Or, perhaps, merely for evidence.'

'But how—' Mary began and then stopped and said. 'Oh. But—he *can't*!'

'I don't think he'll take any real risk,' MacDonald said.

'But you do think he's using the girl as—as *bait*,' she said. 'Like a—what is it?—a sheep or something tethered under a tree. You know what I mean.'

Slowly, he nodded.

'But we can't let him,' she said. 'Surely you
241

see that. Oslen will—he has to keep her from talking. I mean, talking to somebody in authority. Giving evidence. Don't you see?'

He agreed it could be. But he did not seem convinced.

'I'm right,' she said.

'It sounds all right,' he agreed. 'But—if it were that simple I don't think the captain would—well, experiment. Conduct a controlled experiment. Plan to make something happen.'

He was told that he was very trustful; that he had great faith in Captain Heimrich. 'Whom,' she said, 'you don't really know at all.'

'Listen, Mary,' he said. 'Think a minute. Haven't *you* confidence in him? I'll admit I have. I'll admit I don't know precisely why. And—haven't you?'

He looked at her intently. She started to speak; somehow his gaze made her hesitate, made her think again.

'I suppose I have,' she said, finally. 'But—do we just sit and watch?'

'Yes,' he said. 'I think we do.'

'But it's so simple,' she said, and the words were a protest. But she met his eyes again, and then she said, 'Isn't it, Mac?'

'I don't know,' he said. 'I think perhaps it isn't. You know what Heimrich said about making the character fit the crime. I think that's it. It—sticks in my craw. I think it does in the captain's.'

'Why doesn't Oslen fit?' she said. 'I think you're both—well, being fooled. Or being too subtle. Look—assume the story she told, Rachel Jones I mean—is true. You do assume that? Heimrich does?'

'I do,' MacDonald told her. 'I think he does.'

'Then,' she said, 'Oslen's a party member; a member of a conspiracy. He's under orders. And—there's nothing he'd stop at to serve his end. You have to give them that. It's what makes them frightening, isn't it? A kind of inhumanity.' She paused. 'Or,' she said, 'I suppose you could call it a kind of dedication. Anyway, why doesn't the character fit? Wells was working against them. Perhaps he could stop what Oslen was doing. We don't really know how important that was to the party, or how important Oslen thought it was.' She shook her head again. 'It's really all very clear,' she said. 'I don't see why you don't see it.'

But now there was a question in her voice.

'I wonder,' he said, 'if you don't half see? Because—'

But then they were interrupted. A boy in a red jacket stood at the head of the stairs leading down from the dining room to the cocktail lounge, and said, 'Doctor MacDonald, please. Doctor MacDonald.' MacDonald beckoned; the boy came down the stairs. He reported a long distance call. MacDonald said, 'Damn,' and 'I won't be a minute,' and followed the boy. Mary sat with what remained of her

243

drink. She looked out into the patio, and now the scene there had changed.

The western sky still was faintly light, and the palms were silhouetted against it with improbable clarity and now, at their best so, with astounding grace. By day, some of them looked, she had once or twice irreverently thought, like over-used shaving brushes, set on end. But now, moving only a little in the faint stirring of evening air, their heavy fronds made graceful and light in outline, they were enchanted things. There was nothing for it, Mary Wister thought, and smiled faintly at the peculiar trees. They look precisely as palm trees are supposed to look against lighter sky. Since they could not be improved upon, it would be a waste of time to sketch them. It was also an almost irresistible temptation to sketch them.

From where she sat the palms seemed to circle the patio, although she remembered that that was not literally true—it was a trick of light, and of perspective. They seemed to lean down over the whole scene, which now was increasingly one of animation. There was always something charming about tables set up under the sky, at night, waiting people who would come to eat, presumably, food of quite exquisite variety. (It might turn out that the chairs were not particularly comfortable, that the tables did not stand firm on their legs, that food got dusty as you ate it—this last certainly was true of New York's sidewalk cafés. But such facts were unimportant; the charm would not yield to them.) Colored lights reflected from the trunks of palms; colored lights were along the roof edge of the orchestra shell; hung elsewhere in strands. But there were not too many of them, as there might so easily have been. They did not dominate the night, but only accented it, softening the darkness.

And near her, only a little way beyond the window at which she sat, the charcoal fires were leaping gayly, blue and red flames flickering above the strong, deep red of charcoal all alight. Two white-clad men, elaborately capped, presided, and were as yet inactive, although each held a long fork ready, and behind them, on tilted counter, steaks waited in a mosaic, each steak fitted in its proper place, for the approaching ceremony. As she watched, a third white-clad man approached, his cap even higher, more convoluted, than the other caps, and inspected fires and steaks and the acolytes of fire and beef. The three then appeared to stand at attention, and the flames—encouraged by the approbation of the chef in charge—to leap more frolicsomely.

Behind Mary, the cocktail lounge filled. The cheerful clatter of shaken ice was more evident; voices were more numerous; the pretty girl who served the tables moved, in white blouse and bright skirt, at an increasing tempo. Mary turned in her chair and looked around the room. She looked toward the door through which Barclay MacDonald—what *was* she going to call him from now on?—would return. A strange couple was standing in the door, looking around, seeking a table, finding none. The man shook his head and the two went back into the dining room, off which the cocktail lounge opened. Then they went out another door from the dining room and passed outside by the window next which Mary sat, seeking—and this time finding—a table outside at which to sit with drinks.

Mary sipped her own, a little defensively, occupying with diminishing right of tenure a table for two, when tables for two were in demand. Where was Mac, to call him by what came handiest? Where *was* the man? Mary's sudden irritation was, and she realized it was, disproportionate. She was keyed up again, again uneasy. And the feeling of having outstayed her allotted time at a table for two was only the pretext for uneasiness. She turned and her hand encountered the glass and it swayed and almost spilled; she barely caught it, and the metal of a ring she wore tinkled sharply against crystal, the sound harshly loud in her ears.

She looked away from the door, out again into the patio. It was filling, too. The white-jacketed bar waiters were busy—the short middle-aged one, the one who sang late in the evenings for the patio dancers, the singing waiter, was breathing hard and was resolute; as he passed near, Mary could see that liquid was sloshing from the glasses on his tray, that he had the tip of his tongue between his teeth. And now the first steaks were going on the fire, and blue-gray smoke was rising from them, rising on the fire's heat in quiet air. Under the steaks the fire leaped, as fat melted from meat and fell to join fire. And Mary's eyes sought among the waitresses, the people at the tables.

'You're very intent,' a voice said. 'Where's the doctor?'

It had been that obvious all along, then, she thought, and turned sharply and looked up at Paul Shepard, who stood and looked down at her. He was very trim; the black bow of his tie was mathematically exact against the white of his collar. (Mac's will always go up at one end, Mary thought; I know it always will. I'm glad it always will.)

'Hello,' she said. 'I—I wasn't intent.' She remembered what Heimrich had asked; hesitated. But, the more who knew—except for one, and he would arrange to know—the better it would be; the safer it would be. 'I thought I saw the Jones girl,' she said. 'Rachel. But I guess I didn't.' Why she added the last, which was untrue, she did not know.

'Probably you did,' Shepard said, his articulation neat, exact. 'The captain apparently saw her too—and then lost her again.' He shook his head, noting inefficiency on the part of Captain Heimrich. 'Dressed as a waitress, he thought,' Shepard added. He shrugged. 'None the worse for the tennis?' he asked then.

She shook her head.

'You look worried,' he said. 'About the girl?'

She hesitated.

'Not really,' she said. Suddenly she was not—not really. Oslen wouldn't be such—such a fool; wouldn't walk into a trap so obviously baited. He was, he had to be, astute, whatever else one thought of him. He had to be careful; to know how to play a part skillfully. If he had been doing what Rachel said—and if he had not there was no reason for any fear—he was too adept in conspiracy to be so openly conspired against. Heimrich's plan wasn't going to work—not against William Oslen. 'Not really,' she repeated. 'Nobody could get away with—with anything.'

Shepard continued for a moment to look down at her. He smiled, then, faintly.

'You think not?' he said. He looked out the window. 'So much space,' he said. 'So many people coming and going. A resolute man, who was under compulsion to act—who had to act, you know—' He did not finish the sentence, and that was uncharacteristic. Instead, he shrugged again. 'However,' he said, 'you may be right, Miss Wister.' He continued to look down at her. 'Let's hope you are.' He paused

248

for a moment. 'Well,' he said, 'I'm supposed to find my wife. She's with the Sibleys somewhere.' He looked around the room. 'Not here, obviously,' he said. 'Probably outside.' Then he nodded, briefly, and went through the door leading to the patio. At the top of the short flight of stairs he paused and looked around, evidently seeking Penny Shepard and Judge and Mrs. Sibley. He went down the steps, then, and around the corner of the building, still obviously in quest.

And Mac did not come. (Clay—that was what she would call him. Clay, for Barclay; also for clay-foot. For a man stuck somewhere in the mud, when he was wanted.) She turned again from the window, looked again, with hope, at the entrance from the dining room. This time nobody at all stood there, nobody looked around for tables. People were going directly to the patio, now; drinking there if they drank. Mary looked at the backs along the bar; there, she had found, the more resolute drinkers still congregated, lined on stools.

Then, at the far end of the bar, a man swiveled on one of the stools; an anonymous back became a recognized man—became William Oslen, alone and through with drinking. He was off the bar stool, looking momentarily around the room. Instinctively, Mary Wister looked away, looked out again into the patio. There, on the walk just outside, Rachel Jones was standing. She was dressed as a waitress still, in white blouse and gay skirt. But she was motionless in the hurry around her; her hands were empty. She was looking into the Penguin Bar.

But she did not seem to see Mary Wister, who sat so near. The eyes of the slight, vivid girl looked beyond Mary, into the room behind her. Rachel's dark eyes were wide, fixed. As Mary watched, the other girl turned, as if a decision had been reached, and started moving away along the crowded path, past those coming along the walks for dinner in the patio. She moved quickly.

Mary did not need to look to know why the girl's momentary inaction had turned so abruptly into what was almost flight. She did not need to look to know that, behind her, Oslen was moving his big body with resolution among the tables, toward the door which opened on to the patio. But she did look, just as he passed her; watched him as he reached the door. He did not hesitate at the top of the steps. It was very evident that he did not need to search, as Paul Shepard had searched, for the person wanted. He did not appear much to hurry as he went down the stairs and along the walk which led around the corner of the building—which led away from the people and the lights, away from the animated scene, from the brightness of the friendly fire, playing under the broiling steaks.

All confidence, all assurance, left Mary's

mind as, for the moment motionless, she watched him go. She had fooled herself; believed what it was pleasant to believe, reassuring to believe. Knowing that a path was trapped, that a deadfall was somewhere along it, a man might still follow the path because there was no other—might be compelled along it, might have no choice between evils and be forced to put faith in resolution, and in skill.

And Mac was not there. Heimrich—how could she know where Heimrich was? Her hands clenched momentarily, until the knuckles whitened. *There isn't any trap*, she thought. *Not really any trap*. There would be only men to watch, and they were not watching. Only—

She was on her feet, then. For an instant she stood at the table, looking once more—looking now with a kind of desperation—at the door through which (how long ago!) Barclay MacDonald had walked behind the boy in a red jacket. She knew, when the door was empty, that she could not wait for Mac—not even for him. Not for anybody.

She went, then; she hurried; did not quite run. She was through the door to the patio, and her heels were clicking on the cement path. She brushed past people, was brushed by them. She could hear her voice saying, 'Sorry. So sorry,' and hear the breathless quality in her voice. She knew that, having passed her, men and women stopped and looked after her, curiously. But she looked only ahead, along the walk and beyond its turning at the far corner of the hotel; sought with great anxiety to pierce the comparative darkness of the lawn, laden with the heavy shadows of the palms. As she walked—and now almost ran—her eyes grew accustomed to the dimmer light.

She was out of sight from the Penguin Bar when Barclay MacDonald entered it, hurrying down the stairs from the dining room; stopping abruptly when he saw the table empty.

'Damn!' said Barclay MacDonald, with feeling, and, being a practical man, sought out the girl who served the bar.

CHAPTER ELEVEN

The walk along which Mary Wister hurried, avoiding (or not quite avoiding) those who trickled through the warm night toward the soft brightness of the patio, toward the flames which darted under broiling meat, traversed the length of one of the arms which The Coral Isles reached out toward the sea. At the end of the wing, the path divided. One could go to the left, around the end of the wing and so to the sheltered porch which faced the water. One could go right, along a cemented path which curved among palm trees, toward the beach and the cluster of buildings which housed locker rooms, solariums, the tennis shop, even a small motion picture theater. That way, it was darker; where the path curved to circle the far end of the tennis courts, only the colored lights at the bases of palm trees, and the still faintly persisting light from the west, where the sun had set, fought with the shadows.

Where the path divided, Mary Wister stopped suddenly, and at a loss. She had begun pursuit without thought; she followed Oslen, who followed the dark, vivid girl, with only the determination to follow. But now, since she could not anywhere see either the heavy largeness of the man nor the vibrating quickness of the girl, assurance was abruptly pulled out from under her. She could only stand where the walk divided, and look first in one direction and then in the other; could only try to see and, failing that, to guess.

On the path to her left, several people walked, unhurried—a man and a girl; a couple in late middle life, moving slowly, as if urgency long ago had been spent; a man, alone, who walked with purpose, as if already he were late for something. But all of these, and the group of four which was some distance farther along the walk, were moving toward her and among them was no one she knew. It could be assumed, had to be assumed, that they were merely people going, at their leisure, to their dinner. The other way, although it led into relative darkness—and why would Rachel run

253

from a frequented place, rather than toward one?—was almost certainly her way.

She could not, she thought, be far behind Oslen; she had left the Penguin Bar only a few minutes after he had left. He had certainly come this way; he was certainly not in sight on the path toward the porch. Her unobstructed view along the other path was short and, that way, the palms were more numerous. Some of them—a good many of them, indeed—were large enough so that even a large man, wishing not to be seen, could step behind a bole and be hidden. It was not a particularly encouraging thought; starting down the path to the beach, Mary went with less haste, and with considerably less assurance. She was, sanity insisted, doing a very foolish thing.

The point was, however, that it was a thing which needed doing, and which, so far as she could see, no one else was attending to. If Rachel was the bait in a trap where, except for herself—an adequate young woman in a green linen dress, but only that—was the trap? There appeared to be none; it appeared that something had gone desperately wrong, some contingency had been left unprovided for. I don't want any part of this, Mary thought, going down the path with an uneasy eye for each thick trunk of palm; not any part at all. And I'm not really responsible. But that was the trouble. She could say that. She could say it over and over. But she could not believe it.

So she went on, straining her eyes for sight of Oslen, fearing to find him and determined that she would—afraid and unwillingly resolute and above everything else, furious with all the rest—with, most of all, Dr Barclay MacDonald, who had vanished when most needed; who might now, for all she knew, be contentedly finishing a drink at the table in the Penguin Bar, waiting placidly her return from what he would inevitably assume to be a moment of retirement. *Damn Mac!* Mary Wister said to herself, and thought she saw movement behind a great palm close to the walk, where the walk turned at right angles to round the tennis court.

She stopped, and now, for the moment, there was only fear—a kind of cold tingling which absorbed mind and body. She waited for the movement to repeat itself—waited for William Oslen, not now a large, youngish man in the mold of an Eastern school—*now a man who killed.*

But the movement was not repeated. She waited, trying to make herself go on, and her whole body and most of her mind said, 'Go back, you little fool! Go back!'

So, after a second, Mary Wister went on. She did not look at the tree; could not. She walked past it, and could not breathe, and waited as she walked, the muscles of her neck tightening. Only after she had taken half a dozen steps, and those into increasing darkness, did she dare look back. Looking, as she did, toward a lighter area, she could see clearly enough. There had been no one behind the tree. But there were trees ahead, and the buildings among which the shadows were darker still.

She stopped again, but this time to listen; to hold her breath and listen. She heard the sea then, the heavy rustle, the deep obbligato of the great waters. It was always there, all lighter sounds, all human sounds, lived on its surface, by its sufferance. Yet for hours one did not hear it. Now she did, and for a moment heard nothing else. She tried to force the deep sound below the level of perception, and after a moment was successful. Then, in the shadows ahead, where the cement walk went among the frame buildings, passed the beach house and the tennis shop, she heard the sharp click of a woman's slipper heel on pavement. The sound was single, not repeated.

For a moment, Mary found it hard to explain. Then she guessed that someone—and surely Rachel!—had crossed the walk, but found it too wide to cross at a single stride, had had to risk the sound of leather heel on ringing surface. Mary realized then, also, how noisily revealing her own progress must have been along the whole length of the path. The thought was frightening; almost more than that, it was embarrassing. I'll have to remember afterward how many unexpected feelings you can have, when really you're scared to death, Mary Wister thought, and then thought, which was even more absurd in such terms, that she hoped she would have the opportunity.

Still she waited, hoping for—and at the same time fearing—further sound from the pursued, or the pursuer she herself pursued. She listened and watched and was conscious, rather belatedly, that she herself was lost in shadows and that the others, if Oslen also was near by, unrevealed, would be waiting for further sounds from her, surely having been warned, and long warned, by the sharp staccato of her own steps.

There were two of them, almost certainly there were three, standing silent in the warm night, sheltered in the deepest shadows, waiting for movement, for disclosure.

Very carefully, Mary Wister stepped from the paved walk onto the grass beside it. She could move there almost silently. She moved forward. She felt, without seeing them, without hearing them, that others were moving with her, moving around her in the shadows.

She reached, and sought for shelter, the side of the long, rectangular motion picture theater. Dark, deserted, it was nevertheless a refuge to Mary Wister, who from pursuer had come to feel herself a fugitive. With a wall at your back, there is a kind of safety—a feeling of safety.

There she remained for what seemed a considerable time, but was in fact only a minute or a little more. She found, then, that she was breathing more quietly; realized, then, that for no reason (save the shadows, save the click of a heel on pavement) she had come near to panic. Not only a fool, but a frightened fool, Mary told herself; a woman, and a grown woman, thrown into panic by nothing, and, she became increasingly convinced, to no purpose. She had been so quick to move, accepted with so little thought a belief that she could do something which had to be done. So, in the shadow of a long frame building, in the shadow of palm trees, she was cowering against a wall, and listening tensely—and nobody knew she was there, or cared where she was. She threatened no one, and protected no one.

But when she moved, she moved as quietly as she could, listened as intently, tried as anxiously to see into the shadows around her. She moved along the windowless wall of the improvised theater, away from the walk by which she had come. She would, she realized, be moving diagonally toward the shuffleboard court; there was, she remembered, another passage to it from the other side of the building. Remembering this, she moved the last few feet very cautiously, and almost soundlessly. When she reached the corner, she stopped, held her breath, and again listened.

She could hear nothing, and see nothing, although here it was lighter. She did not at first understand this slightly greater light, and looked for its source.

She was looking across the shuffleboard court, across a pingpong table beyond it, at the wall of the triangular building they called the water shed—at the great cistern. Midway along the wall, a single electric bulb, set into the concrete, burned dimly. Beyond the light, there was a rectangle of blackness against the wall.

It took Mary Wister a long moment, standing tight against the wooden wall of the theater, two or three feet on the safe side of the corner of the building, to realize that the black rectangle was the door which led into the water shed—no, since it was black, the doorway itself! *The door was open.*

It would not normally be left open. That thought was clear, and sudden, in Mary's mind before she remembered that, when she had before looked at the wall, the door had been closed. It was set three or four feet up the wall—too high for a small child to clamber to. The picture was clear in her mind—it was a sliding door, one which slid vertically like— like a portcullis. *Or like the door of a trap!*

Now it was open. It was open because—

Mary drew in her breath quickly. The water shed was a trap—a great, triangular trap. A big man—a man as big as Oslen—could force a smaller person into it—a girl as small as Rachel Jones. The water would be deep enough there; the walls thick enough. Perhaps from season's

259

end to season's beginning, no one ever looked into the water shed. A body might be hidden there for months, grappled under black water. Or floating on black water. And who would look?

Almost convulsively, Mary started forward. But then she stopped. Someone was moving along the intersecting side of the building against which, now again, she flattened herself. The sounds of movement were clear; there seemed to be no particular effort to diminish them. She shrank back.

She watched, from the shadow, while William Oslen came to the corner of the building and then stepped away from it—mercifully with his back to her—and stood for a moment. He looked up and down the blank concrete wall beyond the shuffleboard court as she had done; seemed to seek, as she had sought, the source of light. Then he saw the open door and, seeing it, made an odd, soft sound. It was wordless; its meaning beyond translation. Then, moving quickly for all his size, he crossed the shuffleboard court, circled the pingpong table, made for the open door in the thick wall. Mary could only watch.

He reached the door and stopped for a moment before looking into it. Instead, he looked from right to left, and back again, along the wall. Only then, apparently satisfied he was alone, did William Oslen go to the door and lean into it.

He stood so, peering in, for several seconds. Then, with no preliminary movement, as if suddenly compelled, the big pianist hoisted himself from the ground, hung for an instant, and lifted himself into the doorway. It was a low door, and he crouched in it. His body was in strange perspective; menacing. The single light threw his shadow along the wall. Then he was gone.

Mary started instinctively toward the water shed and then, as if her muscles had frozen, she stopped. That was not the way, her mind told her—her mind commanded. Alone, she could do nothing; alone in the darkness which must be deep in the cistern shed she would be helpless. She had done what she could. Now— *surely now!*—the others would come. She would scream out for help now. Now silence was without meaning. Now there must be strength and quickness; sudden, open violence now! She filled her lungs to cry out.

And then, from the shed, she heard a woman scream. The sound was muffled by the heavy walls. Within it might reverberate, echo from concrete, from the surface of dark water. But here it was a frail sound, muted, dim in Mary's ears—dim and terrible. Then Mary Wister ran, and ran toward the door in the concrete wall, knowing there was no longer time to wait. But as she ran she called into the night—called, *'Here! They're here!'* and called, *'Help! Help!'* But she felt that the night swallowed her voice, that the heavy sound of the sea overwhelmed it. As she ran across the shuffleboard court she was not calling loudly, although still she thought she was. She was saying, '*Mac! Mac!*' but the words gasped in her throat.

Then she was at the little, high-set door; she was standing in front of it, her hands on the high sill, as before her Oslen had stood. And inside, at first, was only darkness—heavy darkness. After a second, there was faint light—barely perceptible light, trickling from a distant, tiny bulb set in the ceiling deep in the cavern.

The light reflected darkly from the surface of water, perhaps four feet, perhaps six, below the sill level. The surface of the water was almost as much to be felt as to be seen; it was not as if there were water there, the substance of water, but as if there, a harder darkness, was the far limit of vision made manifest. Yet as she looked longer—and now time was measured not as by a clock, but could be counted by the quick breaths she snatched of heavy air—the surface of the water was a dark, faintly moving mirror, which sullenly reflected the little light.

She looked at the water first, and breathed the air. The air was heavy, odorous. It was oppressive air and the odor was strange, sweetish—the odor of darkness, and of vegetation which was robbed of light. In the warm night, Mary felt coldness, and found it hard to breathe, and for a moment could not move.

Then, deep in the darkness, a woman cried out again and here the sound was shapeless and frightening; here it was repeated, seemed to be everywhere in the spreading darkness within. First the cry was the wordless cry of fear. Then the woman—the voice had no identity; it was only a voice of fear—cried, '*No! Don't! Oh—please! Please!*'

Then Mary Wister lifted herself on her hands, hung for an instant against the wall, and found the sill with her feet. She stood in the doorway, not needing to crouch as Oslen had done. Then, far along the inner wall, and to her right, she saw them—two moving shadows. They seemed, at first, to be pinned against the wall, above the black water.

That was illusion, and held only for a breath. Above the water, there was a ledge, perhaps two feet in width, jutting from the wall. It was wet and perilous; she thought that it did not project at right angles from the wall, but that it sloped toward the water. She pulled off her shoes against the edge of the shelf, and heard soft splashes in the blackness below her. Then she started along the ledge, leaning as close as she could to the wall, toward those she had seen—toward the shadows she had seen. She became, herself, a shadow creeping against the cold dank of the wall.

She had no plan and could make none. She could merely move along the slippery ledge, seeking to overtake the others, who seemed to be moving away from her, but slowly—hope that, somehow, she could delay Oslen until help came. For help must surely come—even over the deep note of the sea on coral shoals, her cry must have been heard. She had to believe that. There was no alternative to that belief; she clung to it as she tried to cling with her shoulder, with her hands, to the damp concrete on her right, with her stockinged feet to the cold ledge under them.

The two farther along the ledge, almost a hundred feet farther along the ledge, appeared not to have heard her. At least they continued their slow progress, one shadow toilsomely leading the other along the ledge above the evil water. It was, Mary thought, surely flight and pursuit, but flight reduced by darkness, by the treachery of the ledge, to a plodding hopelessness and pursuit almost equally slowed. Yet the second shadow, she thought, gained on the first. And both were silent now.

She could not, in the faint light, identify the shadows, but there was in her mind no doubt as to their identity. The first, the smaller, the one who so slowly fled, was Rachel Jones; the larger, Oslen. The light played tricks; the pursuer seemed smaller than she would have expected, and a part of her mind—the part which could never leave such problems quite alone—tried to reason out the pattern of light and shadow which so distorted truth. Actually, seen as she saw them now, Oslen seemed a man of only ordinary size.

Mary tried to increase her speed. But as she did she slipped, and felt herself falling away from the wall, and clutched frantically and found no handhold. She swayed, her body twisting. She must fall—and did not fall. She had caught herself. She went on again. But she realized, more clearly than before, why Rachel, for all the terror she must feel, moved so slowly in her flight along the ledge.

The two reached the corner of the cistern shed, where two walls met at an oblique angle. There Rachel did try to run, and slipped and almost fell. The other clutched for her, taking advantage of the angle, which for a moment, while he was a few feet short of the sharp corner and she had passed it, brought her almost within reach. Shadowy hands clutched at the fleeing girl, and seemed to graze her, and for a moment both swayed and were about to fall. The man spoke, sharply, but his words were lost to Mary. The girl went on and the pursuer jumped from one ledge to the other, cutting off the tip of the angle, and gained. They had been, at a guess, a dozen feet or more apart, now they were barely ten. Then Rachel started again to run. She ran unsteadily, half turned so that both hands seemed to cling, to try to cling, to the smooth, wet wall. Still she did not cry out.

Then Mary did.

'*No!*' she cried, and her voice was strange, unlike her own, echoing from walls, from water. 'Leave her—!'

She did not finish. The pursuing figure stopped, and she thought turned to face her. Still it was only a shadow, without a face. But as she realized this, Mary had suddenly a strange conviction of something wrong, something incongruous. It was, as in a dream, one person faded into another, or seemed to fade, became—

But now, and seemingly out of nowhere, there was another shadow. This was beyond the girl, coming toward the two on the ledge. Now Mary stopped and looked across the black water, and saw three converge, the girl between her former pursuer, who now had turned again to face away from Mary, had begun to advance again, and the new—the *larger*—man who came toward her, seeming to scuttle along the ledge.

Against the wall, the three were like figures in bas-relief; it was as if such figures had come to life and to play out, in motion, some drama which was incomprehensible, yet fearsome.

The girl was motionless, now, as the two came toward her. The smaller man, who had been behind her, reached out for her. She leaped away convulsively. But then the larger man reached too, and she seemed, as convulsively as before, to seek to avoid his outstretched hands.

She staggered a moment, and twisted her body to regain balance on the ledge. She failed and fell toward the black water, and as she fell she screamed.

For an instant, the two left on the ledge seemed to be rushing toward each other, reaching out toward each other. For a moment they grappled. Then the smaller fell away from the wall and in the darkness there was only the sound of churning water, loud in the echoing cavern.

Then, without warning, bright light struck across the cavern, and the two in the water were in a brilliant circle. Paul Shepard's face was white and staring in the light. He held Rachel in one arm and now, after an instant when his face was blank in the light, he began to pull himself and her through the water with his free arm. He began to swim toward the light, which had its source behind Mary.

Mary turned then. Two men stood on the ledge just inside the door—which was an unbelievably short distance from where she stood, although she felt that for hours she had toiled along the ledge. One she did not recognize; the other, tall and thin, holding the electric torch, was Mac. Then a third man came with difficulty through the little door, as if he were being helped from behind by others. The third man had another torch, and as it went on, before it swept a beam around the ledge, the light caught for a moment the

267

blackness of a sling against a white jacket.

'She's all right,' Shepard called, chokingly, from the water. 'I've got her. I've—'

But then the girl he held seemed to writhe under his arm, as if in panic. She escaped from him, as he clutched at her desperately, and for a second both went under the water.

'Get her!' Heimrich said, sharply, and the man who had stood beside MacDonald dived into the water.

The new swimmer churned toward the struggling two, along a path of light from the torch MacDonald held. The beam from Heimrich's light swept along the ledge. It found Mary Wister and for an instant hesitated, it went on, past the corner, to William Oslen. Oslen stood on the ledge, his back to the wall, the palms of his hands pressed against the wall. His face was white in the light, without expression.

The man who had been beside MacDonald had reached Shepard, now. He reached out a hand and seized the other man, pulling at him. Shepard turned toward him, and then Rachel Jones came up out of the dark water beyond Shepard and began to swim, with a kind of desperation, toward the light.

'I'm all right!' Shepard shouted. 'Get the girl. He tried—'

'Now Mr. Shepard,' Heimrich said, and his voice harshly filled the great room. 'We've had enough!' Shepard's suddenly turned-up face was white in the merciless beam of the light. 'It's all over, Mr. Shepard,' Heimrich said, and his voice was as without mercy as the white light was.

Heimrich's light stayed on William Oslen.

'You come along too, Mr. Oslen,' Heimrich said, and his voice was not noticeably more cordial.

Then Barclay MacDonald spoke, for the first time.

'And you, Mary, come here to me,' he said.

'You—' Mary heard herself start to say, with a kind of inchoate anger in her voice.

'Come *now*,' MacDonald said.

Mary Wister went back along the precarious ledge. It did not seem so difficult, now. It took almost no time at all.

CHAPTER TWELVE

Dr Barclay MacDonald said that he was very sorry. He said it had been a matter of some sick mice.

The two of them were stretched on cushioned seats on the sun porch of The Coral Isles. The late morning sun was warm on their legs.

'Mice,' Mary Wister said. 'Mice of all things.' She turned to look at Barclay MacDonald. She was pleased to see that he had, somehow, managed to get a good deal of sun. By the next day, she thought, his forehead would begin to peel. 'Sick mice.' She shook her head against the cushions. 'I hope,' she said, 'that they are doing as well as can be expected.'

'Oh,' he said, 'they're all dead by now. But they did do better than we expected. Much better, really. It was suggestive, I think. Freddy's quite excited about it. That's why he telephoned. Of course, Freddy's young, but still—' He stopped speaking and regarded her. 'I'm afraid you'll find I'm a good deal interested in mice,' he said. 'Hamsters too, for that matter.'

'Mice and cations,' Mary said.

'Fruit flies, too,' Barclay MacDonald said.

'Not in the house,' Mary said. 'Where were you, Mac?' The search for a better name could wait. 'Where was everybody?'

'Almost exactly two minutes behind you,' Mac said. 'Probably it seemed longer, but that's what it was—two minutes. Incidentally, the captain says you yelled in his ear. Not in mine. I had to run. Running is counter-indicated at the moment but—'

'Mac!' she said. 'You didn't—?' Her tone was anxious. She looked at his face, saw his smile. 'If you think,' she said, in another tone.

'It's always seemed to me that the way to get sympathy is to ask for it,' Mac told her, with gravity. 'Otherwise, how are one's nearest and dearest to know?'

270

'You!' Mary said, with force.

'However,' Mac said, 'I'm feeling quite well today, you'll be glad to know.'

'No doubt,' she said, 'because the mice behaved so suggestively.'

'Not entirely,' he said. He looked at her carefully. 'Not even very much,' he said. 'As you know, of course.'

'Because you guessed right,' she said. 'You did, didn't you? And I was wrong?'

'It's always gratifying,' he admitted. 'However—how do you feel, my dear?'

She paused a moment; looked at him a moment.

'All right,' she said, 'I feel wonderful. I'm very glad about the mice, too. Although it's too bad they're dead on—on such a fine day.'

'The mice,' MacDonald told her, 'were in New Haven. It snowed heavily in New Haven yesterday, Freddy told me. I love you, Mary.'

'Of course,' Mary said. 'But there was a time last night I hated you.'

He nodded.

'By the way,' he said, 'I like what you did. It wasn't particularly bright. I should prefer you not to do anything of the kind again. But I like your having done it.'

'There wasn't anything else to do,' she said. 'Apparently it didn't make any difference. I could just have waited in the bar and—hello, captain.'

Captain M. L. Heimrich stood in front of

271

them and regarded them; he managed to keep his eyes open. He was urged to pull up a chair; he did so. He sat in it, with the sun on his back. He did not seem inclined to speech. But they waited. He opened his eyes.

'Mr. Shepard isn't talkative,' he said. 'The assistant state's attorney isn't pleased. Keeps urging Mr. Shepard to co-operate.' He closed his eyes. 'An interesting term under the circumstances,' he said. 'One can see Mr. Shepard's point, naturally.'

'Will it make any difference, in the end?' Mary asked. Heimrich opened his eyes; he shook his head; he said he shouldn't think so.

'Miss Jones can testify he tried to drown her,' Heimrich said. 'Make the jury wonder why, naturally. He'll find it difficult to explain. Probably he'll say he was protecting her from Oslen. But—Oslen wasn't there yet. The chief deputy and I can testify to that. So, the jury'll want to know—why?' He paused, as if he had concluded.

'It isn't very clear,' Mary said.

'Now Miss Wister,' he said. 'Why isn't it?'

She merely shook her head.

'It seems very clear to me,' Heimrich said. 'We invite a certain action. The invitation is accepted. The evidence is—arranged.' Heimrich closed his eyes. 'I'll admit Oslen was an added starter. As you were, Miss Wister. However—'

'Now captain,' Dr. MacDonald said. 'Quit

having such a good time.'

Heimrich opened his eyes; he seemed a little surprised.

'Was I?' he asked. He considered. 'Perhaps I was,' he said. 'All right—first, we know it's Shepard.'

'But—' Mary said.

'Now Miss Wister,' Heimrich said. 'Of course we know. But we can't prove. So, we enlist Miss Jones's help.'

'By "we" you mean yourself,' Mary said, and got, 'Now Miss Wister. The chief deputy, too.' Then Heimrich went on.

'We count on Mr. Shepard's character,' he said. 'A very decisive man; a man who hates loose ends. Likes quick, final movements. Takes things into his own hands. As you must have noticed when you played with him yesterday, Miss Wister. Not a man to wait around. We offer him action—we offer him Miss Jones, come out of hiding, available.'

'But Miss Jones didn't—' Mary began, and then said, 'Oh.'

'Precisely,' Heimrich said. 'She didn't threaten him. She threatened Oslen. So, if something happened to her, we went after Oslen. You see, we'd have had to—whatever we thought. We would have had to dig up Oslen's record—the FBI had enough of it, thanks largely to Miss Jones. A jury wouldn't have left the box.'

'Why would you have had to?' MacDonald

273

asked.

Heimrich hesitated.

'The deputy sheriff would have had to,' Heimrich said. 'The state's attorney. They're in charge, you know. As a matter of fact—' He stopped. He seemed uncharacteristically ill at ease for a moment.

'Look,' MacDonald said, 'did your deputy sheriff—Jefferson, isn't it?—know *who* your trap was set for?'

'Now doctor,' Heimrich said. 'Now doctor.'

'Well?'

'I don't,' Heimrich said, 'remember that I told him in so many words. Didn't think it was necessary, naturally. However—'

He paused a moment.

'Shepard had already tried it once,' he said. 'After he saw me talking to García's sister, found out García was on the loose, he pretended to try to kill me. Assuming we'd lay it to García, which would have been reasonable. As a matter of fact, the sheriff did want to settle for that. I—persuaded them. Pointed out that I might be thought to threaten a good many people.' He closed his eyes. 'A very helpful man, Mr. Shepard,' he said. 'A quick man with red herrings. So—'

Shepard had been offered another opportunity. If Rachel Jones were found dead, or injured—'more probably the latter,' Heimrich said. 'He didn't really try to kill me. He did only what he thought necessary'—

Oslen would be obvious. Rachel had been persuaded to act as bait, assured she was in no danger.

'Did she know who you were after?' Mary asked.

'Now Miss Wister,' Heimrich said. 'Perhaps not. I don't remember telling her.'

'For a sieve,' Mary said, 'you forget to tell a good many people a good many things, captain.'

He considered that. He nodded. He said that he might be getting absent-minded.

'So,' he said, 'we arranged for Miss Jones to show herself just as it got dark, and arranged to be around, not showing ourselves. She was to run, but not too fast; we were to close in. But then—'

Then Oslen had injected himself into proceedings otherwise going according to plan. Rachel had seen him and panicked; had run for the shelter of the water shed. 'It's hard to have faith in protection you can't see, naturally,' Heimrich said. 'It's understandable she lost her nerve.'

Heimrich and the sheriff's men had not, Heimrich admitted, seen Oslen as soon as Rachel had. They had been following Shepard. They did see the girl go into the shed, and see Shepard go in after her. They were about to close in when Oslen appeared and followed the others.

'Then, of course, it wasn't urgent,' Heimrich

275

said. 'Oslen would take care of Shepard, see the girl wasn't hurt, naturally. He was the last person to want her hurt. Then you showed up, Miss Wister, and went into the shed too.' He looked at her. 'Very unexpected, that,' he said.

'A complication,' she said. 'I'm sorry.'

'Now Miss Wister,' Heimrich said. 'Not that, exactly. An impartial witness. Witnesses are always welcome, naturally.'

'It was all confused,' Mary said. 'Dark—uncertain. I—I'm afraid I didn't understand what was happening, captain.'

'No,' he said. 'Well, Shepard's scheme didn't work. He wanted to get her in the open, knock her out. But, as it was, she saw him. So—he would have had to kill her. But Oslen blocked that—he went around the shorter two sides of the triangle, you know, and intercepted them. So Shepard pushed the girl in the water, knowing you were there but that you couldn't see clearly, and jumped in to "save" her. It was the best he could do, by that time. Actually, of course, he tried to drown her. That would have left it between him and Oslen, and take your pick. You couldn't have, with any certainty, could you?'

'No,' Mary said.

It was fortunate, Heimrich said, that Rachel Jones would have no trouble. So—

Again, he seemed to consider his explanation finished.

'You knew it was Shepard,' Mary said.

276

'Yes,' Heimrich said. 'Oh yes.'

Mary and MacDonald waited.

'The point,' Heimrich said, 'is to have the character fit the crime. Have I said that?'

He was assured that he had. He nodded; he closed his eyes. It was obvious, he said, that Shepard's fitted. He was told that that was not enough; that there must have been more. He agreed. There had been a few things; not many, most of the answer had been visible in character. But—

'A package of cigarettes, of course,' Heimrich said. 'Two lies, one provable and the other probably provable. Of course, Shepard wasn't the only one who lied. Both the Sibleys did, as they later admitted. Oslen did, when he said he had come here to rest, and only that, before going on a tour. That was obviously a lie—pianists practice before a tour. He hadn't made any provisions to practice—admitted it. Naturally, I didn't believe him. He'd come to see Wells, as Miss Jones said. Things like that helped—and, of course, hindered. However—'

The cigarettes found in Wells's pocket after he had been killed helped, Heimrich told them. It was obvious they had been put there purposely, not by Wells himself. 'Because,' Heimrich said mildly, 'Wells didn't smoke. Told us all that the other night—or told anyone who was listening, and who remembered. Shepard didn't, apparently.' The only conceivable purpose in planting the cigarettes would be to indicate that Wells had been away from the hotel, in the town. The only conceivable reason for indicating that would be to involve García. Therefore, García was innocent. Naturally. It became necessary to consider only those at the hotel.

Heimrich ticked them off; Shepard, Oslen, the Sibleys. 'You two,' Heimrich said, and nodded at Mary and MacDonald. 'I didn't take you very seriously, Miss Wister. To be honest, I couldn't tie you in. You were different, doctor. You did tie in but—' He shrugged. It hurt his shoulder and he made a slight face. 'I've always found revenge difficult to believe in,' he said. 'You're a research man and hence a patient man. Violence seemed out of character.'

That left, for major consideration, the Sibleys, Oslen and Paul Shepard.

'Not Mrs. Shepard?' Mary asked, and Heimrich looked surprised and then shook his head. He did not then explain.

He had, Heimrich said, ruled Oslen out—at any rate reduced him to an outsider—after he had heard Rachel Jones's story.

Mary looked blank at that; MacDonald looked at her, then at Heimrich, and waited expectantly.

'But,' Mary said, 'I thought you believed her?'

'I did,' Heimrich said. 'Furthermore, I checked, in so far as I could. I do believe her.

278

So, naturally, I decided Oslen probably wasn't the man we wanted.'

Mary had only, 'But—' to say. She said it.

To make Oslen a probable suspect, Heimrich said, it was necessary to assume him to be an active, and professional, communist—a disciplined member of the party; a participant in the party's under-cover work. But when you made that assumption, as you did on believing Rachel Jones's statements, you, paradoxically, more or less eliminated him as a suspect.

'But,' Mary said again, 'they'll do *anything*. We know that.'

Then Heimrich shook his head. He said she was confusing a lack of moral scruple, which he would willingly grant, with a lack of considered intention, which he would not. The very deviousness of Oslen's activities proved, if proof were needed, a calculated program—*and one not to be upset by any personal considerations*. The last, he pointed out, was inherent in the philosophy. The individual had no importance.

But the threat Wells presented was a threat to an individual—to William Oslen. Revelation that the party employed agents provocateurs would hardly damage the Communist Party; that it did had been widely guessed at, and in one or two cases proved. Oslen would be damaged—his usefulness to the party, in that particular activity, would be eliminated. As a professional musician he would be hard hit. But it would be the *individual* who would suffer, not the 'cause.'

But murder, by a provable communist, of a man like Wells, would badly damage the party's program. Not primarily in the United States, perhaps. But the United States was not, for the moment at least, the major battlefield. It was in Western Europe, and in Asia, that the two sides fought for men's minds. And to men and women in Western Europe and in Asia, the communist program was to present our side as the side of violence, of ruthlessness, of suppression of minorities; theirs as the side of patience and of peace.

'Oh,' Heimrich said, 'they kill their opponents. We all know that. But only where they themselves are strong, not where they are weak. They think the end justifies the means, but there is a corollary to that. The end *must* justify the means. And it must be the party's end, not a party member's. There is no area for individual—indignation.' He opened his eyes. 'If you are a communist,' he said, 'you don't kill a man just because you're mad at him, or because he threatens you. That would be, I imagine, some kind of deviation.'

'So,' Mary said, 'you eliminated Oslen?'

Heimrich nodded.

'With,' he said, 'very considerable reluctance, Miss Wister. With great reluctance.'

He had been left with the Sibleys and with Paul Shepard. The Sibleys had obvious motive. But—'Well,' Heimrich said, 'Wells was a vigorous man—physically, as well as mentally. Neither the Judge nor Mrs. Sibley is—well, athletic. They're rather old for violence. I doubted either to be capable of it.'

Then, under pressure, Shepard had lied. He had said he had completed arrangements for Wells to do a radio commentary, sponsored. He said this, Heimrich pointed out, only *after* Wells was dead. But—investigation had proved that he had no sponsor. It had been proved, subsequently, that no one else at United Broadcasting Alliance had heard of the proposed commentary. 'Several of them,' Heimrich said, 'were very much startled at the idea.'

An explanation had to be guessed at, but could be guessed at. Suppose that Wells had knowledge of some incident in Shepard's past which would make Shepard subject to a species of blackmail? Perhaps Shepard had belonged, at some time, to a 'wrong' organization, and that Wells could prove it. Shepard was in a very 'sensitive' industry. 'Which meant,' Heimrich said, 'that Shepard would go out on his ear.' Heimrich seemed slightly surprised to hear himself say this. But then he nodded.

'So,' he said, 'I supposed that the commentary was Mr. Wells's idea, not Mr. Shepard's. That Mr. Wells was using pressure.

That Mr. Shepard was the kind of man who would not accept pressure, would not be pushed around—a man, in short, who made his own decisions—and could be ruthless.'

'He plays tennis that way,' Mary said.

'Yes,' Heimrich said. 'He does indeed, Miss Wister.'

But there had been something else—something equally revealing.

'I asked him if his wife used sleeping pills,' Heimrich said. 'He reacted with—well, with a great deal of violence. But Mrs. Shepard had, talking to Mrs. Sibley the other evening, said something which could only mean she did take them. It isn't a sin to take sleeping pills, it isn't disgraceful. Then—why the denial, why the violence? The assumption was obvious, naturally—a person under the influence of, say, nembutal isn't likely to wake up when another person goes in and out of a room. So, without his wife's knowing it, Mr. Shepard could have gone and returned—and killed once while he was gone and stabbed once, not to kill. So—'

There was silence for a moment. Then Barclay MacDonald said there still seemed to be a good deal of guesswork in it. Heimrich, who had closed his eyes, opened them.

'Now doctor,' he said. 'There is, naturally. There often is. That's why it seemed best to have Mr. Shepard take action. Now, of course, we know where to look for the rest.' He paused. 'That's quite often the case,' he said then. 'One relies on character. Evidence sometimes has to be arranged.'

He sat for a moment longer, his eyes closed. Then he said that he thought he might go down to the beach and sit in the sun.

'That's what I came for, naturally,' he said. He shook his head as he stood. 'Peace in the sun,' he said, and then that he would see them. Then he went away, out into the sun, a very solid man, looking like any solid man.

'It seems—' Mary began, turning toward Barclay MacDonald. But then a boy in a red jacket came onto the porch and spoke Dr. MacDonald's name in soothing tones. He reported a long distance telephone call. 'Damn,' said Barclay MacDonald and got up. He looked down at Mary.

'You wait here,' he told her. 'Right here.'

'Yes,' Mary Wister said. 'I'll wait, doctor.' He looked at her. 'Give my love to the mice,' Mary Wister said.

She settled herself to wait in the sun.